The Indian Cowboy
Part 2

The Hunter

AF124882

The Author:

Brita Rose Billert was born 1966 in Erfurt, Germany. She is a specialized nurse of critical care and respiratory care. A fact that also competes well in her novels. She spends her spare time with her horse in the Kyffhäuserland, Thüringen. She has made many friendships with Native Americans in Utah, South Dakota and British Columbia through her trips to the United States. This fact, the love for the horses and her job inspires her to write. Fourteen novels have already been published.

Home page of the Autor:

www.brita-rose-billert.de

Brita Rose-Billert

The Indian Cowboy

The hunter

Novel

Bibliographische Informationen der Deutschen Nationalbibliothek: Deie Deutsche Nationalbibliothek verzeichnet
diese Publikation in der Deutschen Nationalbibliogra-
phie; detaillierte bibliographische Daten sind im Internet
über dnb.d-nb.de abrufbar.

TWENTYSIX
Eine Marke der Books on Demond GmbH

Herstellung und Verlag:
BoD - Books on Demond, Norderstedt

ISBN: 9783740712334

Übersetzung: Bruno Winkler, Swiss
Korrektur: Natasha Lynn Anderson Wallace, Utha USA
Satz und Layout, Coverdesign: Robert Billert

Every single one of us fights for his existence, for his survival and for his dreams every day. No matter where on this earth and in very different ways. This book is dedicated to all these people.

Don't give up and don't forget to smile whatever happens.

Brita Rose Billert

Chapter 1
Time of the dawning

Around ten in the morning, Sergeant Ryan Black Hawk was led from the detention cell into General Major Barkley's office. Ryan stopped in front of the desk behind which Barkley, Taylor and a young lieutenant had taken a seat. Barkley announced his decision in just two sentences.

"Sergeant Hawk, you are dishonestly released from the service of the U.S. Air Force with immediate effect. Due to the damage you caused to people, the company car, the refusal to obey orders, unreliability and desertion, I see another affiliation as indefensible. Now that you are a civilian on military grounds, the lieutenant will accompany you to your room so that you can pack your things. Afterwards he will accompany you directly to the exit."

Barkley's words sounded like shots fired. Ryan's blood froze. He took a deep breath. With no emotion he showed what he felt. Although he had hardly expected Barkley's judgment differently, he felt the ground shaking dangerous under his feet. Every word was superfluous. Since he was no longer under command, the Lakota turned without a word of greeting and went out the door. The lieutenant jumped up to follow him in a hurry.

Barkley's grim look followed the men. Hardly audible, Taylor said: "He was my best man. I will never find one like him again."

*****

Dark clouds piled up over the land around the Black Hills. Dawn dominated the day. Oppressive sultry announced the approaching thunderstorm. It was incredibly quiet. Not a bird sang and the thick air swallowed the engine noise of Highway 90. A young man came from there on foot. He didn't seem to be in a hurry, but he didn't stroll. A black bag hung over his shoulder and although it wasn't necessary, he wore sunglasses. No road, no path, led in this direction, in which he walked purposefully. It seemed as he knew where he was going. He had put the shirt in his belt. It dangled in time with his steps. Ryan Black Hawk knew exactly where he was going. He knew the way. Not the first time he put it back on foot. After about two hours he had reached the edge of the forest in the Back Hills. In the mountains he would find shelter from the thunderstorm that was coming up very quickly. The jeans stuck to the skin and the tongue to the palate. Even the dark forest offered no cooling relief. A fire seemed to be burning in his sneakers. Ryan ignored all of this. His face looked petrified and his thoughts tormented him. Finally, he put the glasses away. It was dark in the thick forest. Here, too, the Lakota did not follow any track. His feet touched the soft mixed forest floor, rotting needles, withered leaves, moss and branches. It smelled of it. A barely audible sound that didn't belong here made Ryan stop and listen. He clearly heard a human groan. Ryan grinned at the corners of his mouth and waited.

Silence.

Then someone groaned again. It came from above, from the slope. Ryan left the bag behind, crawled up and finally lay on the floor. His grin widened when he realized the cause. Another miserable moan came to his ears. Ryan got up. Although the Lakota always avoided interfering in other people's affairs, it seemed extremely necessary here. A white-haired man, wearing only his underpants, was hanging upside down on the lowest branch of a tree. His head hovered above the ground, while his arms hung in a large anthill. The animals bravely defended their dwelling and did not agree with the intruder. Ryan took out his knife and cut the rope. The old man flopped in the crawling pile and croaked. He swore weakly and tried unsuccessfully to get up. The old man waved awkwardly. Ryan grinned mockingly at the strange, ridiculous creature and turned to go.

"Hey you!", the old man suddenly snorted. "You can't..." He groaned as he laboriously tried to get on his legs "... leave me here. goddam!"

Ryan paused and looked back.

"Maybe you didn't deserve it any other way", he replied unaffectedly.

"I'll kill those cursed skunks! Ungrateful people!"

The old man had enough air in his lungs to swear heavily. On all fours he crawled out of the bunch of brave little animals and kept stroking his fiery red arms. Some dead bodies fell to the ground. When he thought he was safe, he leaned against a tree and took a first look at his rescuer. The little old grinned, coughed and said in a hoarse voice: "Thank you! I owe you something."

Wind came up and drove into the leaves of the trees. It rustled. Ryan looked up.

"I can feel something prowling. I noticed it last night in my old, rotten bones. I'm Samuel Gabriel Anthony Williams by the way. For you, Sam. If you give me your name?"

Ryan looked down at him skeptically and eyed him. He

was small, stocky and had short, crooked legs. His white hair stuck in all directions from his head. But the beard made an extremely meticulously groomed impression. His big nose was reminiscent of a potato and his eyes blinked curiously at Ryan.

"Ryan", he finally said.

Sam laughed in a smoky voice. "I like you, fellow. You're Indian. Looks like an Air Force cut on vacation. No one else would have had the stupid idea to roam through this godforsaken piece of forest. My luck. Otherwise the ants would have gnawed off my bones."

Old Sam changed his mood from an unfriendly snarling to an idiosyncratic humor. He laughed and beckoned to Ryan. "Come on boy! Help an old man get on his feet. My skull is humming from the twisted world."

Ryan took a step forward and held out his hand. The old man grabbed his wrist and pulled himself up. Then he took the first stiff steps.

The wind grew to a storm.

The thunder rumbled.

It was high time for Ryan to go to the cave. Again he turned to go.

"The lightning should hit me that I drop dead imme-diately if I'm a liar. I am a businessman and have always been honest with everyone!" Sam screamed through the loud roar of the storm.

Branches cracked menacingly. One fell to the ground. Ryan remained indifferent and continued on his way.

"Why should our creator send you to me on your way? To save my life! He didn't want me up there yet!" The old man shouted after him.

"Ever heard of hell?", Ryan shouted back without stop-ping. He heard the old man croak behind him.

"The devil is afraid of me."

Ryan disappeared down the slope. The storm played furiously with the tree tops. The howling whistle grew louder and the rustling leaves sang. Ryan reached for his bag. Now he would have to hurry to reach his shelter on the rocks. Maybe he would have to spend the night there. When he threw the bag over his shoulder, he saw the old man, who called himself Sam, limping hurriedly towards himself. He stopped right in front of him. Ryan didn't move. His petrified expression looked indifferent.

"Come on boy. My cabin is nearby. I invite you. If you support me a little bit, both we could still make it."

The strange old man seemed to mean it honestly. He looked worriedly at Ryan and waited for an answer.

Ryan finally nodded. "Okay."

When the two men reached the log cabin in a clearing, lightning flashed through the darkness. Ryan recognized a shed by the house in front of which a relatively new off-road vehicle was parked. The two men had just reached the door when the rain pelted down. The drops of water jumped over the hard floor like pebbles. Sam tossed the door behind him and turned on the light. He breathed heavily. The path had robbed him of his last strength. He laboriously dragged himself to the table and sank onto one of the chairs.

"Sit down, Ryan."

Ryan stood at the window and looked out. The masses of water drummed against the windows and onto the roof of the log house. Then he sat down at the table with the stranger and pushed the bag underneath his chair. In silence, he eyed the room, which was appropriately furnished and decorated with all kinds of frills. His eyes roamed a desk on which a computer was standing. Next to it was a narrow metal cupboard. Ryan's eyes finally caught on an old Winchester. In addition to skins, pictures and some hunting trophies, she adorned the wooden wall. Sam watched him.

"I'll find something to wear and start the fire. And I'm incredibly hungry", he said. Sam rose and disappeared through the door into the room beyond.

Ryan examined the stove that would have honored any museum. In a basket lay chopped wood and next to it some large, stacked logs. When Sam entered the living room, the fire was already burning. He nodded gratefully to Ryan and slid a cast iron pan onto the stove.

"Coffee or tea?", he asked.

"Coffee. Black", Ryan replied.

"I hope you like turkey?", Sam asked while he was making coffee.

"Yes, I do", Ryan replied shortly.

Sam shook his head. Then he cut turkey meat into strips and squeezed them into a pan. Ryan's thoughts deviated. He was trying to find out, why he was sitting here now. *What does that mean? Why did Wakan Tanka send me to this stranger? The old man would surely not have survived the day without my appearance. And now I'm in his house...*

Sam interrupted Ryan's thoughts, as he pushed a large coffee cup in front of the Lakota.

"Thanks", Ryan replied shortly.

The smell of roast penetrated his senses and brought him completely back to the present. The old man now made a very civilized and well-groomed impression, which was in contrast to his appearance in the forest. The old man put the food on the table without saying a word. Then he muttered a prayer.

Ryan felt peculiar emptiness deep inside him. Fear and anger were gone. Suddenly he didn't care. Only the feeling of hunger, with the smell of roasting, came into his consciousness. For a long time, he had enjoyed nothing like it. The old geezer was actually a good cook and host. Ryan smiled.

"Thank you. The food is really very good", Ryan politely thanked his host.

The old man's eyes lit up when he smiled openly at Ryan. "I'm glad, boy", Sam croaked.

The storm raged outside. Stormy gusts lashed the rain against the house. A loose shutter rattled at the shed. The thunder sounded like the rolling ball of a bowling alley and discharged in a loud crash.

When Sam had cleared the dishes, he got a bottle of whiskey and two glasses. He poured without asking. Without a word, he took his glass and drank it in one go.

"Sometimes that's good. Then you know, you're still alive", Sam said softly.

Ryan hesitated. Finally, he reached for the glass and drank it in one go. Sam was right. It felt good to feel the burning in the throat. It was probably the best whiskey he had ever drunk. No comparison to the cheap fluff without taste, which had only eaten holes in his stomach for years. Ryan took a deep breath, as if taking a deep puff on the cigarette. Sam poured coffee and looked directly at Ryan.

"You are the first stranger who was ever allowed to enter my claim. I don't like strangers sniffing around here. You saw where that could lead."

Ryan had to grin.

"Do you like the Winchester?"

"Yes."

 13

"I'm giving it to you."

Ryan shook his head. "I don't need a gun that decorates a wall."

Sam laughed roughly. "So? What do you need?"

Ryan said nothing.

"Are you in the air force? You look like."

Ryan contemptuously twisted his mouth.

Sam watched this very carefully.

"Pilot?"

"No."

"There are dozens of different jobs at the Air Force. But you don't look like a cook and you don't look like one from the cleaning squadron either. I can't explain it to myself, but when I look at you, I don't want to have to face you with a weapon in hand."

A mocking smile now played around Ryan's corner of the mouth, which looked almost snooty. "Driver", he finally answered.

Sam raised her eyebrows. "Then I would bet my holy claim that you were the one, they hunted for two days. They told it on the news. You must have made them angry." Sam indicated the bandage on Ryan's arm. "Shot and escaped the FBI with their jeep", Sam giggled. "And then the US Army fired you after you turned yourself in?"

Ryan was amazed at the old man's knowledge.

"So it is", he nodded.

"What the hell did you screw up?"

"You ask too much, Sam."

Sam raised his hands in defense.

"All right. It's none of my business."

Ryan took the coffee cup in both hands and drank. Sam got up heavily, limped to the desk and rummaged around. Then he pushed a note to Ryan.

"Maybe that's something for you."

Ryan stared at the piece of paper on which a number was written in blue ink in accurate writing.

"What's that?"

"If you're looking for a damn well paid job, call. I think you can handle weapons, drive a car and track down people like me that nobody else can find."

"I can do that."

"Okay. But now the hitching come in, buddy. Can you track down people who don't want to be found at all?"

Ryan raised his head and looked at Sam. A suspicious wrinkle formed on his nose. "Bounty hunter."

Sam nodded slowly.

In silence, Ryan shoved the note into his pocket. Flashes of lightning twitched in front of the windows. Tree branches crashed and a tree seemed to break under the force of the storm. The storm still whipped the rain against the house. Thunderbolts crashed like cannon shots.

"You stay here tonight", Sam decided. "Tomorrow morning I'll take you down to town."

Ryan nodded in agreement.

*****

The sun was just over the ridges of the Black Hills when Ryan got in the car with Sam. He liked the black Dodge truck. In contrast, the old man looked like a dwarf. A few feather clouds stood in the blue sky. Nothing reminded of yesterday's thunderstorm. The air was pleasantly fresh and clear. The RAM rolled down the forest path to the paved road. The sunlight shimmered through the treetops. The road twisted through the mountains like a flattened snake. Country music sounded from the radio. For a moment, Ryan thought the world was back in order. The appearance was deceptive. He knew that. When the car left the forest in an easterly direction, the sun was dazzling. Grumbling Sam made his face and lowered the sun visor. The city of Rapid City was right in front of you. The road now led straight ahead like a ruler. A little later Sam steered the truck into a driveway. He opened the roller door from the car with an electric remote control. It closed automatically behind him.

"Here we are. Come with me, boy", Sam said and got out.

Ryan smiled because the old man kept calling him *boy*. It was Sam's way, but Ryan didn't blame him. He inexplicably liked this strange and idiosyncratic old man. Ryan was amazed when he followed Sam through the depot. He sensed what business Sam was doing. When he entered the store, his assumption was confirmed. Sam had a gun shop. Ryan looked around. Weapons of all kinds and for every taste, many packed, some in the display under glass.

"Pick up a good one. I don't want to be in your debt forever. You saved my life, boy." The old grinned, for he hadn't missed the Lakota's amazement.

He looked at the weapons in silence. His eyes moved from one to the other.

"Take your time. I only open in half an hour."

Sam switched on the computer and sorted the mail. From time to time he laughed croakily or cursed quietly.

"I thought of a small, handy and with a short barrel, semi-automatic. What do you think of that one?" asked Ryan finally.

Sam came up and shook his head. "Toys for people who want to impress. You can scare chickens at most", Sam laughed. "I will show you the professional tool."

Sam put a few boxes on the counter. "Colts are somewhat out of fashion, although they are of course technically acceptable. These are semi-automatic pistols, self-loading, caliber nine millimeters from different manufacturers. Very popular with police officers and agents. All are inconspicuous to wear and easy to operate with one hand. The more mature gentlemen often rely on Smith and Whose or Browning. The young customers prefer Beretta or Glock", smiled Sam. "For your purposes this one seems to me to be optimal. It's practically invisible and has the same impact as its big sisters. High shooting speed. The best life insurance in the skilled hand. And absolutely no stoppages."

Ryan picked up the pistol, looked at it from all sides, and checked the position in his hand.

"It's yours and a thousand rounds of ammunition."

Ryan put the gun back on the table.

"Waste", he nodded.

"Waste", Sam grinned and also nodded.

Then he carefully put away all the other pistols. He treated the weapons like raw eggs.

"Do you think I can show up in the bank with the pistol?"

"Boy! You don't want to ...", Sam whispered in horror.

Ryan laughed amused.

It was the first time since he was released that he laughed. And it was the first time Sam heard him laugh so boisterously. Without scorn and without mockery. Sam let himself be infected by it.

"No I do not want to. I just need something cash."

"I can give you the money too. Credit card? How much?"

"Five hundred and please give me a shoulder holster and the little black backpack there."

Sam nodded and gave Ryan what he wanted. "I would be happy to see you again sometime. You're always welcome to me, boy. And you know where my cabin is."

Ryan packed everything in the new backpack.

"You know, the most worthy way for a man to die is to fall asleep by the fire in the evening or to be shot in battle. Never tell anyone that you cut old Sam off the tree in such an embarrassing situation."

Ryan pressed his lips together and narrowed his eyes into small slits.

"Which tree?", he grinned.

Sam accompanied Ryan to the door and opened his shop. Ryan walked down the street without looking back.

*****

A little later, Ryan showed up at his sister's house, Carry Crowman. The noise of the children playing could be heard from far away. His niece, who played ball with a whole horde of tots on the playground, first discovered him. Joan immediately ran to her uncle and jumped at him. "Ryan! Ryan!", she shouted out and clinging to him. Ryan laughed.

"Hello Jo, you little whirlwind. How are you?"

"Fine, and you?"

"Good as well. Is your mom at home?"

"Yes, she is in the house. She's just packing things up."

Ryan eyed Joan skeptically.

"No fear. Not what you think."

"So? What do I think?"

 18

Joan giggled. "Just a move. That was decided by the great war council."

Ryan grinned.

"Can you play soccer? I still lack a good player in the team. Mason is too clumsy."

"He can't even walk alone", Ryan laughed. "Well then... get off, spider monkey."

Ryan tucked his travel bag into the tree's forks at the playground. Joan beamed when her uncle accompanied her to the field. The field was delimited by the laundry area, pile of sand, wall of a house and a lying log. The other players, all about Joan's size and age, had no objection. The noise roared, louder and jarring than before.

Carry shook his head and smiled as she wrapped the cups out of the closet in newspaper and put them in one of the boxes. She had no idea who was chasing the ball outside the door with the kids.

Ryan shot. Joan enthusiastically screamed *goal! goal!* while Mason was sitting in the pile of sand and putting sand grains in his mouth. Now the children rushed in from all sides to get the ball. Ryan tried to snatch the ball away from them. The little feet got in his way in the fray. He stumbled over it, rolled off his shoulder and caught the ball with his hands. This provoked loud protests from all sides. Joan enlightened him. "That's a foul! You cannot use your hands."

"Okay."

Ryan handed the ball over to the opposing team.

"Wait! That that will be a five meter!", threatened Joan.

"Doesn't that mean penalty?", Ryan asked.

"Sure, but that's too far from the goal!"

Ryan giggled.

The goal was only hinted at, between the wall of a house and a tricycle. With an important expression, a five-year-old attempted and shot the ball. Since no one volunteered to goalkeeper, Joan and Ryan tried to prevent a goal. The ball came flying in a high arc and crashed into the corner of the house. Ryan jumped to the ball and bounced the ball against his chest. The ball jumped to the ground and hopped away. He finally remained in the middle of the field.

"Man! You could have caught him with your hands", Joan shouted.

"You said I shouldn't take the ball with my hands", said Ryan.

"As a goalie for sure", Joan grinned.

"And who gets the ball now?"

"Well, whoever grabs it first."

The unrestrained zeal of the players unloaded again in the battle for the only ball. No one took any notice of the audience that the noise was likely to have attracted. Mason was taken in the arms by Carry and smiled when she spotted her brother in the crowd. Someone had shot the ball with such force that it flew far beyond the field. The children chased him. Ryan stopped and laughed. When he saw Carry, he pulled his bag out of the branch-fork and went to her.

"I was afraid for you", she whispered.

"I was scared too", Ryan replied.

"They didn't put you in a prison. I can hardly believe it. I'm so happy you're here, Ryan. Let's go inside."

"Jo said you are moving."

"Joan!" Carry called as the children ran past her.

Joan stopped and came to her mom. Since she had called with her full name, Joan had no idea of anything good. Mom only called her Joan when she had done something wrong.

"Can you tell me how much sand your little brother has eaten?"

"It couldn't have been that much, Mom. The pile of sand is still as big as before."

Carry gritted her teeth to stay serious. When Ryan laughed, she finally had to laugh too.

"You little cheeky toad", said Ryan.

Joan giggled.

"You can keep playing, but with Mason.

Joan didn't move a muscle of her face. "Yes, mom." She took the little brother with her.

Ryan and Carry went inside. Boxes and laundry were piled up in the apartment.

"Jo said you're moving", Ryan resumed the conversation.

"Yes, back to the reservation, to Kyle", Carry confirmed as she cleared the kitchen table.

"Sit down, dear brother. I can barely make coffee."

Ryan sat down.

"Alex's parents need help and I never really felt at home here. Jo is going to school soon."

"That soothes me. You'll be better off there. How are father and mother, grandmother and my brothers?", Ryan asked.

"Good. For real. They are healthy, also mother."

Ryan breathed a sigh of relief and nodded in satisfaction.

"They miss you. They too were afraid for you. They always ask me about you."

Ryan pressed his palms together. His body tightened like a bowstring. He seemed to be looking for words.

"I'm out, Carry. Dishonorably released for things I've never done. But at least I didn't get a charge of murder

 21

even though I killed three men. Don't ask why. Now I'm sitting here and I don't know what to do. I can't go home. Without a job, without money and without a face. No!", he said softly and took a deep breath. "Two men offered me a lot of money for a job that nobody wants to do. Both valued my skills, although they were the first time in my life. That confuses my senses. My path was always in one direction and I knew where I wanted to go. But now my path seems to be dividing and I no longer know what is right."

"What kind of job, Ryan?"

"Bounty hunter."

Ryan noticed his sister's startled look. He did not avoid.

"I have no choice, Carry. I will have to do it. This is my dance. If one day I no longer come home, you cancel my account and bring the money home. I had your name registered at the bank. Don't tell anyone about it. The less you know, the better for everyone."

Carry felt the big lump in her throat, which took her breath away and prevented her from speaking. Her eyes shone treacherously.

"I can't go back now. My life has become a struggle, a rodeo, my dance. Everything else is not in my hands."

Carry nodded bravely.

"I can understand you well. Take care of yourself, Mi-shunkala, my little brother. I will pray for you."

Ryan pulled the black backpack out of his travel bag and shoved the cash he had withdrawn over to Carry.

"Take what you need. Give the rest to mom."

Carry nodded. "Thank you."

"There is only dirty laundry in my pocket. Can I leave it here?"

"Of course. I also have some from you. You can take that

with you."

Ryan smiled weakly. "Everything that fits in my back-pack. I will hardly need more."

"Where will you live?"

Ryan shrugged. "Everywhere and nowhere. Can I use your phone? I don't have any more."

"Of course."

Ryan got up and went to the phone. The decision was made. His decision and it was not easy for him. Carry went next door to continue packing. Ryan stopped at the kitchen window and looked out. The children were still chasing the ball. He punched in the number on the slip of paper. A male voice answered immediately.

"Yes?"

"Ryan here", he said without hesitation.

"Oh! This is Thompson speaking. You've changed your mind? I'm glad to hear that!" Thompson's voice was actually pleased.

Ryan was surprised and not when he heard the black wolf on the other end of the line.

"Yes", he replied shortly.

"Good. Let's meet for a coffee."

"At the gas station at the Farmer Store."

Thompson laughed. "Okay. In two hours."

"I'll be there."

Ryan hung up and took a deep breath. His features were petrified. Lost in thought he watched the children play. Carry silently stepped behind her brother and put her hand on his shoulder. Slowly he turned to her.

"We will meet in two hours."

Carry tried to smile. "Your decision will be the right one, Ryan. Wherever your path goes one day he will take you home."

 23

Ryan took Carry in his arms and hugged her. She held him tight. It was good. Carry didn't dare tell him she was afraid for him. She said nothing. He knew it anyway.

Chapter 2
The Hunter

Ryan walked the way back on foot. Almost two hours without marching baggage was a no-brainer for him. He was wearing aviator glasses. The sun was shining. He was sweating. There was a constant coming and going at the gas station. A few men stood together, talking, drinking coffee, chewing fast food out of the cardboard. Ryan got coffee, sat in the shade on a curb and sipped it. The black backpack was stuck between his knees. Nobody noticed him. It seemed like someone had dropped him here. Ryan tore open a pack of cigarettes, put a box next to him and the rest away. He smoked almost motionless, his elbows on his knees. About fifteen minutes later a Dodge came up. Slowly he rolled over the asphalt and headed purposefully towards the man who was sitting alone on the curb. It was only when Thompson got out that Ryan got up. Thompson greeted. Ryan nodded to him.

"Jump in. We talk in the car."

Silently, Ryan grabbed the backpack and got in.

"I was pretty sure you were going to call me, Ryan Black Hawk", Thompson started.

"Not me", replied Ryan.

Thompson grinned. "Concerns?"

"No sir."

"You know what this is about?"

"You are looking for a bounty hunter. I don't work for the FBI."

Thompson laughed. "Not for the FBI, Ryan. For me."

Ryan looked skeptical at the black man in the gray suit.

"What's the matter?", Thompson asked.

"Okay. Talk", Ryan replied.

Thompson raised his eyebrows. The glasses of the rimless glasses shone.

"You are my man, my shadow wolf. Silent, fast and invisible. There are only two of us. Forget everything else. You only get your orders from me. You alone decide whether to accept or reject an order. From me you get a laptop and a cell phone with a special microchip. Tap-proof! This enables us to exchange all information, data, photos and so on quickly and easily, and above all without third-party access. As soon as you have accepted the order, you will delete the data. All information goes to me and only to me! In some cases, a meeting cannot be avoided, but it is always associated with a risk. You know. Questions?"

"I understand everything, Sir."

"Okay. Get fon with it. Your account will be checked sooner or later. It is extremely suspicious if no regular payments are made and then suddenly large sums of money come up in one fell swoop. Banks are obliged to report this. That's why I pay regularly. Charged after each order. I take care of licenses and equipment. Do you have a car?"

"No, I have not."

"It will be quite exhausting on foot and the FBI will not let you steal a second car."

Ryan's mouth twisted into a mocking grin.

"Are you sure?"

"No. I'm not sure", laughed Thompson.

Then he started his car. "Let's go shopping, Ryan. A warrior needs weapons and a war pony. Right?", he said as he drove the Dodge to interstate 44.

"If you want to send me to war, Thompson, yes."

"The war is always and everywhere and I'm up to both ears. A shitty job that nobody wants to do. The scoundrels not only wear jeans, but also suits and Rolex. But there are rules, Ryan", said Thompson and the smile faded from his face. "Let's see that we always get our ass out of the line of fire in time."

"Yes, Sir", replied Ryan

Thompson nodded in satisfaction.

*****

Baxter, who was usually in a good mood, slammed his apartment door angrily. He rumbled down the stairs like remote controlled. Panting, he went to his jeep, which was parked on the street. In his anger he neither noticed nor greeted the old lady who came towards him on the sidewalk. Rice had been bullying Baxter non-stop for the past two days. And Rice painted a pretty ugly picture at the former Indian Air Force Sergeant.

"I kill him!", Baxter growled.

Baxter hadn't heard or seen anything about Ryan himself since they fired him. He had just left and the connection was simply broken. That made Baxter angrier. He looked neither to the right nor to the left when he jumped into his Commander, cursing. Just when Baxter was sitting behind the steering-wheel he noticed that the sports car in front of him had obstructed him.

"Such an idiot!", Baxter swore. "I should be pushing you", he roared as he pushed open the driver's door. He would almost have crashed into the narrow figure that was directly in his way. Baxter froze, silent and mouth open, as if seeing a ghost. No word came over his lips.

"Hi Baxter. Everything okay with you?", Ryan asked.

"Where the hell are you coming from," Baxter snapped at him.

"From there", Ryan replied, gesturing with his thumb behind him.

Baxter took a step back and looked his friend up and down. Then he laughed forgivingly and slapped his arm in greeting with his paw. Ryan grimaced in pain.

"I see your head is still on top and everything's still on you. Nice to see you", said Baxter.

Ryan grinned.

"Look at this! What does a stupid think if he puts his show-off car right in front of the bumper of my Commander?", Baxter growled.

Ryan laughed amused.

"I don't know what to laugh about, my friend. Such a fool! Such a asshole, mental defective! Idiot, stupid! I would like to get in and go full throttle", Baxter snorted.

"Do you have to leave urgently, Baxter Bear?"

"What does it mean, urgently. I need to go shopping. My fridge is empty."

"Then it is urgent", said Ryan and offered Baxter a cigarette. "Here, take one! You are loaded like a powder keg. That's unhealthy."

"Hm", Baxter growled and took the cigarette.

"We smoke and then go shopping. I have time."

Baxter took a deep breath and rocked his head.

"Are you coming with me, Ryan?"

"Of course. My fridge is empty."

"Do you have one?"

Ryan laughed softly. "No. Maybe I can use yours."

"Good idea."

Then both were silent for a while.

"You suddenly disappeared without a trace. I really thou-

ght they still locked you up. Tell me."

"It's a long story, Baxter. I'll tell you afterwards if you have space for a mentally deficient, an idiot and a goofy man in your apartment."

Baxter slowly dropped his hand with the cigarette and stared at Ryan in disbelief. "I knew you were crazy...", Baxter shook his head and gave a skeptical look at the dark blue sports car. "That thing is yours?"

Ryan nodded.

Baxter threw his half-smoked cigarette to the floor and stubbed it out with the shoe. Then he crept around the car like a fox around the prey.

"The door is open", said Ryan.

Baxter really looked like a grizzly next to the Corvette. He opened the door and stuck his head inside the car. Then he squeezed into the driver's seat. "Is this shoe box also available two sizes larger?"

"No. But that has the advantage that I can carry the Corvette under my arm in an emergency", Ryan noted. "And it also fits perfectly, almost everywhere." Baxter laughed. His anger was gone. "The little one has a hell of a lot of horses under the hood. If they bolt with you, you lose grip. Where did you steal the thing?"

"From the FBI."

That amused Baxter. He laughed raucousing.

"Aren't their cars black?"

"Camouflage", countered Ryan.

Baxter shook his head again. He struggled out of the driver's seat.

"It's new, isn't it?", Baxter finally said softly to Ryan.

"Yes."

"What the hell are you up to? This way you can't show up on the reservation."

"I'll tell you afterwards."

"Then let's finally go shopping. I'm bursting with curiosity!"

Ryan grinned and rolled his new sports car forward.
Then he climbed into the commander.

*****

The test drive that evening had to be. Baxter couldn't
resist his friend's offer to drive the Corvette. He drove
west on the I 90. The district, Black Hawk, was a bit
outside and was part of Rapid City. Baxter had long
urged Ryan to finally get to know Olivia. The opportunity
was favorable. The deep June sun blinded their eyes.

"When Olivia is not at church rehearsal, she is probably
crouching in front of the TV and watching bloodthirsty
thrillers. Then she can't go back to sleep and calls me in
the middle of the night because a wooden plank has
cracked, Baxter laughed.

Ryan smiled.

"Tell me now", Baxter urged.

Ryan reported on Taylor's orders, Mitchell and
Rodriguez, the trap in the bush and his escape. Baxter
seemed to be speechless because he was silent. Ryan
further reported that he had faced Taylor and also from
his first encounter with Thompson. "You know the rest
of the story. Barkley dishonorably fired me from the U.S.
Air Force and Taylor was silent."

Baxter swore. "I never really knew that your job as a
driver was so dangerous, Ryan. Not even when I polished
the first scratch from the black paint."

"Then be careful, Baxter, what I'm going to tell you
now." Ryan talked about Sam and the gun shop, Thomp-

son and his new job. Baxter listened carefully. When Ryan finished, Baxter blew his cheeks up and blew out the pent-up air.

"Carry and you, you are the only one who knows. Carry will be silent."

Baxter turned his head to Ryan. "That's crazy! That's totally crazy. I can also be silent. Now the sewer rat's gonna be scared shitless. They won't have a chance to escape from you."

"Underestimating your opponents can be your undoing. It's getting tough. As Thompson said, a shitty job nobody wants to do."

"Call me if you're in a fix again."

"Do you know what you're getting into, Bax?"

"Rodeo. Bronc, bareback."

Ryan laughed softly. "No concerns?"

"I think so, but I'm serious!", Baxter said.

"We'll see."

Baxter turned onto Memory Lane and stopped right in front of Olivia Goodman's house.

"Here we are", Baxter said.

"And? What do you say to my war pony?"

"I actually like the little one. It is well on curves, has power and has not stuttered once."

Ryan smiled. "It's a *She*."

Baxter chuckled.

He was still laughing when he got out and knocked on the door. A small, well-rounded lady opened.

"Hallelujah! What do my old, tired eyes see! Is it really you or am I dreaming?"

Olivia Goodman grabbed Baxter, she only reached up to his shoulders, and wrapped her arms around his body.

"Hello mom!"

Baxter raised her and whirled her around his own axis. Olivia giggled unabashedly. Ryan watched them grinning. Baxter took Olivia off after a while.

"May I introduce! This is my friend, Ryan Black Hawk. Ryan, this is the craziest woman in the world I know: Olivia Goodman."

"Oh! Good evening young man!", she exclaimed joyfully. Turning to Baxter, she said softly: "My goodness! He looks good. You should have let me know beforehand. Then I would have made myself chic."

"You're chic enough, mom. Also your nightgown."

"Beast!" Olivia hissed and punched Baxter.

"Come in! I am happy to finally get to know you. I'm Olivia", she said.

"Good evening, Mrs. Goodman."

"Olivia. Only Olivia. I bet you both haven't had dinner yet. Follow me!"

With big steps she went ahead to the kitchen, which was separated from the living room by a counter. In front of it were a few stools. She immediately opened the fridge. Ryan looked questioningly at Baxter. He just waved it off.

"Is it true? Are you a race car driver?", Olivia asked.

Ryan looked at Baxter again questioningly.

"For sure! The best in the world, Olivia", replied Baxter instead of Ryan.

"I never thought that the Air Force would also employ race car drivers. Nothing is impossible. My little one has always raved about car racing. Even when he was still..."

"Olivia! It's enough", Baxter interrupted.

"I kept telling him that it was far too dangerous", she continued undeterred. "But he didn't want to listen."

"Olivia. I am not a race car driver I'm a mechanic. That is a considerable difference and completely harmless. Ryan is not in the Air Force. He drives ... ehm ... freelance."

"But didn't you tell me that you two met at the Air Force?" Olivia doubted and looked at the two young men with wide eyes.

"That was almost four years ago."

"What? Such a long time? They almost starved you!" Baxter laughed.

Ryan was still silent.

"Okay, we have beef, bacon, red beans, corn... what do you think about Texas Pan?"

"Sounds good. Do it", Baxter said.

Olivia noisily pulled a pan out of the cupboard. Then she set up four beer cans in front of her guests.

"Cheers you two."

"Do you have a coke for me?", Ryan asked.

"Are you sick, boy", she asked in astonishment.

"We are traveling by car."

Olivia nodded and gave Ryan a coke.

"Thanks", said Ryan.

"Hopefully you don't want to leave immediately after eating?"

"Depends on how we endure", Baxter laughed.

Olivia shook her head as she added the ingredients to the hot pan. It sizzled immediately, then smelled. Ryan watched the small woman with the deep voice, who accompanied her words gesticulating with her big knife. He actually didn't know many white women, but he thought Olivia was exceptional. He opened the Coke and drank.

Olivia began to rave about the years when Baxter was a child. She told what a talented boy he was and who took responsibility in the house since his father disappeared. Baxter seemed embarrassed. Finally, he interrupted her.

"It's enough, Olivia. Nobody cares."

She sighed and smiled. "By the way, do you know that he can also sew buttons, bake cakes and cook? That can never harm a confident young man." Olivia looked at Ryan and seemed to be waiting for an answer.

"Yes, he can cook perfectly", he confirmed.

Olivia showed a satisfied smile.

When the food was on the table, she said a prayer. "Thank you for what you gave us and thank you for sending me Ryan. I ask you, Lord, that you never let my two boys go hungry and protect us that we can get together again at this table. Amen."

"Amen", Baxter growled and put the spoon in the food on his plate. "Hallelujah! Is that hot."

Carefully, Ryan pushed the steaming food apart. It smelled delicious, but he preferred not to burn himself.

"Wait! I put it in the fridge for a moment."

"Olivia! You don't have to mother Ryan. He'll be fine on his own", Baxter said gruffly.

"Stupid nonsense! I mother who I want."

Ryan grinned.

"And that's pretty much all", Baxter growled.

Ryan started eating slowly. He wasn't hungry but didn't want to offend Olivia. After eating half the plate, he had enough. It was just too much.

"You don't like it?"

"Very good, for sure. Thank you."

Olivia eyed him as if she expected him to say something else. Ryan said nothing.

"You don't like talking, do you?"

Baxter took turns peering at him and her.

"What would you like to hear, Olivia?", Ryan asked.

"Tell me about you, your family and your interesting

job."

"I'm a Lakota. My family lives in the Pine Ridge Reservation. We breed horses. When I was fourteen I got my first car. We drove street races. Illegal. I was the best in every way. I fought for more than two years to be accepted. I wanted to be a warrior like my grandfather, Black Hawk. I even think this part of the city was named after him", Ryan smiled. "But times had changed. I learned to smoke and drink like a man and smuggled drugs into the reservation. I had achieved everything I wanted. But was that what I wanted? Then, one day two of my friends died in a car accident, drunken, and burned with their car. This shook myself awake. They had brought me home shortly before. I was drunk too, so I couldn't even stand by myself anymore. My father would have killed me that night if my mother hadn't been there. I had lost my face. That night I decided to change my life. That's why I went to the US Air Force. They trained me and gave me a job. My life is a dance and the dance is our ritual. Rituals are our life. I don't want to forget that I'm a Lakota."

Baxter had forgotten to chew while listening to Ryan carefully. His mouth remained open. He stared at his friend with large, round eyes as if he was seeing him for the first time.

"Ah, I understand now", said Olivia.

Whatever Olivia thought she understood, she smiled warmly. "If you want you can visit me at any time, Ryan. My door is always open to you. I have food and always a place to sleep."

Ryan nodded. "Thank you, Olivia. I appreciate it."

Baxter let the pent-up air out of his lungs, raised his eyebrows and scraped the rest of the beans off the plate.

Ryan's cell phone reported a message. While he was reading, two curious pairs of eyes watched him. He put it back without a comment.

"When?", Baxter asked.

"Tomorrow."

Both Baxter and Olivia breathed a sigh of relief.

*****

The sun blinded the eyes. Despite the sunglasses, Ryan lowered the sun visor. He dropped Baxter off at Ellsworth Air Force Base just in time for duty. Now that he was alone in the car, Ryan turned up the radio. With his hand he tapped the steering wheel in time. His destination was Pierre, the capital of South Dakota. Ryan had well memorized the data that had already been deleted. Male, eighteen, colored, black, countless thefts and robberies, weapons unknown. Ryan's search started in one part of town that is best avoided. Gray walls of winding row houses lined the street. A queasy feeling warned Ryan to be careful. The Corvette stood out here. The people loitering here stared involuntarily at the sports car. Ryan was unable to choke his feeling. But that was his mission, his job and it was the beginning. Ryan had no choice.

"Damned!", he hissed softly and looked around. The street was the right one. He just had to find the house. Finally, he stopped behind a rusted mini-van. Ryan put the gun in his jeans and got out. People were watching him. Nobody spoke to him. Ryan entered the house whose address he had been given by Thompson. The hallway was dark and dirty. It stank penetratingly. Ryan went quickly to the stairs and silently jumped up the steps to the second floor. He read the name tags on the apartment doors. Some had none. Slowly he followed his instinct and listened. His thoughts were with the people who had left the reservation, hoping that they would be better off in the city. But the slums were the end of civilization and order. These people fought a hopeless battle for respect and dignity. Most lost, gave up, killed themselves or each other. A vicious circle. Wherever there was not enough for life, theft was part of the struggle for survival. Ryan knocked on the apartment door number ten twenty-three. After knocking a second time, he heard shuffling steps. A woman in a nightgown and dressing gown blinked at him wearily from puffy eyes.

"What up?", she said irritably with a heavy tongue, as if she were drunk.

"Where's Jacob?"

"Who wants to know that?"

"I want to know", replied Ryan.

"Are you a cop?"

"No."

"Killer?"

"No."

"A friend?"

"You could say it like this. Where is he?"

At the same instant, a dark figure hurried through the apartment behind the woman. Ryan slipped between the woman and the half-open door into the apartment.

"Jacob!", he shouted.

He didn't answer. Ryan saw the young man fleeing out the window. He disappeared over the fire escape. Ryan followed him. Jacob was clever and quick. He did not seem to do that for the first time. Only this time he had underestimated his opponents. When Jacob jumped off the ladder onto the asphalt, another hit him with great force. Both fell. Jacob groaned. Ryan put his knee in his back and let click the handcuffs. Jacob swore. Then Ryan pulled him up with a jerk and pushed him against the wall.

"Hey man! What kind of fucking cop are you! I didn't do anything!"

"Then you must have a damn bad memory", Ryan replied. "You'll come with me!"

Ryan pulled his arm. The young man was just as tall as he and athletic in nature. He made no move to fight back. Instead he kept talking constantly to Ryan.

"It wasn't me. Believe me. I just slipped in there and they grabbed me."

Ryan didn't answer.

"Hey. Who are you? Are you one of Kinley's workers?"

Ryan dragged Jacob with him until the Corvette appeared. A whole pack of youngsters surrounded the sports car. Even when they saw the two men coming, they made no move to disappear. They felt strong. They were in the majority. Ryan went on without hesitation.

"Get out of here!"

They answered with laughter and cool sayings.

"I would also like to drive such a thing."

"Hey, where did you steal it, Bro?"

"Let's drive a lab?"

"Hey, don't be a drag, come on."

Ryan drew the pistol, pressed it to Jacob's temple and said softly: "Call 'em back!"

Jacob swallowed.

"Hey guys. Move out of the way. Get out of here."

 38

His voice suddenly sounded strangely shrill.

"If that's a cop, he can't shoot you. Stay cool man."

"This is not a cop. Buzz off", Jacob screeched.

"All right."

The teenagers raised their hands and finally stepped back. Ryan roughly pushed Jacob into the passenger seat and slammed the door. He held the pistol in his hand as he jumped into the Corvette and started. Jacob stared at him.

"Hey man, are you Indian?"

Ryan nodded.

"I didn't steal anything, damn it. Why you don't believe me. The cops are after me because I'm black!"

"I'm not interested. Tell that in courthouse", Ryan said unimpressed.

Jacob kept talking constantly to Ryan. Ryan said nothing. He did not get involved in a conversation and did not show that it worked him up.

Ryan only took his handcuffs off in the police station. An officer took Jacob into custody. Ryan had the reception acknowledged and left. The handcuffs clinked softly against each other with every step. From now on they were part of Ryan's equipment. Ryan smiled bitterly because he understood Jacob's world only too well. From now on he stood on the other side and represented law and order. Ryan got into the Corvette and sent a message to Thompson. Then he started the engine and stuck a cigarette between his lips. His way took him back to Rapid City, straight to Samuel G.A. Williams business.

*****

 39

Ryan parked in front of the rolling gate. Then he went to the entrance of the shop. Two men stood with their backs to the window and talked to the old man. Ryan stopped in front of the barred shop window and watched everything. Then he went inside. He just greeted with a nod and seemed to be interested in the display in the locked glass cabinet. He happened to be able to hear the conversation. These two guys were hard to impress with Sam's advice. At some point they finally reached a deal and presented their papers. Sam shook his head grimly when they finally closed the door behind them.

"They're not all as trusting as you are", Sam laughed croakily. "Hello Ryan. Good to see you. What brings you by?"

"Hello Sam. I need another one."

Ryan put the Glock on the counter. The old man raised his eyebrows and looked at Ryan. "You're taking me to hell's kitchen", he said softly. Then he laughed amused.

"How do you know Thompson?", Ryan asked.

Sam laughed again and coughed. "So you were with him?"

"We met."

"And now you're working for him", Sam noted.

Ryan said nothing. He still seemed to be waiting for an answer from the old one. Sam, on the other hand, seemed to enjoy torturing him.

"Follow me."

Sam picked out some boxes. "Everyone has their preferences. Those of the police attach great importance to things that a private individual would never think of. Then there are some, professionals, after all, who have a clue, but prefer to avoid police weapons."

Sam opened the box and showed Ryan the gun. They were like one another. Ryan nodded in satisfaction. "I'll take this one."

"Did you get a license from Thompson?"

"Yes."

"Then everything is correct. I'll put them on his bill."

"Where do you know him from?", Ryan asked Sam a second time and a little sharper.

"A good choice."

Sam laughed. "He is an old friend of mine. One of them which you can rely on without exception and one of my best customers. But the ones he catches he takes them hard. He doesn't know any friends. Do you understand? They didn't deserve it any other way."

Ryan took the Glock.

"How many bounty hunters does he have?"

"I don't know." Samuel Williams turned and walked slowly back to the shop. Ryan followed.

"Who asks too much lives dangerously and usually not for long."

This time Ryan laughed. "And those who don't ask don't get an answer and living is always dangerous."

"You are right. You talk like an old hand, but you're still so young, Ryan. You could be my grandson. Ammunition?"

"Yes."

Ryan packed everything in his backpack. "Bye, Sam."

"All right", Sam replied and raised his hand in greeting. "May the lord protect you, my boy", he added so quietly that he hardly heard it himself.

*****

Baxter crossed the elbows on the counter and laughed out loud while his friend Jimmy Boy told.

"Two like us are sitting in the pub drinking a beer."

"Several!", Baxter threw in.

"Certainly! One was red, I mean the hair. The other had none. *God didn't want to give you any hair or did he have none left for you?,* asked the red-haired man. Then the bald man said: *Yes, but he only had red ones and I didn't want them.*

"Jimmy Boy!" Baxter laughed with tears in his eyes and patted him on the shoulder. He was a head smaller than Baxter and looked like half a portion against his bearded stature.

"I'll buy you another beer. Dian!"

Dian also laughed and filled two large glasses for the two.

"A guy comes in. Something like me and orders a huge portion of food", Baxter said.

"Just like you?", Jimmy interrupted and laughed.

"Right! And outside in the parking lot is a super truck with chrome trim. An ocean liner is a paddle boat against it, I tell you."

"And then?", Jimmy asked.

"The pub is full of bikers in leather clothes."

"Pub?", Dian asked indignantly.

"Restaurant."

"You're exaggerating", she said flattered.

"Hm", Baxter growled meekly.

"And what about the bikers?"

"If you'd shut up, I could tell you. So the guy, the trucker, pound down. After all, the man is hungry. The bikers next to him start to make fun of him. Someone accidentally hits him with the elbow against the fork, causing his food to fall down. He ignores it freezing cold and keeps eating. Another squirts ketchup from his bottle against his chest." Baxter grinned.

Dian and Jimmy looked at him expectantly.

"He calmly takes a napkin and wipes it off. Then he continues to eat as if nothing had happened. Even he doesn't seem to hear the swear words. With a mild smile, he pays his bill and leaves. The laughter breaks out when he was outside. *Hey, what kind of sissy was that?,* blaspheme the bikers. Dian, now it's your turn."

"But I don't know the man at all", she said in surprise.

"Right! The host said that too. And: *but he can't drive a truck anyway. He just rolled over a whole row of motorcycles while driving away.*"

Baxter, Jimmy and Dian burst out laughing at the same time.

"You have to imagine the faces", Jimmy croaked.

Baxter grabbed for the beer glass.

"Where did you leave your Indian friend?"

"He's now self-employed with his taxi company and constantly on the move."

"Well, he dares something. As a White one that's not without its dangers, but as a Red one it's almost suicidal."

"Oh, he mainly transports animals for the zoo. Oxen, pigs, donkeys, camels, rhinos and what else belongs behind bars."

Jimmy stared at Baxter in disbelief. He seemed to doubt his words.

"I swear. It's the truth", said Baxter, raising his right hand.

Jimmy shook his head. "Greet him from me when you see him. I like this guy."

 43

"I do", Baxter said.

"Dian! Two whiskey for my little friend here and for me. Do you drink one with us, sweet heart? I invite you."

Dian smiled. "Thank you Baxter. I better get a coffee."

As she poured, Baxter asked: "Don't you know a story too, Dian?"

"Let me think about. So... two drunk guys leave my truck stop."

"I hope you don't mean us!", Jimmy interrupted.

"Nonsense!" Baxter said. "Have we ever been drunk?"

Dian giggled and continued: "They staggered across the parking lot and looked for their car. When they found one who looked like yours, the key didn't fit. *Such a crap! Now we have to walk,* I heard him swearing. So they started walking around in circles and always around the car. A highway patrol stopped and asked what they were doing. One said that they were on their way home and got lost. Then the other said: *come on, my friend, we are going back again. I remembered the way.*"

Baxter, Jimmy and Dian laughed. Then they raised the glasses. "Before the whiskey gets too warm, it tastes like horse piss."

"Have you ever tried them?", Jimmy asked.

"Do I look like this? I don't even have a horse."

"Then how do you want to know?"

"Is such a saying from Ryan."

"Oh, I thought he didn't drink something like that?"

"I didn't say he drinks that either, Jimmy Boy. Pay attention, I'll tell you something. A white tourist in Pine Ridge asks a local when he could normally see Indians dancing with feather headdress. *Usually after about five to six whiskey*, he replied."

Jimmy grinned, then laughed. "This one, I think, Is from

Ryan?"

Baxter nodded. "Cheers!"

The door opened and a group of five men in checkered shirts, jeans and cowboy hats came through the door. When they spotted Baxter and Jimmy, they headed for the two and greeted each other.

"Hi! You guys want to go for a game of pool?"

"Of course, why not", Baxter said.

"Don't tear the table open again, like last time", Dian warned.

"Joe is not here. He's tearing up something else tonight, sweetie." The guys laughed. "... and bumps into others."

Dian rolled her eyes and shook her head.

*****

The sun sent warm rays from the cloudless sky. The trees on the side of the road provided shade. Some cars parked there. It was exceptionally quiet that morning, in the neighborhood where a certain General Major Barkley lived. Ryan pressed his lips together and got out of the car. He tried in vain to erase Barkley from his memory. There was a large garden in front of each house. A sprinkler system that someone had probably forgotten to shut down, sprayed. In blue jeans, sleeveless shirt and sneakers Ryan jumped over the curb. He was wearing his pilot glasses and a black cowboy hat. It was a rather idiosyncratic combination, it seemed. He did not avoid the water from the sprinkler. Ryan rang at the front door and waited. When nothing moved, he rang a second time. Nobody seemed to be there. He waited. With one leap he finally jumped over the fence to get behind the house. He found himself in a large garden with a short lawn in lush green. A woman lying in a deck chair by the pool had her eyes closed as if she were sleeping. The pale-skinned woman was no longer a young thing. Her hair was almost as red as the bikini she was wearing. Countless freckles adorned the nose and cheeks. Startled, she flinched and stared at the stranger with wide eyes. Ryan was ready to put his hand on her mouth, but she didn't scream.

"Who are you and what's the meaning of this?", she hissed.

Ryan stood up. "Hawk, Madam. I need to speak to your husband."

The woman pushed the sunglasses up and eyed the intruder skeptically. "And why don't you use the front door like every normal visitor?", she asked not un-pleasantly.

"I tried that. Nobody opened it", Ryan smiled.

"Do you have an appointment?"

"No. I love surprises."

The woman smiled strangely at Ryan as she slipped the sunglasses over her head so that she served as a hair clip.

"Is Mr. Homes in the house?"

"My husband will come home soon."

"I'm waiting", Ryan decided. He settled on a white stone by the pool and calmly pulled a cigarette out of the box. The woman leaned back in the chair. She was still looking at the stranger who had entered her property.

"You are a brazen burglar. Do you know that? I could scream for help."

"Correct, Madam." Ryan smiled charmingly.

"Do you work for him?"

"No."

"What do you want from him?"

"He missed an important date."

The woman straightened up in the chair and put her feet on the floor.

"Are you from the police?", she asked skeptically.

"No, madam."

"For whom do you work?"

Ryan noticed the fear in her eyes. Her voice became uncertain and harsh. Slowly he pulled on his cigarette and blew smoke through the narrow crack of his lips. He didn't think about answering her question.

"He is not here and I won't tell you anything", she said defiantly.

Ryan nodded. "I know."

Undeterred he continued to smoke. The woman felt for the phone. Ryan watched that.

"You know he's in trouble."

"Three months ago, he was arrested in his office. It was an embarrassing mistake. He was released the next day."

"Yes. On bail", Ryan nodded.

The last drop of blood seemed to be leaving the woman's already pale face. She stared stunned at Ryan and held the phone in her hand.

"You know what that means. Where is he now?"

"On business. Since yesterday evening. I do not know where he goes. He doesn't talk to me about it. John is a businessman. He didn't do anything to anyone."

"Then nothing will happen to him."

Ryan pulled the cigarette one last time and stubbed it out on the stone. Slowly he got up and turned to go.

"His office is on eighth Ave", she said flatly.

Ryan turned again. "Really?", he asked and smiled.

The woman stared at Ryan, speechless.

 47

Ryan's path led him to the address Thompson had sent him. *Johns Car Service-sales, repairs and car service* was on the billboard at interstate 44 in Rapid City. Ryan knew he wouldn't find John here, but he hoped for information. What Mrs. Holmes had told him didn't really help a headhunter. Ryan headed straight to the open workshop door and started a little small talk with the men. They seemed pleased with the variety and were actually impressed with Ryan's knowledge of vehicles. Therefore, they willingly answered his questions. Ryan learned that the boss had gone to Denver last night.

"He usually sends one of us to get the rental cars back", said one of the young men, shrugging his shoulders. "But he's the boss."

Ryan laughed softly. "Don't you need a car transporter to do this?"

The man nodded.

"One of this he has. I also told him that I would come to help him. I mean, Holmes is more of a theorist."

The men laughed.

"When did it start?"

"Around five last evening."

"Then he could be back here around four today", Ryan affirmed.

"Not John Holmes. He is rarely at work before ten o'clock. He won't be finished loading before noon", grinned the man who answered him.

"And then he will surely go to lunch with his business partner. Before two there is no wheel moving on the truck", the other laughed.

"Can I contact Holmes by phone?", Ryan asked.

"For sure. You can call from the office. Susan is in there.

She has the number."

Ryan thanked him and headed straight to the office.

"Hi. What can I do for you?", the young woman asked gently as she looked up from the desk.

"Hi. I need to speak to Mr. Holmes urgently. The boys outside told me he's in Denver and you, Susan, could call him there."

The young woman smiled. "Of course, Sir."

Ryan nodded with a smile.

"Just a moment please. I'll try it."

"Thank you very much."

Ryan turned his back to the reception counter and leaned on it with his elbows. While Susan was connecting to Denver, Ryan looked around the office. It was relatively small and primitive. Two advertising posters and a large calendar adorned the light gray wall. The air was stuffy. Susan's floral perfume smelled weakly on Ryan's nose.

"Mister Baker is on the line. This is our business partner in Denver", Ryan heard Susan's voice and turned around.

"Thank you", he said and took the phone.

"Hello, Mister Baker. My name is Hawk and I'm in John Holmes office. He must have forgotten our appointment. Is it possible to speak to him?"

"No, unfortunately not. He is already on the way."

"With the car transporter, I hope."

"No. With a rental car. The van is on the courtyard."

"Loaded?"

"May I ask who you are and if you work for John?"

"I'm his business partner and I'm urgently waiting for the rental cars he wants to bring me", Ryan replied indignantly.

Susan looked up in surprise and gave Ryan a questioning

look.

"I'm sorry. He said he had an important appointment."

"That can happen, but he should have contacted me by phone."

Ryan heard Baker take a deep breath on the other end.

"Do you know where he went?"

"He just said downtown", Baker replied irritably.

"Denver? When?"

"Hm. About an hour ago."

Ryan checked his watch. It was just a quarter past ten in the morning.

"Maybe he has a cell phone?"

"It's possible."

"I got the number", Susan interfered.

Ryan nodded. "Okay. What car and what license plate?"

"Are you from the police?" The man at the other end of the line asked in amazement.

"No. I just urgently need my cars."

"Uhhh ...", Baker hissed into the receiver. "Okay. He has a silver-gray Chrysler that is currently licensed in New Mexico", the man replied.

"Do you have a pen and paper for me?", Ryan whispered.

Susan gave him a pen and notepad.

"Okay. I hear."

Ryan wrote the license plate down and thanked him. Then he hung up, tore the sheet off and put it in. Susan gave him her boss's cell phone number.

"Thank you Susan", said Ryan and went to the door.

"No problem. I'm glad I could help you."

Ryan turned around and gave Susan a smile before leaving.

"Goodbye", Susan said as the door closed behind him.

"And?", the men asked when they saw Ryan.

"Your boss has just exchanged the truck for a silver-gray Chrysler."

"How boring. I would have taken this one", said one of the men.

Ryan laughed. "The Corvette?"

"Well ..."

"I like the pickup truck over there much better. I'll trade the Corvette for it at some point", Ryan meant.

The men laughed with amusement. Ryan said goodbye. He had to hurry. Holmes was definitely on his way to Mexico, Ryan thought. When Ryan was on the highway, he called Thompson.

"What's up?" he asked.

"He drove one of his car transporters to Denver yester-day to get four rental cars back. The transporter is currently standing on the courtyard, while our bird has been traveling with a silver-gray Chrysler for about an hour. Do you think what I think?"

"He wants to go to the Mexican border and he has an inconspicuous car and surely a random choice of number plates. I inform the boys at the border."

"Okay. Send me a usable photo of him and by the way, I will get in trouble with the highway patrol."

Thompson laughed softly into the receiver.

"You have permission to fly, Falcon. I'll handle it."

"Okay. I will get in touch."

"Okay", Thompson answered too.

Ryan put the phone away and accelerated.

At one hundred and sixty miles an hour, he stayed in the fast lane. He was amazed at the power that was in the engine of the small sports car and no less that no patrol car had yet discovered him. Ryan smiled when he felt a feeling of freedom that he had never felt before. It was completely different from the feeling of the illegal car racing he had driven. It was different from when he was on the Air Force. It reminded Ryan of the times when he raced out into the grasslands with his black stallion. He gradually liked Thompson, who granted him freedom of action and his influence on the system that the young Lakota had previously only patronized. Ryan's thoughts returned to his assignment. If there was a chance to put Holmes before the border, it was this. Ryan was calling.

"Jumper here. Where does the air burn?"

"Maybe in El Paso. I need your help."

"Truckers call via radio. Help me for a moment, my friend."

"Sergeant Black Hawk out of service. The one with the small, black high-gloss truck without civil radio."

"Ah! Now I know who you are. Without you and your lighter, I would have had to chew the tobacco out of my cigarettes." Jumper laughed loudly into the receiver. In the background Ryan heard the deep hum of the engine. "I'm glad to hear from you. I almost didn't believe it anymore. How can I help you my friend?"

"Where are you?"

"I'm just about a hundred miles southwest of Amarillo toward Roswell, New Mexico. And you?"

"I'm just outside Denver with my nose to El Paso. I have to catch someone before he crosses the Mexican border. But I can't make it anymore. Not even with my Corvette. The lead is too big. Can I send the data and the photo of the guy to your cell phone?"

"That's fine. Listen, I'm giving it to the boys who are floating around in this area. Is he a friend or foe?"

"Bail jumper."

"Wow! Are you no longer with the Air Force, Falcon? You became a bounty hunter. Crazy! You have to tell me in more detail. If we have set up the guy, we'll smoke one together. Do I have your word on it"

"Of course you have."

Jumper laughed.

Ryan sent the data to him. Then he put the cell phone in the holder on the dashboard, started and accelerated.

*****

The man who was sitting in the silver-gray Chrysler was driving at permissible speed. Holmes didn't want to attract attention. Restlessness tormented him and made his heart beat faster. He hardly took any notice of the trucks that were driving in front of and behind him. They belonged to the highways like heaven to earth. El Paso was in front of Holmes and it was only a few miles to the border. He had friends in Mexico who were waiting for him. Holmes smiled smugly. In front of the Chrysler, one of the trucks flashed and switched in the fast lane. Holmes took his foot off the gas and also switched in the fast lane. But the seemingly faster truck right in front of him stayed at the same speed as the one he wanted to overtake.

"Idiot!", Holmes swore and honked.

He switched back to the right lane. For a moment, Holmes thought of dodging on the shoulder. But he was startled when a truck suddenly passed him on the right. Holmes snorted angrily. He still thought the guy was annoyed by his two colleagues, whose trucks were slowing down. But all three remained, like a wall, in front of Holmes. They braked. Holmes swore. Drops of sweat appeared on his forehead. The highway ahead was blocked. Holmes honked several times. Without success. His panicked view was looking for a way out of the trap. He looked behind him confidently and braked until the Chrysler came to a stop. He quickly shifted into reverse to be able to turn. The three trucks in front of him were already there. But also the trucks that were driving behind him had come dangerously close. They braked and stopped on either side of Holmes' car. He swore again. Drops of sweat were already running down his neck as he tried to turn with trembling hands. Three more trucks braked behind the Chrysler and blocked him from every possible way out. Holmes still believed in an insane joke from the truckers who blocked the highway every now and then for whatever protests. He went out of the car. Maybe he could talk to the men. But when he saw himself surrounded by at least eight men at that moment, his voice failed. Holmes cleared his throat.

"Hi guys. Do you have a problem?", he finally croaked.

The men laughed.

"No, we don't, but you!", one of them replied.

Holmes suddenly felt the heat that shot through his body and the weakness in his knees. "If you were kind enough to share a highway with me, gentlemen, my problem would be solved."

The men laughed again in a way that Holmes didn't like.

"Of course. The highway is not just ours. As soon as our bunny arrives, he is free again and the river of metal behind us can roll on", a long guy with a bull neck and broad shoulders grinned. Holmes looked small, dainty and inferior. And that's how he felt. Some of the men dug out cigarettes and started smoking. Holmes looked at the watch for the second time.

"How long will it take? I have a very important appoint-ment", asked Holmes.

"Stay cool, Buddy."

"If you are scared, we will accompany you personally to your important appointment", said another. "And what puppet says is law. We can attest to that."

Laughter was spreading.

Holmes snorted impatiently. That was anything but a joke. While Holmes was doggedly looking for an escape, he heard uncompromising honking. Two of the trucks made room for a car transporter.

"Hey, bunny!", the men joyfully called out and raised their hands in greeting.

Holmes watched it suspiciously. A slim guy with a dark blonde curly head got out of his truck.

"Hi guys! I heard there was a car broken down."

Holmes slowly went to his car and sat in the driver's seat. He took the pistol out of the glove compartment, shoved it into his pocket and made a call. Ron Cortez voice answered immediately. Holmes briefly reported his predicament as he watched the men. They didn't seem to be taking notes from him at the moment.

"Comprende Amigo. I'll be right there", Cortez replied with his unmistakable Mexican accent.

John breathed a sigh of relief. Cortez. Damn, there were only twelve miles left!

*****

Ryan seemed to be flying the Corvette across the highway. He was able to test the sports car to its limits almost unpunished. Thompson had given free flight permission. Ryan was almost there. He left the highway

five miles before El Paso to avoid the traffic jam. The side street was free. There was no traffic jam. Ryan doubted for a moment. Maybe Holmes had won and he screwed things up. The cell phone was buzzing. Ryan pressed the speaker. Neither Jumper nor Thompson answered.

"Hi, Falcon. This is Bunny talking. I have your rat on my tow truck. We are waiting for you, last parking lot on the highway before El Mechico. The highway is clear and clean again."

"Wow! I will soon be there."

Ryan twisted the corners of his mouth and hit the accelerator fully. The cell phone buzzed again.

"Yes?"

"Jumper here. My boys are great, aren't they?", laughed Jumper.

"Oh yes, they are", Ryan confirmed.

"I'm approaching with my truck. I have about eleven miles to the parking lot. See you soon, my friend!"

"See you soon, Jumper."

Three minutes later, Ryan pulled into the parking lot. He headed for the group of men who had gathered between the trucks. They cheered uncontrollably when Ryan got out of the Corvette. He smiled and greeted. Ten men greeted the Lakota in their middle as if it were an old friend they had been waiting for. The yellow-blue car transporter was immediately noticed by Ryan. The silver-gray Chrysler was properly loaded.

"So you're Hawk Jumper spoke of."

Ryan nodded. "Yes, I am."

"I'm Bunny and this is my son, Dan. We drive the truck. And this one", Bunny thumbed to the men, "these are my friends: Tedd, Cloud, Fluff, LG, Bump, Dummy, Doll and Screw loose."

The men laughed.

"By the way, LG is a full blood Choctow. His name is unspeakable. Welcome to our family."

"Nice to meet you guys and thank you for your help", replied Ryan. "Where's John Holmes?"

"He lies in his car and takes a nap. He didn't want to admit that he had a breakdown. Then he started to argue with a gun. Before the cops could become suspicious, LG kicked it out of his hand, Bump caught it and Fluff removed the magazine. Well, things like that sometimes develop a spontaneous life of their own."

Ryan grinned.

"I hope the guy doesn't sue us. Doll wasn't particularly fond of him when he laid him flat. Holmes has a huge bump."

The men laughed and Ryan with them. He liked the conspiratorial gang. They were rough, but honest. Then Ryan went to the truck and climbed up. Through the tinted windows he saw the man lying inside. Holmes seemed to be coming back to reality from his dreams and was moving. Ryan reached for the door opener, but the door was locked.

"Better safe than sorry", Bunny yelled.

"Hey, catch it!", LG called and threw the key to Ryan.

Holmes again sensed an escape opportunity. When Ryan opened the car door, he kicked against it from the inside with full force. Ryan was thrown a bit backwards with the door, but stayed on the loading space of the car carrier. Holmes jumped out, stumbled, caught himself again, and swiftly balanced past the car to the rear. The truckers had crossed their arms and watched the spectacle. There was still no reason to intervene. Ryan, who immediately slammed the door shut, quickly caught up with him. He grabbed the fleeing man by the neck and turned him around with a swing, so that he landed roughly with his chest and chin on the rear of the car. The dull thump let the truckers pull the air through their teeth. Ryan handcuffed Holmes before he was able to do anything about it.

"Looks like you're not fast enough for me", Ryan said.

"I want to talk to my lawyer right away", grunted Holmes.

Ryan grabbed Holmes and pulled him to his feet. The truckers applauded.

"Are you crazy!", Holmes shrieked when he saw the tips of his shoes over the loading space.

"Come on sweetheart, cut me a break", shouted Doll and positioned himself right below the nervous man. "It is not that high."

His own scream followed Holmes down. Puppet, the strong man with the bull's neck, caught Holmes. The laughter flared up again when he put the much smaller man down on the asphalt with care and straightened his jacket.

"You are crazy! All of you! You belong in...."

Holmes didn't get any further. Doll had taken a step towards him, leaned over and cut off the word.

"Think carefully about what you want to say now. Do you know what they do in prison with people like you?"

Holmes swallowed and said nothing. Ryan had jumped off the truck and stood next to Holmes. The headhunter calmly took out his cigarette box, pulled out one and then passed it around. Only when the clouds of smoke rose from the group of men did the words and laughter rekindle. Ryan listened carefully to their reports. At some point a deep honking sounded behind him. A motor roared and then went out with a hiss.

"Jumper!", Bunny called.

A giant appeared between the tractor-trailers, making great strides towards the group of men.

"Hi guys!", Jumper greeted with a broad grin.

The men greeted each other with drivel and handshakes until Jumper finally stood in the middle of the cluster in front of Ryan. He held out his hand to the Falcon.

"Hello my friend. Nice to see you again."

Ryan shook on it.

Jumper gave him a warm hug, like an old friend. When he let go of Ryan, he eyed Holmes.

"The guy looks almost harmless. What did he do?"

"A headhunter never asks what or why someone did what. I only have an order. Not more. But without you and the help of your friends I wouldn't have made it. Thank you, Jumper. I am deeply in your debt."

Jumper waved it off, pulled out his cigarette packet and held it out to Ryan. He took one.

"Do you have fire?", Jumper asked.

Ryan laughed and gave him his lighter. "Keep the lighter, or do you plan to switch to chewing tobacco?"

Jumper made a face and spat. "God forbid!"

Ryan looked at the tips of his shoes and grinned.

"As I have heard, you are already part of our family. We stick together like thick as thieves. If someone needs help, we are there. If someone is in trouble, we take a hand if someone have a break down, we get it, but if someone has a problem with women, we stay out. That's too dangerous for us. That's the law."

The others nodded and laughed in agreement.

"Now tell me guys! I want to know everything exactly", Jumper grinned.

Ryan and Jumper listened attentively to the report and found out in a very amusing way how the truckers had found the silver-gray Chrysler and finally had him over the barrel.

"What are you up to with the guy?", Bunny finally asked.

"I will deliver him to my client."

"And the car?", Doll asked

"You can keep it."

"Thank you, my friend, but I can't use a toy car."

The men laughed.

"Hey boys. Let's go over to the truck stop. The best far and wide. We have something to celebrate!", Jumper decided.

"And what should we do with this one?", Tedd asked, pointing to Holmes, who stood silently in the middle.

"We'll take him with us", Jumper decided. "After all, someone has to pay."

Laughing, the men started to move. Jumper stayed next to Ryan.

"I don't need any attention", he whispered to jumper.

"No fear my friend. So we have him under control. Your prey is safe with us and is guaranteed to shut up. Trust me", grinned Jumper and winked at Ryan.

*****

The leaves on the trees around Sam's claim, as he used to call his possession, had already formed a dense, light green canopy. The constant drizzle of the past few days had soaked the forest floor, which soaked up all the moisture like a sponge. It smelled of damp moss and earth. A squirrel scurried between the trees as if it couldn't choose one. Finally, it jumped up one of the deciduous trees and set higher and higher from branch to branch and disappeared into the thicket of leaves. The daylight barely came down to earth and spread a strange aura. The engine of a sports car rumbled softly, rolling to the shed at a walking pace and stopping there.

The Lakota got out and stretched. He looked very large next to the Corvette. Ryan put on his fur-lined denim jacket and looked around. Delicate clouds of smoke in his breath moved before his mouth and nose. After a long, hard winter, spring had hesitantly entered the Black Hills. It was the time when the Lakota once left the winter quarters in the mountains and moved to the prairie to hunt buffalos. Ryan's great-grandfathers and great-grandmothers called this time the moon of sore eyes because in March strong winds and storms blew across the open grasslands and caused inflamed eyes. It was still like that today.

Ryan sucked the fresh forest air deep into his lungs. Sam's hidden claim had become his home since he was released from the US Army last summer. Nobody could find him here. Sam's off-road vehicle was not there, and neither was the old one, usually at this time. The locked door of the log house was no obstacle for Ryan to enter. He knew where to find the key. When Samuel Williams entered his hut about two hours later, the fire crackled in the oven and it smelled of coffee. The young Indian sat at Sam's computer and immediately turned.

"Hi Sam."

"Hello my boy. Have you already made progress?"

"It's amazing what you can do with such a box", smiled Ryan, who had used the long winter to learn and try out different technical things. His training in the Air Force and with the shadow wolves had been very useful, but also one-sided.

"Google will ask me for advice in the future, Sam."

"For all I care. But don't encroach on my activities. That's taboo for you."

"I will be careful! Far too dangerous", Ryan grinned.

"Do you have to go into hiding again? Is someone after you?"

"One? Hundreds, Sam."

"Aren't you exaggerating just a little bit?"

Ryan laughed. "I stay overnight. Can you take the letter to the post office?"

Sam came over and looked at the envelope. "For your family, hmm", he said. "Why don't you even visit them?"

"Too dangerous at the moment. You know, a man with a family can be blackmailed."

Sam nodded. "It's fine."

"Thank you."

Ryan nodded toward the fridge. "I did a little shopping."

"Hmm, perfect. Then I will immediately rattle pots and pans. I'm starved."

Sam took two cups out of the cupboard, placed them next to the bags on the table and poured them.

"Come on, Ryan. Give your electric friend a short break."

Ryan got up and sat at the table with the old man.

"What about your friend, that bearded monster down in the city? He skillfully siphoned out from under me a Glock three weeks ago. The guy blackmailed me and insisted it's the same as you have. If I hadn't known exactly that you had sent him on my neck, he would never have got it."

Ryan nodded. "He is my friend and partner."

"Something catchier, would be appropriate for his paws, but he absolutely didn't want to be convinced, the stubborn. I hope he can handle it."

"His name is Baxter and wherever he strikes, there's no grass growing so fast anymore. But sometimes the arm is not long enough."

"But does he also hit with the gun?"

"Every man can do it, Sam. The only question is where."

Sam laughed croakily. "Maybe he will smash someone skull with it."

"He'll learn it, Sam. If Baxter has to cover my rear, my life depends on it."

Sam nodded. "You're absolutely right. Did Thompson, the old crook, contact you again?"

"Yes, we have been talking to each other again for two weeks."

"An order?", Sam asked.

"No, Sam, he invited me to his grandmother's wedding", Ryan countered.

Sam laughed that his eyes were watering. Ryan joined the old man's laughter. There was little reason in Ryan's life to laugh as exuberantly as right now. But it was the only chance to live. It was the secret to survive. Not only the Indians who lived in reservations or slums knew that. Ryan had finally regained his sense of humor, albeit often in a sarcastic way. But it gave him the air to breathe and the strength to continue fighting for his dream. His new job was tough and dangerous. Ryan was glad to have found old Sam in the forest. Perhaps he had been right when he claimed that the Creator had sent him to old Samuel Gabriel Anthony Williams for good reason. Sam had become a good friend, like Baxter Goodman. Ryan did not resent Sam for treating him like a son, occasionally like a greenhorn. The old man had gone through life cleverly, had a good reputation in his industry and knew how to make himself invisible. Ryan studied him and he made no secret of it to Sam. He would have seen through it anyway.

"So, so…", grunted the old man and wiped the tears from his eyes.

*****

Baxter spat in his hands. Then he pulled the rear wheel of an old pickup with all his strength. With the following jerk, Baxter staggered back a few steps and finally found his balance. Then he sent a pitying look over the old car.

"I'm sorry, little one. There is nothing left to save. But I promise you to treat your individual parts with particular respect. In this way you become immortal", said Baxter while loosening the wheel nuts on the other side of the vehicle.

The big bearded man, whom his friend called Mato, which means bear and couldn't be more apt, had finally thrown in the towel. Baxter had given up his friendship with the Air Force four weeks ago because he couldn't turn Rice's neck around. Now Baxter was working on a junkyard in the south of Rapid City, where he had no fixed working hours and no deadlines. The cars that arrived here could wait. It didn't matter whether they were stored in their entirety or correctly sorted into individual parts. Ronny, the owner of this rather lucrative small company, didn't mind either. If Baxter was there, it was okay and if not, it was okay too. He knew exactly that Baxter would show up at some point. Baxter enjoyed his new freedoms.

Baxter was rolling the last wheel to the tire stack when Ronny appeared behind him.

"Hello Baxter. Who are you talking to?"

"With the pickup here."

"Do you tell that to every heap of junk you take apart?"

"A few comforting words can't hurt."

Ronny looked skeptically at the pickup that lacked the wheels.

Baxter picked up the wheel nuts and threw them into the box. "So far I have always repaired the babies and made them ready to go. They pawed their hooves before they started. These one have done their job. So you should have a reasonably worthy finish."

Ronny grinned.

The small, sleazy guy didn't make the brightest impression, but he knew a lot about the scrap and spare parts trade and was very business-minded.

"I've never met a crazy guy like you, Goodman, who talks to cars", Ronny said and shaking his head.

"After all, they're just poor creatures", Baxter said. "We take everything without asking and when we no longer need it we just throw it away carelessly."

"There's enough of everything, Baxter."

Baxter waved it off, sat in the driver's seat and removed the dashboard. At some point his cell phone rang. He got it out of the pocket of the overall.

"Junky here. Who disturbs?" Baxter nodded into the phone as if his interlocutor could see it. "Hecetu yelo", he finally said and put it in his pocket. "I disappear for a few hours. See you later, Ronny."

"What are you always doing so mysterious when you're not here?"

"Rodeo. Bronc, bareback", Baxter grinned.

Ronny stared at him in disbelief. "What? You?"

"Why not? I'm natural talented."

Baxter washed his hands and disappeared into the Commander with a short *bye*. There he took his headset and fumbled the little plugs in his ears. "Okay, Ryan. Tell me!", he said and started.

"Three weeks of hard work, Bax. Now I have it where I wanted it."

"I hear."

"At the Rapid City Regional Hospital. He has just got out of a car and is going to the entrance. Someone is still sitting in the car. Seems to be waiting for him. The hospital has several exits. So hurry up."

"I'm flying", Baxter ended the call.

A short time later the black Jeep rolled into the parking lot of the hospital. Baxter looked around and saw the Corvette. He parked in front of it and got out.

"The black Shelby. You see a piece of him. He is parking in front of the gray Ford, to your left. If someone gets out and goes in, you tell me, or when the car drives away. I'm going to get Charlie now."

"Sure, Ryan."

Baxter never took his eyes off the Shelby.

Ryan determined went to the City Regional Hospital. He used the elevator until the second floor, like all visitors. Charlie's brother was in the emergency room and Ryan had already researched which room. Some people were moving in the hallway. Hospital staff, patients and potential visitors. They ignored each other. Ryan silently opened the door and slid through the crack like a shadow. Nobody noticed him. He closed the door behind him just as silently.

"Hello Charlie", Ryan said softly.

The person mentioned jumped up from the chair, visibly startled, and turned to Ryan.

"I'm coming with you, but on one condition", the young man said as he gasped. He seemed to know exactly who the Lakota was and what he wanted.

Ryan stood with his back to the door and eyed Charlie. Charlie was white, almost the size of Ryan, but more muscular. Ryan knew that Charlie had previously been a boxer and therefore classified him as unpredictable and dangerous. Charlie wore jeans, a shirt, and high athletic shoes. A black jacket hung over the back of the chair. The scalp shimmered through the short stubble hair, which began to shine with the sweat beads.

"No handcuffs!"

"An attempt to escape and I shoot", Ryan answered coolly.

Charlie's brother was lying in bed with his plaster foot on the ceiling. He looked skeptically at the Indian, then at Charlie, and again at Ryan.

"Don't worry, little brother. Everything will be fine. I promise to you."

From the microphone in his ear, Ryan heard Baxter's voice quietly. "The guy got out of the Shelby and is headed for the entrance."

"Okay! Let's go", Ryan urged Charlie to hurry.

"Hm", Charlie just did and took his jacket.

"Bye. I will be back soon. You can rely on me", Charlie said goodbye to his brother.

The man in bed nodded weakly.

Out in the hallway, Ryan spoke a few words in Lakota as he pushed Charlie forward briskly. It seemed like Ryan was talking to himself.

"What did you say?" asked Charlie. "I did not understand."

"I will aim at your eggs if you make the wrong move.

Then you survive. Go faster!"

Charlie went faster.

The two men disappeared into the stairwell through a glass door. There they were alone. On the ground floor, he had Charlie open the front door of the stairwell. Charlie went outside first. Maybe he thought about escaping for a fraction of a second. But at the same moment a strong paw grabbed his upper arm and Charlie stared into the bearded face of a tall, strong man.

"Hi Charlie", Baxter smiled.

"Who is this?", croaked Charlie, who looked like a school kid next to Baxter.

"Goodman. And as my name suggests: I'm a good man", laughed Baxter.

Charlie tried unsuccessfully to free himself from Baxter's grip and finally reluctantly allowed himself to be pushed into the passenger seat of the black commander.

"Buckle up!", Baxter ordered.

When Charlie hesitated, Ryan said: "Charlie, as you like. Then I handcuff you."

Charlie quickly pulled the strap over his chest and buckled up.

"Good boy", Baxter said contentedly.

Ryan took a seat on the back seat.

"Let's get out of here", Baxter growled and started.

"Where should it go?", Baxter asked.

"Two songs straight ahead, Baxter", Ryan grinned.

They were forced to stop at the next traffic lights. Charlie grew restless. Ryan watched him carefully. Charlie's thoughts seemed to be working at full speed.

"Do not even think about it!", warned Ryan. "You know that I stand by my word."

Charlie grimaced.

"Just don't shoot the guy in my Jeep! The last time I had to scrub it for three days. The brain stuck to the windshield like special glue, even if it was just a bird brain. Not to mention the mess with the blood everywhere, as if a bottle of ketchup had exploded." Baxter was clearly enjoying himself.

Ryan chuckled as he watched Charlie's eyes widen in panic. Sweat dropped from his head down his neck and he fidgeted uncomfortably on his seat.

After about twenty minutes, the Commander parked in front of the police department, Rapid City Regional Prison.

"Doesn't look very inviting, but there is full board."

Baxter got out.

Ryan put the pistol in his belt and also opened the door. Charlie took his last chance. He expected to surprise the two bounty hunters, who now seemed to be weighing themselves in safety. He jumped out of the Jeep and ran like a deer startled by the hunter. Ryan responded immediately and followed him.

When Baxter had overcome his moment of shock, he jumped back behind the steering wheel and started at full throttle. He had just seen them on the street. Then they were suddenly gone. "Damned shit!" Baxter angrily hit the brakes. "And now?"

"Hey! I'm not hearing impaired", he heard his friend's panting voice on the headset. "Second street. Step on it, Bax!"

"All right!" Baxter immediately stepped on the accelerator and jerked the steering wheel around so that the rear wheels broke out. Baxter brought the Commander back under control. "Hey ey ey."

69

Baxter felt the heat. In front of him he saw Charlie jumping across the street. Ryan was close behind him. The guy was actually still fit. He jumped over the banister and disappeared down the steps to the park. Ryan followed. Baxter braked hard. Even before the jeep stopped, the wheels struggled forward again. "Oh sorry Baby. But you can do it. You're an SUV after all", Baxter murmured.

He made a quick decision to turn the steering wheel to the left and bumped down the stairs. *A jeep has to get over the few steps,* Baxter thought. *Just don't lose two pedestrians again.*

The park path was paved. Baxter accelerated. The few people jumped to the side. The two men ran across the lawn. Baxter drove right next to the two and lowered the side window.

"Come on, Ryan! You have him right away. Grab him!", Baxter cheered on his friend.

Charlie's strength was obviously weakening. Ryan stayed close behind him.

"We'll handle this in a sporty way", shouted Ryan.

"Well, Charlie. Do you need a ride", Baxter shouted, and laughed.

He didn't answer. He panted, gasped, and dodged. Baxter laughed and let the Jeep roll alongside him and Ryan.

"You lost a lot of speed. Only ten miles an hour", Baxter commented. "Are you running backwards?"

Nobody answered.

Charlie gave up a few minutes later. He fell in step, then stopped and leaned forward, panting, hands on his knees. Ryan stopped behind him. He too gasped.

"Your condition has dropped Charlie", Ryan said.

Baxter got out. "What a pity. I thought Charlie made it

easy to get back on foot. Now I have to play garbage truck again", he growled.

Charlie stood up straight and started running again. Quick-witted, Ryan put his foot in his way. Charlie stumbled and fell on the grass.

"Hey, I'm not escaping anymore. I just wanted to get in the Jeep. So don't worry", gasped Charlie as he staggered to his feet.

"I'm not worried either. Maybe you should be worried", Ryan said, pulling Charlie's hands on his back and handcuffing him.

"It was self-defense. I didn't want to shoot the guy, but he had a rod pointed at me ..."

'Well, well", Baxter said, raising his eyebrows. "If I was you, I would have kept that to myself, Charlie. My friend here can't take a joke. He basically kills killers straight away and doesn't just take them to prison. This saves a lot of washing up, trouble and tax money."

Charlie couldn't see Ryan's face because he was behind him. "You are a cop. cops are not allowed to shoot."

"I'm allowed to shoot."

"But don't kill!", Charlie screeched.

"What makes you so sure that I'm a cop, Charlie?", Ryan asked amused.

"Are you a contract killer?", Charlie shrieked a sound higher, causing his voice to roll over.

Ryan laughed when he saw Charlie's uncertainty. "I'm allowed to shoot and I'm allowed to kill. It's actually written in my contract. Nobody will sue me if I have to kill you. But, if I deliver you alive, I get more dollars for you."

Baxter, who was standing right in front of Charlie, nodded approvingly. "I can testify."

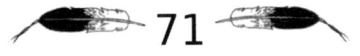

"You both are crazy guys!"

"Correctly. A normal person wouldn't mess with something like you", Baxter said.

"Get in, Charlie!", Ryan ordered.

He did so and wrapped himself in deep silence.

*****

While Charlie was waiting for his trial in prison relatively unscathed, Ryan completed the formalities. Then he informed Thompson and left the Police Department Rapid City. Baxter waited below the entrance.

"All done?", he asked when Ryan got in.

"Yes, everything is done."

"Boy, I never thought that the guy would dare to escape from the front door of the police station."

"Never underestimate your opponent, Bax. It could be fatal."

"Did you underestimate him because you didn't chain him?"

"That won't happen to me again!", Ryan growled.

"In any case you are still in great shape. Now I know why you measured the base every morning at a run. How many miles do you have on your speedometer?"

Ryan laughed. "No idea."

When Baxter and Ryan arrived at the hospital, it was already evening. The Corvette was parked. Baxter stopped behind.

"What are you doing now? Do you already have the next order or are you free?"

"Available."

"If you have nothing better to do, come to me. We could cook something or visit Dian."

 72

"Thanks for the invitation, my friend. But first I want to go up the mountain. The sun will go down soon."

Baxter stared at Ryan in wonder, but didn't dare to ask. "Okay. I'm waiting for you."

Baxter waited for Ryan to get in his sports car. When the Corvette drove off the parking lot, he spontaneously decided to follow Ryan. Ryan left the city in a northerly direction and drove towards Sturgis. He didn't seem to be in a hurry and must have noticed that he was being followed. *What does he want here*, Baxter wondered, glancing at the Black Hills, from which both vehicles were moving further and further away. Baxter automatically picked up the radio. But when he put the earplugs in the pinna, he paused as if he had to hold his breath. Finally, Baxter took it out and put everything aside. *Ryan will know what he's doing*, he thought.

A single mountain appeared directly in front of them. Baxter knew the Bear Butte. Like a giant, sleeping bear, its shape rose from the plain. When Ryan pulled into the parking lot at the visitor center, the commander parked next to the Corvette. They were alone. At this time, no tourists strayed here. The Indians used these times to be undisturbed. Ryan smiled as Baxter hesitantly got out.

"Come on", Ryan requested him.

Without comment he followed the Lakota, who ran up the mountain. Baxter soon regretted his decision because he quickly got out of breath and had trouble following Ryan. But he didn't dare to whine. With panting breath and sweaty clothes, he did his best. Ryan must have noticed and never moved further than his friend's sight. The way up seemed endless to Baxter. Dawn was already entering the valleys. The dark yellow fireball stood above the horizon. Finally, Ryan had reached his goal and remained motionless on a plateau. Baxter waited a few steps behind him and watched his friend. His panting breath and heart calmed down.

Ryan looked across the wavy grassland to the setting sun. The wind played with his hair, which he had let grow since he was released from the army. Baxter didn't dare to bother. He cautiously felt for his cigarette box. The last three cigarettes were crushed and when he tried to light one, it broke in his trembling hands. He swore silently, sucking the air through his teeth. The tobacco crumbled to the ground. The wind blew the rest out of his hands. Baxter waited and was put through a long test of patience.

His friend finally pulled some scraps of fabric from his jacket and tied them one by one to the dry branches of a tree. The tapes were blowing in the wind. Red, yellow and blue, like little flags. Then Ryan raised his arms, staring at the setting sun. He seemed to be praying. At some point soft words came to Baxter's ears. The Lakota words he didn't understand sounded like a melodious murmur. At some point when Ryan moved out of his rigid, he took one of his cigarettes. He did not light it, but crumbled it so that the tobacco was carried away by the wind. Baxter stared after the tobacco as if to catch with his eye. Finally, Ryan sat down and held out his cigarette packet to Baxter.

"Thank you."

Baxter pulled one out. Ryan lit it in silence. Both smoked. His friend still said nothing. Baxter asked nothing. As long as he knew Ryan, he knew when it was time to speak and when to be silent. Ryan had always counted that on him. Baxter had started to understand the Lakota. He had finished smoking the cigarette when he heard Ryan's voice.

"I had to do this because I don't want it to die in me. The years have come and gone and I'm far from what I used to be." Ryan didn't look at Baxter. He talked about the dry, yellow blades of grass and the valley and the wind carried his voice away with him.

"The Holy mountain", said Baxter softly.

Ryan nodded. "The only thing to find the middle of me again. You are nothing alone. I'm a Lakota. All I have left are the words, familiar words, prayers and my thoughts. Not even dreams send me back", he said softly. Ryan's voice sounded sad.

"You are not alone, mitakolà. Tell me how I can help you."

Ryan turned his eyes to Baxter and smiled a little as he narrowed his eyes. "You already have. You understood a lot, more than usual a Wasicu that I have ever met and you have learned to speak and understand some Lakota words too. Now I can tell you what my father said about you. Now you will understand. Wakan Tanka sent me a Wasicu as a friend, but he's obsessed with the spirit of a rogue. That's good medicine."

Baxter grinned and scratched his head. "Hmhm", he said embarrassed. "Why don't you just sign up with Thompson for a week or two and go home? He will survive."

"I heard Mitunkasila's voice, Baxter. It can bring disaster to them, because my path that brings me back is not over yet. It's like sitting on a rodeo horse. Then you have to give your all to stay up as long as time runs out." Ryan paused for a moment, then added: "I would like nothing more. But it's too dangerous at the moment. I have too many enemies."

"Understand. But when do you think the right time will

be? Thompson won't let you out of his hand anytime soon. Not in the next thirty years."

Ryan laughed softly. "When the time comes, I will know, Baxter. But thirty years are definitely too long for me."

Ryan's way of thinking and acting seemed increasingly clear and logical to Baxter. Even now he saw his own world with different eyes. As if Ryan had guessed his thoughts, he said: "There are things that no human tongue can put into words. You just have to feel it."

Baxter nodded. "That's the way it is."

The sun touched the earth, bathed the horizon in orange and red flames and finally took all the colors with it when it disappeared. Smoke-blue fog remained. The air became uncomfortably damp and cold. People left the mountain. The light of the stars and the moon accompanied them down.

*****

The foliage on the trees began to color and heralded the end of summer. Life was in an everlasting circle, in which there was no beginning and no end. The sun's rays sparkled through the canopy of the forest. They still warmed the earth during the day. But the nights were cold. The moon was fully rounded and shone like a yellow lantern over the old man's wooden house. Sam's car stood next to the shed when a small sports car parked next to it. The man who got out, looked around and silently closed the driver's door was dressed in black. A strand of hair had come loose from his braid and was hanging over his nose. It didn't seem to bother him. The Lakota moved swiftly to the log cabin, the door of which was a crack open. He drew his pistol and carefully pushed it all the way open. The wooden door creaked unmistakably. Ryan paused. When nothing happened, he carefully entered Sam's house. The light of the moon shone through the windows so Ryan could look around the room. Overturned chairs and torn-out drawers, the contents of which lay on the floor, confirmed his suspicion that something must have happened to the old one. He hadn't been to his house for two days, nor to his business in the city. Ryan could no longer reach him. He sneaked carefully through the chaos so as not to make any noise. It didn't look any better in Sam's bedroom either. Even the mattress was on the floor. Someone must have been very angry here, Ryan thought. Sam did not live harmlessly because he sold weapons. Sam had a lot of secrets. Too many how it looked.

Ryan pushed aside the heavy chest of drawers that stood behind the door in the bedroom and knelt on the floorboard. Ryan systematically tapped the wooden boards. Where it sounded hollow, he loosened the planks with his knife and lifted them out. Then he got something out of the hollow space. It was wrapped in a black cloth. Ryan put it in front of him and unpacked it. His eyes fell on a rifle and a pistol. Ryan switched on his tiny flashlight, which looked like a pen, and examined the weapon. His mouth formed an O and his eyebrows rose. *That's two sizes too large for you, Sam*, he thought.

The serial numbers were missing. Ryan grimaced. He looked around cautiously and listened, only to make sure that he was actually alone. Then he unfolded two sheets of paper and read. He shook his head in surprise. Ryan sat down on Sam's computer. He hadn't turned on the light. His eyes had got used to the darkness in the house. Ryan listened when he heard the sound of an approaching car. The light from the headlights roamed in through the half-open door, through the window panes, and continued to walk on the wall until the car stopped. Ryan smiled.

The headlights went out and the engine fell silent. Ryan was already standing at the window, watching the tall figure climb out of the jeep and head for the wooden house door. The man stumbled and fell with a muffled noise to the ground. A scream of horror choked the loud curse that followed when someone suddenly grabbed him and pulled him away. At that moment a stone fell. Exactly where Baxter had been before.

"You sneak up like a herd of buffalo and walk with your feet instead of your eyes", Ryan whispered.

Baxter gasped and stared wide-eyed at his friend. The fright was obviously in his eyes and limbs. The Bear struggled to his feet. He staggered for a moment, caught himself and shook his head, like a freshly bathed dog.

"I had always thought of Sam's automatic firing system as a joke", Baxter growled.

Ryan laughed softly and turned to go. Baxter glanced skeptically at the missile and followed his friend.

"Did a tornado go through here?", Baxter asked as Ryan turned on the light.

"Something like that", said Ryan and sat down at the PC. "Sam has no friends. He is a businessman and this is obviously a disagreement with customers."

"Well, you should look at the people before you trust them."

Ryan laughed softly. "Sam was always very careful. He doesn't just look at people, Bax. He checks them because he doesn't trust anyone. This will break his neck if nobody helps him."

"Okay. Speak."

"Look at this." Ryan pointed to the computer screen.

"Sam for the two weapons including the papers or we kill him ...", Baxter read murmuring.

"This is extortion!", he outraged himself.

"An ultimatum!"

"And where?"

"The coordinates say twenty miles southeast of Crawford. Down at Niobara."

"Then they will soon have an old, dead man and still not what they want", Baxter said. "What is so special about the weapons?"

"They are newly developed prototypes without any serial numbers. These are semi-automatic rapid-fire weapons made of carbon, Bax. NASA developed this feather-light and odorless plastic. They recognize neither the scanners at airports nor the tracking dogs. These weapons are invisible, to say to least. The ammunition however not. The cartridges are covered with steel. They go through everything like butter. Highly illegal high-speed bullets with high penetration, contraction compensation and, Baxter, damned unerringly."

Baxter stared at Ryan with wide eyes.

"It's like a car. Anti-lock braking system, anti-slip and stability compensation. That increases safety and success, even if the driver is not the best", explained Ryan.

"Aha", Baxter finally nodded.

The manufacturers are proud of it, sense the big business and there are enough customers. Even the US Army was interested, but also many gangsters. Even a blind man hits the target with these things. You just fire at it."

"And you will definitely hit something. Hopefully not the wrong ones", Baxter doubted.

Ryan grimaced and looked his friend straight in the eye. "A bullet that misses your arm a few inches apart can still kill you, Baxter. A specially developed ammunition explodes in the air, even if it does not hit it anywhere. Then countless, tiny fragments penetrate deeply through the skin into the muscles and organs at undiminished speed. You have no chance, even if you can throw yourself on the ground. Even a glancing blow makes your blood clot immediately."

Baxter blew his cheeks and let the air whistle slowly through his teeth. "Let's get out of here quickly, my friend. The fire brigade in Rapid is also looking for men", he finally said.

"Shit-scared?", Ryan asked.

"What the hell does the old skimpy want with these things? How does he get something like that?"

"No idea. Sam has been in the arms trade for almost fifty years. He had a big business and this time he got the wrong people."

"Or he stole them from the wrong people who want them back at any cost", Baxter mused.

Ryan nodded.

"We're going to Nebraska and you're exchanging Sam."

"Wait a minute!", Baxter interrupted Ryan. "You want me... me send me to handover? Did you stick your nose in Thompson's handbook for hostage release? Why don't you inform him? I planned to stay alive for a few more years", Baxter croaked nervously.

"That's why. If you gave the weapons to them, they will put Sam and you in a row and pierce with a bullet."

"You are totally crazy!"

"Do you realize that only now, Baxter?"

"And you?", Baxter snorted.

"I'll watch your back. We're starting tonight. Before that I break into Sam's shop and get a good rifle with rifle scope and ammunition."

"Then you'll end up in jail tonight", Baxter said confidently.

"I know how to turn off the alarm system." Ryan typed something on the keyboard until an encrypted code covered the monitor and connected the PC to his cell phone. Then he entered a number combination and pressed again on the side of the cell phone. Sam's computer screen showed the code for the alarm system within half a minute. Baxter shook his head in disbelief. Ryan turned off the computer.

"Here we go!"

"You really want to give the weapons to this assholes?"

"Not necessarily, Bax. First Sam must be safe. The guys are professionals. They control the weapons precisely when they are handed over. One mistake and we're all dead."

"Explain to me", Baxter growled.

"If it is too dangerous for you, then...."

"Hell. I'm a man of my word!", Baxter interrupted his friend gruffly. "Even if I'm scared. That might be allowed."

Ryan grinned and nodded.

"And then? We have Sam and we watch how the guys with the weapons taking the coward's way out?"

"If all goes well", Ryan grinned and rose.

Baxter started to protest, opened his mouth and closed it again without saying a word. He just gasped and gave his friend a scathing look.

*****

 81

The sun burned on the desert sand of Nevada. Here it was still in the high eighties during the day. Hot wind blew through the silence of the steppe. The devil's breath blew the dust over the earth. On a bump there was a human body, which the wind had covered almost entirely with sand and dust. The clothes did not differ from the color of the sand. Even the head was covered with the bright cloth. The figure was completely merged with the desert. Not even the griffon vulture circling high above would recognize the motionless figure as long as Ryan Black Hawk was not moving. The dry air irritated the mouth and nose and burned in the trachea with every breath. Thirst began to torture Ryan. Drinking was out of the question. The eyes burned. The sunglasses had to stay in the car. The light would be reflected on the glasses and reveal its location. Ryan narrowed his eyes to protect them. The rifle was in front of him, horizontal on the device. He had covered it with a cloth to camouflage it and protect it from the grains of sand. The scout waited patiently for his deployment, while Baxter waited in his Commander, which was only a point on the plain.

Ryan pricked up one`s ears when he heard a barely audible sound. Rotor blades cut through the wind. Then he spotted the black dot on the horizon. Ryan watched Baxter get out. The helicopter went deeper and circled over the area before landing near Baxter. Two men got out. One of them came up to Baxter and talked to him. Baxter nodded. The other remained at some distance and supervised the deal.

Where's Sam? In the helicopter, I hope, Ryan thought without saying it. Baxter did a good job. He handed one of the two weapons to the man. He controlled the pistol.

Now the men seemed to be discussing with Baxter. But he kept shaking his head.

Good thing, Ryan thought.

In response to a sign from the stranger, two other men climbed out of the helicopter, the rotor blades of which kept stirring up the dust. One of them was unmistakably Sam. The other led him to Baxter. Ryan had his finger on the trigger. He watched the happenings like a hawk his prey. Adrenaline flowed through his body, made him sweat and sharpened his senses. Ryan had to wait for Sam to sit in Baxter's Commander. Everything seemed to be going according to plan. Ryan had his sights on the men. Only the one who had the gun went to the helicopter. The other two aimed their weapons at Baxter and Sam, who were about to get into the Jeep. Ryan aimed at the helicopter when he instantly felt the metal of a barrel of a rifle on his neck. Ryan held his breath.

"Look at that. Who do we have here? Get up, Sergeant Hawk!"

Ryan followed the order. Major Cox from the US Army Nevada Training Camp stood in front of him.

"Hands behind your head!", he ordered.

Ryan brushed the cloth off his head. He hid his surprise, his restlessness and his defeat with difficulty. The adrenaline in the body followed its own laws. The heart was racing and longing for oxygen. Ryan breathed quickly.

"Nice to see you", Cox grinned. "Did you think you are the only one who knows about such things?"

"I never thought that", Ryan replied hoarsely. The dryness burned in his windpipe.

"Strange how the circle sometimes closes."

Someone fired a couple of warning shots directly in front of the moving Jeep so that it stopped.

"It doesn't look too good for you and your friends", Cox noted.

"You have to know when a game is lost", Ryan replied.

Cox laughed. "Forward!", he ordered.

Ryan moved. "Why such trouble? You got what you want", asked Ryan.

"The rifle is missing. I know you're smart and I like to play, Hawk. Just a shame that we are not both in the same team."

"We used to be, Cox."

"Hmm..."

"Is this your part-time job or do you do it full-time?"

"A pretty lucrative part-time job. The army doesn't pay very well, as you know. I also have to use my skills so that they do not wither. Desk work is for veterans. And you? You're not here on behalf of the Air Force?"

"No, the Air Force fired me. I found a new, pretty lucrative job."

"The Air Force fires a specialist?", Cox doubted. "Did you do crooked business?"

"Just killed a few guys who wanted my scalp."

Cox laughed amused.

"Maybe I should bring you into our team."

"I am my team, major. No orders and no regulations."

"Why do you protect the arms dealer?"

"In doubt, for the accused."

"Uhhh. You represent law and order", Cox stated.

"No. I'm a hunter."

Cox laughed. "Okay. And who is the other one?"

"An auto mechanic from Rapid. Once he repaired my car."

Ryan and Cox had reached the helicopter.

Weapons were aimed at Baxter and Sam. Both stood in

front of the Commander with their arms raised and did not dare to move.

"Let's clarify the matter like professionals and play the game among us. You got me, Cox. Let them go", Ryan said, hands still clasped on the back of his neck. The arms began to tingle.

Cox seemed to be considering.

"Your offer excites me. You owe me a revanche anyway. The old one comes with us. And the other one", said Cox and eyed Baxter. "You will bring me the gun. Today! It is exactly nine hours and twenty-three minutes until sunset. Afterwards you will be able to bury your two friends in the desert. Understand?", Cox asked.

Beads of sweat stood on Baxter's forehead. The hands trembled imperceptibly. His wide eyes and intense breaths seemed to amuse Cox. Baxter was afraid for his life. Ryan couldn't help him. Cox put on the gun. Baxter held his breath and closed his eyes. Okay, that's it. A thousand thoughts whirled through Baxter's head. Shots crashed. He counted two, three, four. Then Baxter heard the men laugh. He carefully opened his eyes.

"Your cell phone remains here. You can go", Cox finally said.

Baxter gulped down the chunk of dust that had stuck in his throat. He didn't dare say a word and didn't dare move. Stunned by the shock, he was under a spell that made everything impossible for him.

"Hey, You! You can go", Cox repeated.

Baxter cleared his throat and let the arms sink exhausted. "Tha... thank you Sir", he stuttered.

Then he twisted on the spot. Baxter desperately sought his friend's look. Ryan tried to tell him something with his look. But what?

"Get out of here!" Ryan nodded. "Go on."

Baxter turned to go. He heard Sam's tormented cough. Finally, Baxter got into the Jeep and said softly: "Don't worry, my friend. I'll get you out of there. Promised."

*****

Even the fan in the office seemed useless. He just stirred the stuffy air. Thompson the stress drove sweat out of the pores. Since yesterday he had no connection with Ryan for whom he had a new order. That made the man angry, who otherwise could hardly get a rest. He had all hospitals, prisons and motels checked. Without success. This morning Thompson had decided to issue the man-hunt for him.

"Come on In!", he called when there was a knock on the door.

A young man in jeans and sneakers entered. He wore a gray jacket. Mirrored sunglasses blocked his view. "Good morning, Chief", he said and sat down without being asked.

"Take the damn glasses off if you want to talk to me", Thompson demanded grumpily.

The one who sat across from him obeyed.

"William's gun shop was broken into last night. A neighbor allegedly noticed and reported this. No traces, nothing damaged and it seems that no stealing was done. We are still looking."

"This is peculiar. Who breaks into a gun shop that is equipped with a highly sensitive alarm system so that nothing can go wrong?", Thompson said, shaking his head.

"It was off, Sir. Even more strange is that the owner has

not been in his shop for two days. We wanted to talk to him, but he disappeared without a trace. All data on his computer has been deleted."

A chilly shower passed through Thompson. So Ryan and Sam were disappeared. There had to be a connection. But what ..., Thompson mused.

"Duncan, send me a computer specialist who can restore the deleted data."

The young man grinned and nodded. "Is already on the way, Boss. By the way, I found a man who could know something. His name is Baxter Goodman, he is twenty-seven and lives in Rapid City. He is a mechanic and was until recently technical manager of the Ellsworth Air Force fleet. He was definitely with Hawk a lot. We don't know yet whether he knows old Williams or is a customer of him.

"Well then go there!"

The young man Thompson had called Duncan jumped up. With an *okay*, he disappeared through the door. Thompson watched him go. Then he got up and got a coffee from the coffee machine in the hallway. As always, he had the change in his pocket.

*****

Ryan inhaled and exhaled calmly as Sam struggled with his dry cough.

"Get in the helicopter", Cox ordered.

"Too little audience?", Ryan asked.

"No. But if I left you in the desert, even naked, you would escape me and eventually get in the way."

Ryan laughed. "May I take my arms down, Sir?"

"One wrong move and you're tied up like a parachute."

"Got it, Sir", Ryan replied.

He glances at Sam, who also lowered his arms. He looked exhausted and weak-willed.

"I can still recruit you. Think about it, Hawk."

Ryan slowly lowered his arms. They were stiff and their
hands went numb. He smiled and looked at Cox.

"Does the army actually take back people who have
previously dishonoredly fired them?", Ryan asked in astonishment.

"You don't believe what is possible and crazy people like
you with any brains at all in your head are damn rare. I
know you too well and appreciate your skills. It would be
really unfortunate to lose you. The army itself stands in
the way with its pencil-pushers that make decisions they
have no idea about. Get in, Hawk. I'm in a hurry. My business partners don't like to wait."

Ryan nodded and got into the helicopter with Sam and
the men. The helicopter turned to the southwest. Ryan
looked at the old man sitting across from him.

Sam had never dared to say anything before. He looked
small and vulnerable when he looked at Ryan. The hair
stuck out from the head, as it conformed to his
constitution. Ryan noticed Sam's pleading look, revealing
his fear. Ryan grimaced.

*****

Baxter's powers weakened. For what felt like an endless
time, he was now running through the desert. He no
longer swore, because that only dried his throat more
than it already did.

*You have never let me down in my life. Why now of all
times? I know it was just the tire. It isn't on you, buddy.*

I'll take you home. I swear that to you and Ryan and also to this old forest man, without whom we would never have come here, Baxter followed his thoughts.

The pictures blurred before his eyes. The water bottle was long empty and useless. Baxter Goodman was thirsty and hungry. His leaden limbs no longer wanted to obey him and the skull throbbed. Spotting the wind on his face reminded him that he was still alive. In the distance he saw the highway that led straight through the desert. No, it was not a fata-morgana and not a hallucination. It was real, the trucks drove in both directions. The highway was Baxter's rescue and the only chance to escape the dilemma. When he felt the asphalt under his shoes about half an hour later, the highway was deserted. Not a point in the distance that was moving towards him. Baxter was desperate. He had to choose a direction. Sometimes it could take a long time before someone came along. Waiting here was insane, walking on foot too. But it made Baxter feel like doing something. He thought of his friend. He did not want to get the picture out of his head how he had stood with his hands on his neck next to that scoundrel. Baxter wondered if Ryan was scared as much. Ryan had looked at him as if to say something to him. Baxter hadn't been able to see fear in that look. Rather an expression of pride and superiority.

"Oh shit damn it!", Baxter swore. His thoughts tangled together. He couldn't think of what would have happened if Cox hadn't just shot in front of his feet.

The guy made fun of it and I almost peed in my pants. Maybe I was just lucky. Maybe I owe my life to Ryan. If anyone can help them now, that's Baxter Goodman. Just screw up nothing now!

A truck approached. The unmistakable sound shook Baxter's senses. He turned and signaled to the driver with his arms raised that he needed help. The colossal giant stopped when he past Baxter a few feet. Baxter opened the passenger door. A guy who looked almost exactly like Baxter grinned at him.

"Hello brother. Can you take me to civilization?"

"Get in", the driver laughed and accelerated.

"Thank you. I'm Baxter, Baxter Goodman."

"Frank Anderson. I am always happy to have a visit and a little entertainment. So: what happened? I have never seen a car with a breakdown."

"My Jeep is in the desert. Maybe you have a phone on board? My friend urgently needs help."

"Is in my jacket. Find out for yourself"

"Damn shit! I don't have the number at all", Baxter swore. He sounded desperate.

"Maybe by radio. Who do you want to call?"

"Thompson. He works for the FBI."

"Are you kidding me?", Frank croaked and stared at Baxter in disbelief.

"No, I don`t! And that's not a joke either. My friend was taken hostage and if I don't reach Thompson, I don't even know him, he'll be dead soon."

"Hm", Frank did and picked up the radio.

"Hi guys. This is an emergency call. I urgently need to speak to the FBI in South Dakota."

"One moment please. I do my best", snarled a tinny female voice.

"Hopefully quickly", Baxter growled softly.

Frank grimaced.

"What was the name?"

"Anderson, ma'am."

"I'm sorry, but there is no Anderson registered with us."
"Thompson!", Baxter yelled. "He has to sit on the executive floor. Lost his number. It's an emergency."
For a while the device just cracked and rustled.

*****

The helicopter landed less than ten minutes later. Ryan took a look out of the window. The swirled dust blocked the view.
"Okay, get out!", Cox ordered.
Two men pulled towels over their mouths and noses. They jumped out and aimed the weapons at Ryan and Sam. Another bumped Ryan hard on the ribs. Ryan also jumped into the cloud of dust and sand caused by the rotor blades. The eyes burned and watered immediately. The dust crunched in the mouth. Ryan heard the old Sam cough suffocatingly. They were practically blind while the armed men dragged them with them. Ryan blinked. He vaguely recognized buildings in the veil of tears in his eyes.
"You'll be waiting for us here", he heard Cox's voice. "It will not take long. If you are clever, Indsman, you will survive."
Ryan blinked and was silent. He heard Cox laugh softly next to him. Then he felt a hard blow to the skull, which brought him out of balance. Ryan felt the strength wane in his knees and the pain that robbed his senses. Darkness and silence remained.

*****

About an hour before noon there was another knock on

the door to Thompson's office. A little older lady stuck her head in the door and smiled friendly.

"What's up, Dawson?", Thompson asked.

"Your medicine and a me asked sage, just for you personally."

She came in and put a small tray on the desk. "The message comes from a certain Goodman. Unfortunately, I did not understand which department he is from. I thought it was a macabre joke", she said as she poured the tea into the cup. Thompson, who usually never looked up from work during this daily procedure, looked at his secretary questioningly. She put a note on the desk. Thompson pulled it towards him. "What's that?"

"Coordinates or something, the man said on the phone. I could hardly understand him. The connection was not very good."

"Why didn't you put him through to me, Mrs. Dawson?", Thompson asked angrily.

"He was afraid that the connection would break down completely before he could deliver his full message", she dismissed the accusation. "He said he was acting on behalf of a Falcon. You should send your people to this place immediately." She pointed to the note. "And he urgently needs a taxi to sing sing. Those were his words."

"That was all he said?"

The white-haired lady smiled and added: "But a little quick! Then there was radio silence."

"Thank you, Mrs. Dawson."

"You're welcome!", she said and turned to go.

Duncan jumped in immediately as he knocked on the open door. Dawson closed the door behind him.

"Tell me!", Thompson ordered while opening Nebraska's map on his screen.

"This Goodman has also disappeared since yesterday. However, it was not exactly unusual for him, said the junkyard owner. Goodman comes and goes as he pleases, but he would have no problem with that."

"Hmmm", Thompson said. "And he didn't tell him where he was going?"

"Never."

"Well then we have a perfect trio that wants to play games, I can't get rid of the feeling." Thompson stared at the monitor, making the impression that he was thinking hard. Duncan said nothing.

"I got them, Duncan", Thompson triumphed. "Goodman called here recently and ordered a taxi."

Duncan raised his eyebrows in disbelief. Thompson turned his head and grinned confidently.

"Who do you have?", Duncan asked.

"I don't know yet. Come on!"

Thompson hurriedly pulled his jacket from the back of the chair and went to the door. Duncan followed.

"Imagine that one of my hunters hunts without a mission, but he wants me to get my prey", Thompson explained as he hurried down the hall.

"And where?"

"Maybe twenty-two miles southeast of Crowford towards the Niobara." He gave him the note.

Duncan just shrugged and stayed hot on Thompson's tail.

*****

Like two big bats between parachutes the two men hung from the ceiling. Sam cursed the guys. Like back then in the forest, he hung upside down. His hands dangled above the floor. The blood accumulated in the skull, which threatened to burst under the pressure. The feet tingle painfully. He could see Ryan hanging in the same way. His silence made the old man angry.

"I think they are gone. What did they say? How long will it take for all the blood to blow up the skull?", Sam croaked laboriously.

"I won't wait that long."

"What are you up to?"

Ryan didn't answer. He tensed his muscles, lifted his head and upper body towards his feet, pushing his arms, whose wrists were tied on his back, past his buttocks and now piece by piece to the back of his knees. There he stopped briefly and took a deep breath before struggling upward. Sam watched him. He made no attempt to move.

Ryan pressed the wrist cuffs against the soles of his feet to hold on. It was impossible to bring them forward. Again he took a few deep breaths. Then he grabbed the rope, he was hanging on, with both hands. That was connected to a steel girder in the roof structure. Due to the many parachutes, the building had to belong to an old airfield. Bit by bit Ryan caught up and kept pulling himself up. His knees pulled close to his body, he now got hold of the strap and pulled himself up. He sat there exhausted as he took a deep breath. Cox had found the knife and taken it from him. The lighter does not. Ryan grinned triumphantly. When he had freed himself from the shackles, he balanced on the construction to Sam.

"Give me your hand, Sam. I'm pulling you up", Ryan whispered, bent over to Sam.

"Are you crazy. We'll both crash!", he hissed.

"You can't crash. You're roped. Come on, Sam."

"I'm afraid."

Ryan took a deep breath and looked around. Then he climbed down carefully on one of the parachutes. Maybe there was a guard at the door that was out of sight. Ryan knew that the game wasn't over yet. Cox would show up again soon, so as not to miss the final. He had to expect not finding Ryan hanging dead on the rope. Cox knew exactly what the Lakota was capable of. When Ryan was convinced that only a guard posted about fifty feet away from the building opposite and smoked, he pushed two large boxes right under Sam, placed them on top of each other and climbed up.

Sam groaned.

"Shh! Hold on tight to me. I burn the rope and let you down slowly."

Sam groaned again. When he finally sank to the crate weakly, Ryan released Sam's ankle cuffs. "Come on, Sam. The dance is not over yet", Ryan whispered.

Sam agitated and blinked around. Then he coughed suffocatingly. "At least not an anthill."

Ryan nodded.

"The same trademark. The same men?"

"Yes, Ryan. Let's just get out of here!"

"So that the guys will hang you up again somewhere at the first opportunity?

"What are you up to?"

"Put a stop to their game once and for all time."

"You want to kill them? Are you crazy!", the old croaked in horror.

"No. I'm a hunter, not a killer."

"Just don't let Thompson know I'm in on it!", Sam murmured.

Ryan scowled at Sam. "Maybe I should hand you over to

him right away", he said hard. "Right for everyone, Sam and you don't ask which side."

Sam kept an embarrassed silence. Finally, he took a deep breath and said: "I'm a businessman. I never ask what someone is up to with the thing. Who asks too much does not live long."

Ryan laughed bitterly.

"In this case it was of no use to you."

It stayed quiet outside. Sunlight shone in through the hangar's open gate.

"Where are we?"

"Bush airfield. No military, just an old biplane and two gliders. At the moment it doesn't seem to be anybody but us here. Apart from a security guard on the hangar opposite."

"Let's take the biplane and leave."

"Can you fly that thing, Sam?"

"No. But you were in the Air Force."

"I just got the low-flying ticket, Sam", Ryan grinned. Then he looked for two ropes that he rolled up like Lassos. "I put the man over there out of action. They will come back soon and we need weapons. So we have to come up with something. There's a lot of stuff around here", Ryan said.

He came back two minutes later and searched tool boxes and spare parts. He took two spanners with him. He knotted one each on a rope. Sam crouched on one of the boxes and watched Ryan.

"There were three men and Cox. We have no weapons, so let's use this." Ryan held out one of the coiled ropes to Sam. "You swing it like a Lasso with all your strength and aim at the heads. If you hit, they will be on the floor and will have a terrible headache in the next few days."

"And then?"

"The FBI is responsible for illegal arms deals. Thompson should decide what he does with the guys."

"And how are you going to transport them all to Thompson?"

"He'll get it", Ryan smiled.

Sam eyed Ryan in surprise with his old vulture eyes. Under no circumstances did he want to be found here by Thompson. Ryan knew that exactly. He grimaced at a mocking grin. When they were hiding for the moment of surprise, the sound of a helicopter came to Ryan's ear. He peered out the gate and saw him appearing in the distance.

"They are coming. Hide", Ryan said.

Sam disappeared.

Ryan watched the helicopter landing. Then he also pulled away from the gate.

*****

Three men entered the gate. Cox wasn't with them. The men automatically looked up. At that moment something whirred through the hall. Two of them were hit hard on the skull before they could register what was happening. They immediately went down. The third threw himself to the ground. He immediately drew the weapon and fired blindly in the direction from which the attack came.

Ryan crouched behind the stack of tires and kept his head down. Something whirred through the air from the opposite side. Startled the man spun around. Sam missed the guy only by a hairs breadth. Taking advantage of the instant surprise, Ryan jumped on him. The guy lost his balance. Both fell over. Ryan wrapped his arm around his opponent's throat as he reached for his pistol. Both men rolled on the dusty floor in a fight. The man clutched the weapon so tightly that Ryan couldn't take it away.

"Give up or I'll break your neck", Ryan hissed.

"Forget it!", the man hissed back and rolled his body onto the Lakota.

"Right. That would be too short a pleasure for you!", Ryan replied.

"I'll kill you."

"Cox will be proud of you", Ryan said, as the guy knelt on him and tried to point his gun at him.

"Watch out!", warned Sam.

At that moment something whirred through the air again. The spanner flew past the man's arm. But the tight rope slowed the flight of the bullet, so that the rope wrapped around the wrist. The man didn't drop his pistol, but he couldn't aim either. The shot rang out and whistled past Ryan's ear. Ryan immediately grabbed the spanner and jerked the surprised opponent around. With the face to the ground and the hands on the back, he finally surrendered. Ryan plonked on the guy and took his pistol. "Where's Cox!"

The man moaned softly while Ryan tied his wrists with the rope.

"Where's Cox?", Ryan asked.

The man didn't answer.

"Shoot him", croaked Sam, who had stepped next to the men.

Ryan pressed the wrench to the man's neck.

"No!", the man cried. "I don't know!"

"Too bad. Then we don't need you anymore", Sam cro-

aked.

Ryan tightened the trigger with a click.

"He is on the way to get here."

Ryan knocked the guy out with a short but powerful blow to the temple.

"Hurry up, Sam. Tie the three guys together as tightly as you can", Ryan said as he got up. "And thanks for not hitting my head."

"What do you think about me?", the old one outraged.

Ryan smiled.

*****

Ryan listened when a car stopped outside the gate minutes later. Two doors slammed. Silently two figures appeared at the open gate, difficult to see against the light. Only a soft crack disturbed the silence. Then a thud, an angry scream and a single shot. One of the two had fallen to the ground under the force of the blow. The bullet that was fired flew through the air and hit the pile of tires behind which Ryan was taking cover.

"I warned you!", the bear's voice boomed through the hall. He bent down, picked up the pistol and took the magazine out of the weapon.

Ryan grinned and rose.

"Where do you come from now?", Ryan asked surprised.

"From out there", Baxter replied. "So I had a flat tire and ran through the desert. Then hitchhike to the next gas station. I had to fill up there first. I was thirsty. And then I actually have a spare wheel for my Commander...."

"Okay Baxter. One is still missing at our party", Ryan cut his words off.

"Thompson", Baxter growled.

"He too. Have you reached him?"

"Even though", Baxter beamed.

"Tie the guy up and to the others", Ryan ordered.

Sam did it immediately while Baxter looked around.

"Cox will show up here at any moment."

"Ah, the snake's head", Baxter noticed.

Ryan nodded. "Yes, he is a tough guy and not to be under-estimated. He was one of my camp instructors."

Baxter whistled softly through his teeth.

"Special unit? Magnetic bomb?"

"Yes", Ryan nodded. "How did you find us here?"

"My sleeping friend brought me here. Just when I was changing tires, he appeared. You will not believe...."

Again Ryan interrupted his friend with his forefinger in front of his lips.

"Tell us later. Now we have to think about how to put Cox on the cross."

"OK. Speak! I'm listening."

*****

Ryan sat in the shade, leaning against the hangar doorpost, smoking. He wanted to see Cox coming, wanted to know which direction and how many men he had with him. Ryan kicked out the cigarette and painted pictures in the dust. Grass, sun, two moons and horses. Again and again he blurred the sand pictures and started again. It was only when he lit a second cigarette that he heard engine noise. He got up, leaned back against the doorpost, and continued to smoke. That seemed to keep the adrenaline in his blood a bit in check. A US Army sand-colored Wrangler SUV appeared. Cox drove himself. He had only one companion with him. He didn't seem particularly surprised when he got out and came up to Ryan. The other man followed him and stopped about twenty feet apart.

"You live. I expected nothing else", grinned Cox.

"You taught me to survive."

"You killed my men?", Cox hissed as his grin faded.

"No I have not. They are my prisoners."

"I'm impressed." Cox laughed. "One more reason to recruit you, Hawk. Something could become of you."

"So? What?"

"An extraordinary warrior, a hero and a damn rich man."

Ryan grimaced contemptuously.

"What for?"

Cox cocked his head and eyed the Lakota suspiciously. Then he slowly shook his head.

"Or soon a dead Indian that anyone will find in the desert. It's your decision."

Ryan nodded.

"What about old Williams?"

In the hangar, behind Ryan, someone cursed loudly. A metal part rattled. That caught Cox's attention. He took a step forward. Ryan stepped aside to clear the way. Cox companion didn't move. But he aimed his weapon at Ryan.

"You first!", Cox ordered. "I prefer to keep an eye on you."

Ryan did what he asked for and entered the hangar. Cox stopped at the doorpost and looked around suspiciously.

"Sam?", Ryan shouted.

"Yes", he croaked.

Ryan turned to Cox. A smug grin appeared on his face. Then he also entered the hall.

"So you saved the old one", Cox observed. "What for?"

"So I can hang you, upside down on the steel beam", Sam called.

"Do what you can't let go, old man", Cox replied, amused.

Instantly Ryan heard the telltale whir in the air and put his head down. The bullet flew strait over Cox's head. He too must have heard the whir and reflexively pulled his head down. Ryan pushed Cox down.

A shot was fired outside.

Then it was quiet.

Cox swore.

He was taller and stronger than Ryan. But Ryan was faster. He put a thin wire around his neck.

"One wrong movement and the wire cuts your throat."

Cox hissed, cursing.

"Maybe someone will find a dead arms dealer, killer and traitor to the flag in the desert. Maybe you're smart and survive", Ryan said.

"You won't kill me, Indsman. The price is too high for you."

"Right, but I wouldn't bet on it. As a hunter I have authorities." Ryan saw Sam's boots appearing next to Cox.

"Nobody gave you the order and nobody knows where we are", Cox hissed.

In silence, Ryan also tied Cox's hands with the thin wire on his back. "If you want to live, keep quiet. You know exactly what happens when you move", Ryan said and getting up.

"Damned bastard", Cox hissed.

"That's just what you taught me. Silent, invisible and fast. The only difference was that nobody told me that there should be no prisoners. I made that up."

Ryan heard Sam giggle softly next to him.

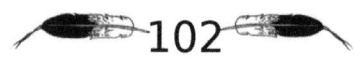

Baxter's figure appeared at the gate. He dragged an apparently lifeless body over the dusty floor.

"So that's it. Come on Ryan. We disappear. The taxi will be here any minute to get the packages."

"Then better tie your last package before the guy comes to", Ryan said.

"One day we meet again, Hawk. Then god have mercy on you, because then I'll kill you", Cox snorted angrily.

"Coping with defeat is a special lesson in life. Every rodeo rider knows them. But I don't know anyone who hasn't gone back up", Ryan replied.

Baxter laughed bitterly.

Sam gave him the rope he was holding and Ryan hadn't used. Baxter knelt on the floor and carefully handcuffed the last of Cox's men. Ryan turned and went out of the gate. Sam followed.

"Sam doesn't want to be caught by Thompson here. So you two get in the jeep and get out of here as quickly as possible", Ryan said when Baxter joined them.

"Why? That's brilliant. We packed the bad guys and serve them on the tray before he even gave you the order. Something is due for that and money is no object to Thompson", Baxter said triumphantly.

"Sam doesn't want to be seen by him here. And no one else can bring him home, Bax."

Baxter nodded.

"Now look at that!" Baxter pointed to the helicopter with which Cox men had come. "We better should have learned to fly at the Air Force."

Ryan nodded. "Get out of here! We meet at Sam", he urged.

"And you?"

"I'm waiting for Thompson."

"He's going to ask questions, Boy", Sam croaked in horror.

"For sure", Ryan nodded.

"What do you want to serve him?" Baxter asked.

"The truth", replied Ryan.

Sam looked at Ryan uncertainly, horrified and fearful. Ryan's face remained frozen when he said: "Get out!"

Neither Sam nor Baxter dared to contradict. The two men, who could hardly be more different, silently climbed into the jeep. The black commander disappeared into a cloud of dust as he drove away.

Not even a cigarette length later, Ryan heard the sound of the approaching helicopter. He looked up.

Thompson.

*****

That evening Sam had to accept that the big bearded man had entered his claim. Baxter Goodman was the second person besides Ryan to be allowed to do this with impunity. After all, he had helped him and he was Ryan's friend. Sam had crawled away from people in the forest many years ago. He had no friends for a long time. None he could trust. His emotional world was now completely confused. It suddenly felt good not to be alone, especially not now. Sam still eyed the big stranger suspiciously from his old vulture eyes while he opened his front door.

In silence, Sam contemplated the chaos in his house and started his coffee machine.

"Well, then...", Baxter started undecided.

"Let's make a fire and drink coffee", Sam muttered.

"Okay. Ryan will be here soon anyway", Baxter agreed,

and started setting up the chairs and table.

"Thank you", said Sam.

Baxter turned to the small old man with the crooked legs and grinned. Groaning, Sam knelt in front of the stove and lit the fire. The air in the Black Hills was damp and cold.

When the fire crackled and the smell of fresh coffee drifted through the room, the gravel crunched in front of the house under car tires. Sam listened.

Baxter grinned. "Does the gravel also belong to your alarm system?"

Sam giggled. "For sure! Not even a Sioux Indian can sneak up anymore."

Seconds later there was a soft knock on the door.

"Come in, Boy. The door is open", Sam called.

Nothing happened.

It was quiet.

There was another knock.

"Are you sure it's the one you expect?", Baxter asked.

"Nobody else knows where my hut is", Sam said a little unsettled.

"Of course! Except for the guys who turned your hut upside down and kidnapped you", Baxter growled.

Sam limped to the door, opened it a crack and called out: "Anybody there?"

"Yes of course! And now finally let me in, Sam. I have my hands full."

"That's what I'm saying", Sam turned to Baxter and grinned triumphantly.

*****

When the three men sat at the table together, Ryan said

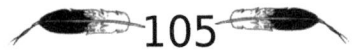

to Sam: "They will show up to tell you that someone has broken into your business. They will ask you if something is missing. The rifle that Cox took from me has disappeared without a trace. There are no traces, nothing in your shop is damaged and nothing has been stolen, it seems. At the moment Thompson is more concerned with this than Cox and he tries desperately to solve the puzzle. He asks himself: Who breaks into a gun shop that is equipped with a highly sensitive alarm system so that nothing can go wrong? Strange. That gives him a headache."

"But why didn't the alarm work?", Sam asked irritated.

"Was turned off", Ryan smiled.

"Who the hell...?", Sam snorted as the color drained from his face. He did not finish his sentence. His thoughts were obviously working at full speed.

Baxter cleared his throat.

"No fear Sam. There will be nothing left on your computer", Ryan said.

"Have you put your nose in my computer? How did you find out my code?"

Ryan was still grinning. "It's a no-brainer. By the way, I deleted all your data."

Sam gasped in disbelief and jumped up from the chair.

"You made what?!"

He immediately started his PC.

Baxter watched the spectacle grinning.

"There were a hell of a lot of people sticking their noses in there for the past twenty-four hours, Sam. Just they will have been very surprised."

Ryan got something out of his little black backpack and held it out to Sam.

"What you have there?", he croaked contritely.

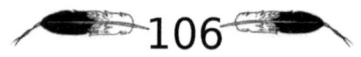

"Backup copy. I learned a lot from you, Sam. The last winter was long."

Sam's face relaxed in relief.

Ryan reached for the coffee cup.

Baxter looked alternately at Ryan and Sam and seemed to understand. "They'll ask me too, Ryan."

"I told the truth to Thompson. He is not stupid and knew anyway that the three of us were there."

"Which is still not entirely clear to me: Where is the rifle now I should bring Cox?"

"In your Commander, Bax."

Baxter stared at Ryan as his jaw dropped slowly.

"The whole time?"

Ryan nodded.

"Ahm ... and now?"

Ryan looked challenging at Baxter. Then he had to grin.

"And you knew that all the time, that I drive the part through the area?"

Ryan nodded.

"You haven't given it to Thompson?"

"What for?"

"Evidence against Cox."

"And against Sam. Maybe against me and the rest of the world. Whoever is keen on this weapon is not doing anything good with it. We will destroy it."

"Oh…", Baxter said.

"And what about Cox and his men", Sam asked concerned.

"They won't be able to hang you anywhere for now. I gave Thompson the copies of the papers on the weapons and also the ransom note. Not only the FBI will be busy with that in the near future."

"Thank you guys. You saved my old, screwed up life and

it would have almost caught you too. I'm getting too old for that shit. Now I owe you both."

"I'll take the Winchester", Ryan grinned.

"What? You want her?", Sam asked in astonishment.

"It's fully functional and I know someone who can get me ammunition for it."

Sam laughed amused and croaky.

Then he looked at Baxter.

"I'll take a good whiskey, or better two", he replied before Sam could say anything.

Chapter 3
Keshia

The ringing of the phone woke Ryan Black Hawk from deep sleep. Dazed, he groped around on the bedside table and accepted the call.

"Hello Ryan! Baxter here. How are you today?"

Baxter's voice boomed in Ryan's head.

"It's okay", he murmured into the phone, hardly understandable.

"Maybe you should go to a doctor after all."

"It's just a flu." Ryan couldn't stop the cough. He couldn't see Baxter's head shake.

"Where are you currently?"

"With Sam."

"It sounds like I woke you up. Sorry. Did you just sleep?"

"Yes, I had."

"You are absolutely right. Right now sleep is the best for you. Can i do anything for you? I would come, but I'm not sure if Sam has mined his claim again or a new self-shot system is waiting for me in the ambush."

Ryan's laugh turned into an excruciating cough. "All right. You won't find me here tomorrow either. I have an order."

"What? You're crazy! You belong in bed! Do you want to kill yourself with all power?", heard Ryan Baxter's angry voice.

"It will be better tomorrow morning."

"I wouldn't be so sure about that. You've been crawling around for days as if you had consumptive on your neck."

"I'm going to the Northern Cheyenne Reservation, tomorrow morning. I just get the Cheyenne, deliver it and lie down in my bed again."

"Call him. Maybe he'll get in touch with you", Baxter grunted.

Ryan coughed again on the phone before answering. "I will. Do you have his phone number?"

"No, but I can give the information a try, or the chief. What's the name of the guy?"

"Black snake."

"Black snake? That sounds damn dangerous. I hate snakes. Ryan?"

"Yes."

"Let me know!"

"Okay, Bax. See you later."

"Bye, little brother. Keep a stiff upper lip."

Ryan ended the call and immediately fell back asleep, cell phone in hand.

Towards the morning he struggled half asleep with his blanket, in which he was totally caught. Finally, he woke up bathed in sweat and freed himself from the terrible confusion. The heat he felt under the covers didn't want to go away. It pounded in the head and the pressure in the skull was so bad that Ryan thought it would burst at any moment. He stood up with glassy eyes. With difficulty he dragged his heavy body to the water bowl that stood on the chair. His body swayed as he shoved the cold water onto his face and neck with both hands. It felt good. Ryan washed himself completely with the cold water and rubbed the skin with the towel so that it blushed. It woke him up. Then he dressed. A few minutes later he was sitting with Sam at the breakfast table.

"Good Morning. Did you sleep well?", Sam asked and eyed his guest skeptically.

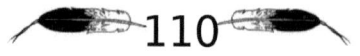

"Yes, like a hibernating bear."

Ryan reached for the coffee cup and drank carefully.

"You might want to eat something", Sam said, when he noticed that Ryan was slowly pushing the plate aside.

"I'm not hungry", he replied, crossing his arms tightly around his body. He could hardly fool Sam that he was shivering.

"The hot coffee is good", Sam said worriedly. He avoided giving Ryan good advice.

Ryan just nodded.

When he said goodbye to Sam, he looked into his worried face. "I'm getting something from the pharmacy", Ryan appeased.

The old man nodded and smiled.

"Do that. if you want to get as old as me, then without that cough", he said with a harsh voice and coughed tortured. "Because that can be a nuisance", croaked the old one.

"Thanks my friend", Ryan said.

Then he climbed into the Corvette.

Sam stood at the driver's door and slowly shook his head. "See you soon son. I hope you come to your senses quickly. The fever clouded your mind", Sam muttered.

Ryan lowered the side window, smiled weakly and started. The old man he could see in the rearview mirror looked after him.

*****

After about three hours, Ryan reached his destination. The head still wanted to crack, but it didn't. It was autumn. The days were cool and sunny, while the nights

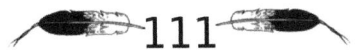

were extremely cold. The forests in Montana's mountains were beautifully colored. The sunlight reflected the colors of the leaves and the wind brought them to life, so that they resembled flickering flames. Ryan perceived it as if it wasn't real. He had passed Lame Deer long ago and a few houses appeared in front of him. Directly on the street he recognized a trailer from which the yellow paint was peeling. There was a fairly large billboard in the parking lot.

Drive Inn - Jimmy's specialties
A typical Indian snack truck in which hardly any strangers got lost. The hub of gossip, Ryan thought.

Hoping to find out something about Black Snake here, he turned off the street and parked directly in front of the trailer. Ryan took the last two aspirins from the glove compartment and swallowed them arduous. The mouth and throat were dry, rough and painful.

I can drink in there.

Ryan was very thirsty. His supplies had long been used up. He got out, slammed the door and went to the entrance. The letters on the billboard next to the front door began to dance and blurred before his eyes. Ryan took a deep breath and went inside.

The air seemed stuffy to him. She laced his throat. Ryan pulled himself together and sat at one of the four tables by the window facing the street. As he watched the parking lot from here, an icy shower of chills seized him. Startled, he spun around when a female voice spoke to him. "Hello, what can I bring you?"

Ryan turned his head and looked at the shadowy, slim figure to which the voice belonged.

"A hot coffee, pleace."

The voice chuckled softly. "Okay."

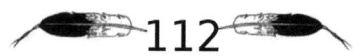

The shape disappeared.

Ryan's eyes slowly cleared. He looked around. The trailer was long and narrow. There were four seats directly at the counter, opposite the entrance. Two men sat opposite each other at the next table, deep in conversation. Painted pictures hung on the opposite wall, where, like Indian artists, they offered tourists for sale. As Ryan wondered if a tourist had ever strayed here, he involuntarily reached for the packet of cigarettes. At that moment the figure brought the coffee.

"Can I do something else for you?"

Ryan forgot about the cigarettes. Contrary to his Indian politeness, he literally stared at the young woman. She was pretty and smiled at him provocatively.

"Do you know a certain Black Snake?", he asked hoarsely.

"What do you want from him?" Her voice sounded icy.

"Help him."

The young woman smiled pityingly. "Oh, I think at the moment it looks like you need help urgently."

"Where can I find him?"

"You don't know him and you don't know where to find him. How do you want to know if Black Snake needs your help, stranger?"

Ryan clutched the coffee mug with both hands and drank carefully. The icy perceived coldness turned into pleasant warmth. But then heat burned through his body, which threatened to burn him and drive sweat out of his pores.

"I even know it", he muttered.

His defiant words came with difficulty over the lips. His hands started to tremble. He put the cup down and hid his hands under the table. The young woman leaned

over to him. "Who are you?"

"Cetan sapa, Lakota", he answered laboriously.

Ryan gasped as the figure of the young woman blurred before his eyes.

"You have a fever", she noticed and put her hand on his forehead. When Ryan reached for it, he slumped willingly.

"Jimmy! Help me Jimmy!", the young woman's voice called from far away.

Suddenly it was night around him. A loud clatter of crockery was the last thing Ryan heard. The blood rushed through his head like a waterfall and suddenly it was quiet.

*****

Slowly the Corvette drove up a narrow forest path into the mountains. She stopped in front of a tipi. Two old people, a man and a woman, came to the strange car. The grandparents had recognized their granddaughter, Keshia. After a brief change of word, they carried the young man into the tent. Bedded on blankets, undress him and cover him with a cotton blanket. The young man breathed heavily in a high fever. Keshia, who worked at Jimmy's Drive Inn, washed the sweat beads from his forehead with cold water and then wrapped damp, cold towels around his calves.

At some point Ryan opened his eyes and blinked around. The heat he felt was unbearable to him. Like fire she burned him. Exhausted, he fell back into a deep sleep.

Keshia cooled the hot body until she finally fell asleep herself.

With the rising sun, Ryan opened his eyes and blinked

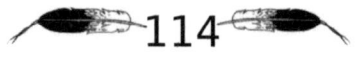

again. He didn't know where he was. His senses were confused and memories erased. On all fours he crawled to the exit, into the cool, redeeming morning air. He took a deep breath. The floor beneath him began to turn and sway. His limbs began to tremble and failed working. The weakness that ruled Ryan's body prevailed over his will.

The old man had watched that. He knelt before the unconscious man and tied his arm with a cloth. Keshia appeared on the other side of the strange man lying in the grass. She looked at her grandfather, startled.

"Take the stick as a gag and twist the cloth as tight as you can, Keshia."

Keshia obeyed.

The old man picked up a scalpel, just as it was used in hospitals. He put it on the fevered arm and pressed the tip into the bulging vein. A slight moan was heard and the weak body twitched reflexively. The blood shot out, ran down and flowed into the earth. Then it went slower. The old man undid the knot and pulled the cloth away.

Ryan's body no longer trembled. The heat seemed to be leaving him. He gradually came to. He felt the cool breeze on his skin and opened his eyes. The old man, whose face he saw first in front of him, smiled contentedly and nodded to him. Ryan's gaze wandered further to the sky, to the tree tops, in the branches of which the wind played with the colored leaves, and finally got stuck on the young woman who knelt beside him on the other side. She didn't smile when her eyes met.

"Ne`a e`she. Nia isch. Thanks", he said hoarsely.

She nodded, got up and left.

At the same moment a young man appeared in front of Ryan. Together with the old man, he helped the Lakota to his feet. They supported him as they brought him back into the tent. Exhausted, Ryan slid onto the ceiling. The wound had stopped bleeding. With his eyes closed, he breathed calmly through his open mouth. Startled, he shrugged when a hand on his shoulder touched him and opened his eyes.

"You have to drink. The water is fresh and cool. It will do you good." Smiling, Keshia put her arm under Ryan's head.

"Wait", he said, leaning on his elbow. With the other hand he took the mug and drank it in one go. It strained him more than he ever wanted to admit. Then he dropped back again. "Thank you."

"I think you've got over it now, Lakota. The fever has gone. You will no longer need me now."

The fog in Ryan's memory cleared slowly. He reached for her hand and held it back as she tried to get up.

"What's your name?"

"Keshia."

Ryan smiled and repeated softly: "Keshia. You are a medicine woman, Keshia. How long have I been here?"

"Since you had coffee with Jimmy yesterday morning. You have lost consciousness."

Ryan nodded. He could remember it.

"You are in good hands with my grandparents. They're actually a medicine man and medicine woman", Keshia smiled

"Will you come back?"

"If you want tonight, after work."

"I'll be here."

Keshia giggled softly and disappeared.

Ryan's weak body continued to fight the infection, demanding rest and deep sleep. The fever did not return. With short breaks, Ryan slept until evening. His dreams kept sending him home to the valley that the brook ran through. He stood at the fence, saw the horses grazing and heard himself speak to Kola. Grandmother and mother were sitting on the bench in front of the house and Andy was training with his piebald stallion. Father John came to him and moved his lips.

"My heart is with you."

Even when Ryan opened his eyes, he still saw his father's face in front of him.

Ryan was alone in the tent and looked around. It was covered with blankets and some skins. In the middle was the fireplace. Something glowed in the ashes. Ryan's gaze wandered over groomed birds, storage containers, bowls, baskets, buffalo horns and a bleached buffalo skull. Feathers and bouquets of herbs, flowers, sage and grass hung from a ribbon and hung up to dry. An idiosyncratic but pleasant smell penetrated his nose.

The old man stuck his head in through the entrance and smiled when he noticed that Ryan was awake. Keshia's grandfather had combed the top section of hair back and tied it with a hair tie. Icy gray, wavy hair reached up to the shoulders.

"I see you are better, Lakota."

Ryan nodded. "My name is Ryan Yes, I'm feeling better. Thank you. Only my skull wants to burst."

"My name is Adam. Did you drink everything, Ryan?"

"Yes, I did."

"Good."

Slowly he turned and looked for something in his storage jars. When he found it, he took some of it in his hand

and gave it to Ryan. It seemed to be chewing tobacco.

"What's that?"

"Peyote."

Ryan did what Adam said. He was familiar with the cactus plant and its effects. Even the Lakota sometimes fetched them from the southern desert areas for ceremonies. You just couldn't get caught with it, because colloquially this plant was not called a drug cactus for no reason. The dried parts tasted hideous. After a few minutes, Ryan felt sick. He quickly choked the mass. The pain subsided, but a feeling of dizziness spread. Ryan closed his eyes and fell asleep again. It must have been a long time he overslept and he had confused dreams.

When he woke up it was dark night. Ryan listened to the steady breaths in the tent. He could see the outlines of the two sleeping people. Ryan came up laboriously and braced himself on his elbow. With the other hand he groped for the water bottle. It seemed incredibly heavy to his weak arm. With a low moan, he pulled her towards him.

"Are you thirsty?", asked a low voice right behind his head.

Surprised, he immediately held up. Ryan knew the voice well. He had not noticed her breaths.

"Yes, I am", he replied just as quietly.

The dainty black shadow of Keshia scurried silently past him and knelt before him. Only the soft splashing that caused the water to pour was heard. Keshia felt for Ryan's hand. The gentle touch touched Ryan in a strange way. She touched his heart and his senses, broke through the hard wall with which he protected himself. Just a moment, then he took the mug of water and quenched his thirst.

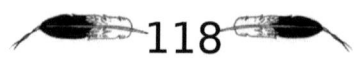

"Thank you, Keshia."

"How are you?"

"Better. The pain is bearable."

"Put this in your mouth. It will do you good."

"No, it works without."

He heard her chuckle softly and saw the sparkle in her eyes.

"This is a sage candy. It is good for your inflamed and dried out mucous membranes. Your voice sounds very rough and hoarse."

Ryan hesitated briefly and took it.

Keshia was right. Silently she slid back behind the head of his bed and went to sleep.

Ryan stared with open eyes at the smoke vent of the tent. A faint glow of light came in through him. He couldn't sleep anymore. *If Black Snake had found out that someone was looking for him by now, he would be over the hill and far away,* the headhunter thought. *And until I am unable to get up, there will be nothing I can do about it.*

Ryan took a deep breath.

"You need a lot of sleep, Lakotaman, if you want to be well soon."

"Yes. But I can't."

It rustled barely audibly behind his head and the dark shape of a head leaned over his. A few strands of hair crawled across his skin. Soft, gentle words came to his ears. He didn't understand the Cheyenne language, but he felt it. The words that Keshia whispered sounded like an old magic song. He felt the touch of her fingertips running over his eyes. Ryan closed his lids and listened. In his mind, Ryan tried to imagine Keshia's face, but he couldn't. He had never really seen it clearly. Ryan sank deep into the blankets. He was still hearing the soft song as a black snake appeared before him in his mind. She came up to him and grew bigger and longer. Her piercing yellow eyes stared at him as she twisted around his body. He wanted to shake her off, but he was unable to move. Ryan thought he felt the breath of death. She would soon strangle him or bite her poisonous teeth. But nothing of the sort happened. The black snake continued to wind and left his body.

Darkness and silence now spread around Ryan.

When he woke up the next afternoon, Keshia's grandmother was sitting next to him. She smiled as she wrung out a towel, washing the sweat off his forehead. Even though he knew immediately where he was, he looked around confused, questioning.

"She comes back tonight."

Ryan nodded. He wanted to say something, but his tongue seemed paralyzed. He resisted leaden tiredness.

"Sit up. You have to eat something. I slaughtered a chicken", said the old woman, and pushed a backrest behind Ryan.

So it was more convenient. The weakness of his body and the feeling of dizziness in his head could hardly be pushed out. His eyes watched Keshia's grandmother at work. The chicken soup worked wonders in the emaciated body. The old woman helped him and held the bowl, which was still too heavy for him. The muscles shaken by the fever still refused to serve him. He ate little of the chicken. The appetite was limited and even chewing was hard. He pushed the plate away from him.

"Thanks a lot. It was very good, but I can't go on. Ne`a e`she. Nia isch. Thank you."

She smiled contentedly and put everything away. Ryan

leaned his head back on the support and closed his eyes. Without wanting it he fell asleep again.

*****

It was almost a week before Ryan could stand up alone for the first time. The dizziness slowly disappeared. His movements were stiff and slow. Every day he walked a little further on foot. Keshia came every evening at the same time. She always asked about his condition and told him about her day. Tonight she led Ryan to a shallow bank on the river.

"Do you want to bathe?", she grinned.

"Only if you come with me. I am a miserable swimmer."

"Maybe another time."

He nodded.

"Well. I will hurry. The sweat has already turned into a sticky crust on my skin", he said and undressed.

Wearing the black boxer shorts, he went inside. Then he dived and swam a little downriver.

Keshia was sitting on the bank watching him. The friendly smile had left her face. There was fear and hard determination on her face. When Ryan was in a fever, she had got his things out of the Corvette. But she had found something else in the little black backpack. Keshia had given Ryan the car key three days ago. He had taken it in silence and he hadn't asked for Black Snake until today. It seems Keshia knew who the stranger was.

When Ryan climbed back onto the bank, he wrung out his wet hair. The water beaded off his skin. In front of Keshia he leaned to the floor and picked up his shirt. Keshia watched his movements in silence and smiled as he rubbed off himself with his shirt. Then the Lakota sat

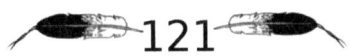

121

next to her.

"You can give me your things tonight. I'll put it in the washing machine tomorrow morning."

"Good idea. Thank you. I feel better now than I have in a long time. You saved me, Keshia. In every sense."

"Grandfather will go to the sweat lodge with you. Your circulation will now be able to handle this."

"You know a lot, little medicine woman. Wakan Tanka meant well to send me to you when I couldn't help myself."

Ryan smiled openly at Keshia.

"You will leave when you're healthy?"

"Before I go I have to find Black Snake", Ryan said matter -of-factly.

"Why?", Keshia snapped at Ryan.

Ryan was silent and stared at the river.

"Do you want to kill him?"

Ryan raised his eyebrows and turned to her in surprise.

"What makes you think that?"

"When I got fresh things out of your car, I looked into the backpack."

"No. I am not a killer. Do you know him?"

"Yes", Keshia replied softly.

"Do you know where he is?"

"Yes."

Ryan took a deep breath. "Here in the Reservation?"

"Yes", she snapped at him gruffly.

"Will you help me find him?"

"What are you going to do with him?"

"I only can talk to him about it."

Now it was Keshia staring into the river.

Ryan took another deep breath.

"Is he your sweetheart, your husband, your brother or

your father?"

Keshia shook her head.

"Go to the sweat lodge and think about it. Maybe it will take you further. Maybe I'll help you find Black Snake." That ended the conversation.

Keshia rose. "Let's go back I'm hungry."

*****

That evening, Ryan and Adam were sitting in the sweat lodge. Ryan kept his eyes closed and breathed calmly and evenly as the sweat came out of his pores and slowly ran down the skin. He thought, but he couldn't sort out his thoughts. Everything was knotted in his head. Finally, he said a prayer so softly that only he could hear it. Familiar Lakota words. Ryan hoped for a vision, for an answer to his questions. But nothing happened. Only Keshia's smiling face was in front of him.

On the morning of the following day he woke up with new strength. He jumped awake from his bed. Dressed only in his black short, Ryan went out. He shivered. The fresh, cool air pulled his skin together. He ran to the riverside and back again. Grandmother watched him and smiled.

The next morning Ryan awoke powerfully and jumped out of his bed. Wearing the black boxer shorts he went outside. He shivered. Then he rushed to the river and returned.

"You're brave", Keshias grandmother said to Ryan and gave him her husband's jogging suit. "It could fit."

He took it gratefully and put it on.

"Nia isch, grandma", he thanked her.

There were only a few words he could speak in Chey-

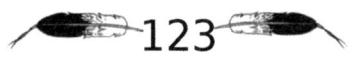

enne. He called her grandmother out of respect. He now knew that her name was Neloa.

"You have a good heart. Keshia knows that."

Ryan smiled at grandmother Neloa and sat with her. She gave him coffee.

"She saved my life and you too. I was so far from myself that I forgot who I really am. I found myself through you."

"That's good, my grandson. That's good", the old woman nodded.

"Your tent, up here in the mountains, is healing medicine. I could get used to it", he smiled. "Are the horses outside yours?"

"Yes, these are ours. My son Matthew, Keshia's father, is a mountain guide for tourists and hunters. Sometimes scout for lost things."

"We also have horses on our ranch. We breed them. But hardly anyone wants to buy them anymore. Maybe someday I will make it a tourist ranch, teach them to ride and ride with them on the prairie."

"That's a very good idea, Ryan. Tourists are curious. Some ask many questions. Some understand the answers, some never."

Ryan smiled as he turned the coffee cup in his hand and finally took a sip.

"My grandmother Lucy always said: *don't think they understand us and don't try to understand them*. But now I know both worlds and I understand a lot. It's important to accept both as it is, I think."

"Yes", Neloa said. "That's how we think and that's how we live. We live in our tent all summer. We feel at home up here in the mountains. But in winter we go down to the place, to our house. Back to the small civilization and

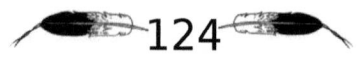

to the people we love."

Ryan stared silently into the coffee cup. *To the people we love*, he heard their words in his thoughts. They touched his heart painfully. Suddenly he felt an overwhelming longing for his family, the horses and the home ranch. He was no longer able to suppress this longing.

"You have a good heart. Maheo knows that", Ryan heard the gentle voice of the old woman who reminded him of his grandmother.

Ryan pressed his lips together and nodded.

"Where can I find black snake?", he asked softly.

"Maheo knows that too", smiled Neloa and rose.

Ryan watched her leave the tent. He had hardly expected it otherwise. He knew that. But if you don't ask, you won't get an answer. He knew that too.

*****

The autumn wind played with the colorful foliage on the roadside. He whirled it up as the Corvette, drove past and slowly danced down. The slopes on both side of the street glowed in flaming red tones. Sun and wind brought them to life. The road wound down the mountain slopes until it finally led straight through a plain. A rushing mountain stream accompanied the asphalt road a bit through the valley. Then a handful of houses and trailers from the Cherry Grove estate appeared. Ryan recognized the yellow trailer. He could remember it. It seemed like an eternity.

Ryan stopped next to two other cars. He went in and silently closed the glass door behind him. The smell of coffee came to his nose. He could remember that too.

Coffee. Hot black coffee. He looked around. He couldn't see Keshia anywhere. A middle-aged and medium-sized Indian stood behind the counter and polished a glass. He looked up immediately.

"Oh hello. Nice to see you. Are you feeling better?", he asks the one who has entered.

"Yes, thanks", Ryan replied.

The man seemed to know him. Ryan couldn't remember him, however.

"I'm Jimmy", he said finally, as if he had read Ryan's thoughts.

"Ryan", he said and nodded to Jimmy.

"I know", Jimmy laughed.

Ryan didn't dare to ask about Black Snake. Some of the tables were occupied. One was free. Ryan sat down exactly where he had sat before. He had time and thought it would be wiser to wait for the right moment. Jimmy came over to the table. "Do you want something to eat?" he asked.

"No. Give me a Coke, please."

"Okay."

Seconds later, Jimmy came with the Coke and sat opposite Ryan. "Are you looking for Keshia?"

"She said she's here during the day."

Jimmy smiled. "She'll be right back. She's just hanging up your clothes."

Ryan nodded and opened the bottle with a hiss. Jimmy got up and went to the other tables. With the dishes he passed Ryan again. He was just putting the coke on his lips while looking out the window. Outside a pick-up slowly drove past and finally turned into the parking lot. Shortly afterwards a young, tall man came in. Ryan watched him skeptically.

Black snake?

He seemed younger than Ryan. He wore his long hair loose and a streak of black hung across his face. There was a hostile expression on his hard features that reminded him of his youngest brother, Andy. The stranger glanced at Ryan with a short, scowl as he passed his table. Ryan's suspicion that the man was Black Snake caught his attention. The guy sat down with the man at the second neighboring table. The men spoke quietly to each other. Ryan watched the two without looking directly at them. He couldn't understand her words. Then he heard soft steps behind his back. Ryan immediately turned and looked into Keshia's smiling face.

"Hello. Well-rested?"

"When I saw your face in a dream in front of me, I was startled from sleep", he smiled.

Keshia giggled and sat across from him.

"Were you afraid of me?"

"You actually seem dangerous to me. You confuse my senses, my thoughts go strange ways and for the first time in life I forget things."

Keshia smiled. "Do you need a strong coffee?"

"Today my coffee needs are met, Keshia. Your grandmother meant very well to me."

"She likes you."

Keshia's eyes wandered conspicuously over the jogging suit. "Couldn't you wait until I bring you your things?"

"I'll wait. On my things and on you."

"Then you will have to wait longer."

Ryan smiled and took her hands in his. "I've always been waiting for you the last few days. Today I'll wait for you here."

"I'll give you something to eat."

"Later. May I use the electrical outlet? My cell phone is dead. I have been cut off from the other world for too long."

Keshia's smile faded. "Naturally."

She got up and left.

Ryan sipped his coke. The two men he was watching rose. While the older of the two passed him, the young man stopped right in front of him.

"Stay away of Black Snake", he hissed. His eyes flashed sharply on Ryan before walking on without expecting an answer. Then the two men said goodbye to Keshia and Jimmy before heading out the door.

Ryan saw them walking across the parking lot. They both got into the pick-up and drove away. Finally, Ryan got up, bought a newspaper and a pack of cigarettes from Jimmy, sat back in his seat and started reading.

Every now and then he picked up interesting scraps of conversation. When the phone was charged, Ryan disappeared outside. The stick of cigarettes was stuck under his arm. The usual Indian cars from the reservation were parked in the car park. No foreign license plates except his own. He tore open the pack of cigarettes and tossed the rest into the passenger seat. He hadn't smoked in a week. *And I'm still alive*, he smiled at the thought. Leaning against the Corvette, he lit a cigarette. Then he followed his thoughts.

Who was this guy? Something is wrong. He clearly warned me. He's not a friend, but maybe Black Snake's friend or himself? Maybe my senses betrayed me, maybe not.

Keshia stood at the window and watched Ryan. He smoked and spoke on the phone. Meanwhile, Jimmy was watching her. What irritated both of them, however, was that he kept laughing while on the phone. What might have amused him?

"He does not know."

"No. But he'll find out, Jimmy. Then what?", Keshia said softly.

"Maybe you should forestall him", he said.

"I'm afraid."

"Should I make him disappear?", Jimmy asked.

Keshia sighed. "That doesn't make it any better."

"Should I talk to him?"

"No", Keshia replied quickly. "No .... I .... I", she stammered undecided.

"Should I tell you the truth, Keshia?"

Keshia turned her worried look to Jimmy.

"The Lakota is a bounty hunter. He's a warrior and he's a man", grinned Jimmy. „You made him loose his mind. He loves you. Even a blind man sees that."

Keshia's cheeks flushed. She searched in vain for words.
Jimmy is right.

Keshia took a deep breath. She watched Ryan motionless until he finally put the phone in his pocket and came to the front door.

Ryan was still grinning as he entered and sat in his seat. Some guests had come and gone.

It got really crowded towards evening. The people here had made a ritual of meeting Jimmy around this time to learn new things. They slid together at the tables. Ryan had cleared his seat and was at Jimmy's counter. Wordlessly Jimmy gave him a Coke. Ryan hadn't given up hope of learning about Black Snake. But at the moment he thought it was unwise to ask the men. They would not give him the desired answer. A woman with a round face came in, greeted and disappeared into the kitchen behind Jimmy. Shortly thereafter Keshia appeared next to Ryan. He eyed her. She had changed her shirt and carried a bundle of things in her arms. "You have remarkable endurance, Lakotaman", she smiled.

"I'm a hunter", Ryan replied with a smile.

Keshia sighed. "Let's go."

He carefully stroked a strand of hair from her face.

"Thanks for the laundry."

Ryan got up. It had not escaped him that he suddenly caught the attention of the men who had been watching him skeptically all along. The voices grew quieter. Scowls met him.

"Bye, Jimmy."

"Bye, Ryan. If you hurt Black Snake even a hair, I'll kill you", he warned.

Ryan looked surprised at Jimmy. Their looks met. The Cheyenne didn't seem to be kidding. Jimmy turned to the others.

Keshia reached for Ryan's arm. "Come on", she said, pulling him out with her.

They went to the Corvette in silence and got in.

"I like your car", Keshia said when he started.

"Me too", he smiled. Then he took a deep breath and pressed his lips together as he drove to the street.

"It seems to me that if I take Black Snake with me, I get in trouble. Your people will declare a war to me", he said without looking at Keshia.

"No. They will kill you and nobody will ever find your body. Unless Black Snake comes with you voluntarily", she replied.

A smile played around Ryan's corner of his mouth.

"You saved my life. Would you do that again?"

"Yes", she whispered.

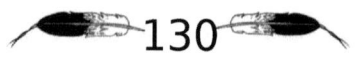

"Who was the young man this morning who came to my table, then talked to you and Jimmy briefly and then drove away with the older man in a Ford pick-up?"

Keshia said nothing.

Ryan looked at her.

She seemed to be in a trance. Her eyes were closed and her chest rose and fell in quick succession.

"Black snake?"

Keshia nodded hesitantly.

Ryan looked back from her to the street.

"Thank you."

There you go. My feeling did not deceive me and my brain seems to be working again.

*****

The sunlight shimmered between the trees and shimmered before the eyes. Ryan and Keshia were silent until the tent appeared in front of them. It was evening. Keshia went to her grandparents without a word. Ryan crawled into his freshly washed clothes. It feels good. They smelled floral. Then he reached for a cigarette. When he wanted to light it, he paused and finally put both away. He slammed the car door shut. Slowly he went to the tent.

"Let's take a walk?"

Keshia hesitated.

"Please."

Keshia sighed. Without looking at him, she slowly came to him. "Okay. Let's go."

"Something is bothering you, Keshia. Maybe I can retaliate and do something for you?", Ryan started.

Keshia didn't answer.

131

Ryan stopped and stood in her way. She stopped in front of him and looked down.

"Look at me, Keshia."

Keshia looked up at him. Her eyes shone as she smiled tortured.

"How are you, Lakotaman?" That was the question she asked him every evening when they were walking together to the river. Ryan looked intently at Keshia. He scanned every part of her face with his gaze before answering.

"I feel things that I haven't felt in years. You healed me in a way I almost forgot. You touched me, Cheyenne woman. I am completely healthy again and I know that I have to go. Nobody asked me what I wanted."

His quiet words sounded wistful. He smiled weakly. Ryan felt his heart beat faster and harder as he reached for Keshia's hands. He did not dare to think about his wish.

Keshia looked somewhat embarrassed. Ryan noticed that her cheeks turned reddish.

"What do you want?", she asked softly, looking at his eyes.

"You", he answered hoarsely. "And you? Do you want me to come back and get you?"

Keshia trembled as if she was suddenly freezing. She gasped and blushed even more than she already did.

"I'm scared", she whispered. "You too, Ryan, threw my life off track. More than you think."

"What are you afraid of?"

"Of you."

There was a lack of understanding in his questioning look and the smile faded.

"I saw the weapons in your backpack, your equipment and you are looking. You ... you are a bounty hunter.

Someone who doesn't care what or why someone did something. You finish your job, collect the money and disappear. Maybe some didn't deserve it any other way. So why would you want to help Black Snake?"

"I still have a week to get him to the trial in time. They think he won't come."

"And what do you think?"

"He will not come."

"Do you believe in the justice of the white courts?"

Ryan let go of her hands and slowly walked on.

"My client believes in it. Otherwise he wouldn't have sent me. There is still a chance for him. If the deadline has passed and Black Snake does not appear voluntarily, it will no longer exist."

"And if nobody finds him?"

Ryan laughed softly. "They have their specialists and methods. It's only a matter of time. If you want to help him tell him to talk to me."

"What happens if the deadline has passed and you have not found it?"

They had almost reached the bank. Ryan stopped again and entered Keshia's away. His face remained serious when he looked at her.

"You know that yourself. The FBI will show up here and they'll take the whole reservation apart. They won't give up until they have him. And then they won't care what and why he did something."

Keshia swallowed hard.

"Yes. I know", she sighed dejectedly.

The water rustled softly on its way into the valley. The wind rocked the leaves in the treetops. A horse whinnied from afar. Dream and reality blurred together.

"What's your full name?", heard Ryan Keshia's voice.

 133

"My name is Ryan Black Hawk."

"My name is Keshia Black Snake", she said determined.

Ryan turned his gaze to her and looked at her intently. She stood motionless in front of him, her face hidden behind an expressionless mask and holding his gaze. The blush had left her face. Suddenly she looked pale under her brown skin.

"You found the Black Snake", she said.

Ryan nodded slowly. "I had such thoughts, but maybe I didn't want to be true."

Ryan took a deep breath.

"You helped me and saved my life, Keshia Black Snake. Will you be able to trust me?"

"If not you, who then?", she whispered.

Ryan sat down, plucked a long blade of grass, and started playing.

"Take a seat next to me. Tell me everything."

"What did your client tell you?", she asked as she sat down on the grass next to Ryan.

"That I should bring him Black Snake before the trial date."

"Not more?"

"A Cheyenne, here in the reservation."

Keshia shook her head in disbelief. Then she started to tell.

"I was a nurse at the Medicine Health Center in Forsyth. I had just passed my exams and had only been able to work on my own for a few weeks. The chief doctor called me one afternoon and asked me to do something for his friend. It was urgent and he could not drive himself. I did it. Multiple times. It didn't bother and it was right on my way. On the twenty-first of June this year the last time."

Keshia took a deep breath before continuing.

"When I knocked, the door was open a splat wide. I went in with the little box and called his name. There was no answer. I was about to put it on the table in the living room when I heard a groan. It came from the bathroom. I called again and went there. When I opened the ajar door ..."

Keshia paused and searched for words. It is difficult for her to speak. "He lay in a pool of blood with several bullet holes and wheezed. The whole bathroom was full of blood. I knelt down to him, believing that I could still help him. He moved his lips as if to say something to me. I did not understand it. His eyes broke and in the same instant I was ... I was surrounded by a whole police unit, which had their weapons pointed at me ready to fire. I was so scared and jumped up. I was immediately over-whelmed. I myself was full of blood and my fingerprints were everywhere. Especially on the small box. They opened it in front of my eyes."

Keshia gasped and bravely blinked away the tears. Dejected, she shook her head. "It was full of small, individually packaged ampoules from our hospital needs. A strong pain reliever containing morphine. Although nobody found a weapon with my fingerprints, they arrested me on the spot. In the pre-trial detention there were rather rough manners and no one believed me a word. Our chief doctor, whose name I had given, of course knew of no package, of no favor and no friend. Somehow our people found the money for the deposit. It was not little. They believed me", Keshia finished her explanation.

"Do you have a good lawyer?", Ryan asked, trying not to make the question look cynical.

"My father is on the way to an Indian lawyer. He has his

address. We cannot afford another and I do not want a white lawyer, a duty defender that I do not trust."

"This doctor, is he still working in the clinic?"

"Yes."

"His name?"

"Richard Hollister."

"I will visit him."

"Do you think he shot him?"

"No. But he can lead me to the murderer."

Keshia reached for Ryan's arm as if looking for it. He took it up, put it around her and gently pressed her to him. She leaned her head on his shoulder.

"I won't go to prison again", she said softly but firmly. "I rather kill myself."

"No, Keshia. You will live and I will do anything for it."

Ryan took his cell phone and made a call.

"Ryan here. We need to talk."

"Where are you?", he clearly heard Thompson's voice.

"In the reservation."

"Do you have Black Snake?"

"We need to talk urgently!"

"Okay. I come halfway to meet you. We meet on the Scenic View Plateau. It will be night before I am there", Thompson agreed.

"I'll be there."

"Okay."

Ryan put the phone away.

Keshia turned her gaze to him and looked into his eyes, fearful and hopeful at the same time.

"I'll be back tomorrow morning", Ryan said.

Keshia sighed.

*****

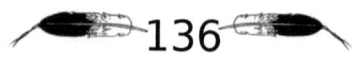

The forest was dark and lonely. Only the headlights of the Corvette wandered over the asphalt of the serpentines and touched tree trunks and bushes. The narrow road screwed up the mountain and ended on a high plateau. Ryan turned off the street and parked his car between the trees in the shelter of some bushes. He turned off the engine. At first he couldn't see anything on the moonless night. It took a while for the eyes to get used to the dark. From here he could observe the plateau without being seen. Ryan got out and put on the black blouson. It was cold. In the silence of the night the leaves rustled softly in the wind. Some fell heavily and noisily on the damp floor. Ryan's breath evaporated into smoke in front of his mouth and nose. He lit a cigarette and sat on the warm hood. He cleverly hid the embers of the cigarette with his hand. The smoke mingled with that of his breath. When he took the last puff, he heard engine noise. A Dodge rolled slowly into the parking lot of the Scenic View Plateau. Ryan kicked out the cigarette. When he recognized Thompson, Ryan revealed himself.

Thompson opened the door.

"Jump in. It's too cold out there for me."

Ryan got in.

Thompson's glasses glittered at Ryan in the dark. "Tell me!", he asked Ryan.

"Why did you make me think Black Snake is a man?"

Thompson laughed softly. "I never said that."

"But you knew it", Ryan hissed.

Thompson cleared his throat.

"You're right. I should have told you. Is she pretty?"

"Guess what", Ryan hissed.

"Oh, Ryan. The first time I experience you angry. It gets

complicated."

"You can bet your bottom dollar."

Thompson sighed deeply.

"Okay, I hear", Thompson replied, lighting a cigarette.

Ryan told Thompson everything he could find out. Thompson whistled softly through his teeth. Then Ryan set out his plans to Thompson.

"You have to leave the Black Snake case to me, Ryan. You are not a cop. I will reopen the investigation."

"Hm", Ryan grumbled.

"Believe me. I've always stood by my word, Ryan. You know that."

Ryan didn't move. He thought.

"Give me three full days before you send your men", he finally said.

Thompson lit the second cigarette and kept silent for a while. Ryan waited patiently for a decision.

"That's against the rule. You are hunter. It's not your job to clear up the cases."

"I know that. In that case it will decide whether to live or die."

Ryan noticed Thompson shake his head. The glasses mirrored the shimmer of the embers.

"It was a mistake on my part to send a Lakota to bring a Cheyenne."

"No, Thompson! It was a mistake myself to ask. A head-hunter is not concerned with what and why someone did what."

Thompson sighed loudly and extensively.

"Oh my God. You fell in love with her, Ryan", Thompson said.

"And when, Thompson. I'm a man and she's a woman. Sometimes that can happen", Ryan said cynically. "By

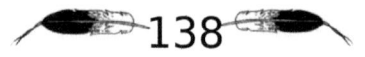

the way she's called Keshia. She has been fooled, abused and scared. Before she has to go to prison for something she hasn't done, she'll kill herself."

"We will prevent that."

"By taking away the shoelaces and belt from Keshia?" Ryan hissed angrily. "She will do it."

"How come?"

"She is an Indian, a Cheyenne and she is a medicine woman. Things that no white person understands. But you, Thompson!"

Thompson hesitated before finally nodding.

"I can't approve of you. I'm not allowed. I don't know what you will do in the next three days. You'll bring me Black Snake to trial. I know that. My trust and my job is in your hands."

"We'll be there. You have my word on that."

"Does she have a lawyer?"

"Yes. I hope that he will be there in time."

"OK. See you next week."

Ryan smiled at Thompson in the dark.

"See you soon", he triumphed and got out.

Thompson started his Dodge and drove slowly away.

*****

The morning sun shone through the window panes onto the floor. The shadows of the frames formed patterns. For more than two hours an Indian had been waiting in the corridor of station B in the Medicine Health Center Forsyth. He had settled on one of the chairs. With his eyes apparently closed, he leaned motionlessly against the wall with his head, so that one could think he was sleeping. Through the tiny crack of his eyelids, Ryan

139

watched the waiting ones. Emerging and disappearing sisters, a cleaning lady and a man who was picked up by a taxi driver. What was particularly interesting for him was the office behind the glass wall, which enabled him to watch the sisters at work. So far it has been pretty uninteresting. Ryan was waiting for the doctors and especially for Hollister.

All chairs were now occupied. At some point two doctors caught Ryan's attention. A younger and an older came running down the hall. They reported to one of the sisters. She immediately took a stack of documents and a small device, similar to a cell phone, and followed them. Ryan got up and accidentally nudged her, causing some of the sheets to fall out of her hand.

"Sorry", he said to her and stooped to pick it up.

"I have an appointment with Doctor Hollister today and have been waiting here for a long time. Is he there?"

"Yes. But he's very busy right now. Please wait in the waiting area."

The older of the two doctors turned around and called impatiently: "Where are you? We are in a hurry. Can't you be careful?"

"I'm coming, Doctor Hollister."

Ryan hadn't turned directly to Hollister so he couldn't see his face. But Ryan had Hollister's face and the voice well memorized. Then he went to look for Hollister's office. Nobody prevented him. Not even the door was locked. Since Hollister was very busy at the moment, he would hardly appear here anytime soon. Ryan pulled on the gloves Keshia had given him so as not to leave fingerprints. Then he locked the door from the inside.

First Ryan started the PC. The program asked for an access code. Ryan's eyes fell on the family photo on the desk. He looked at its back, but found no clue. Ryan took his cell phone and connected it to the PC with his wire. Then he picked up a ballpoint pen and tapped it several times on the cell phone's keyboard. It took a few seconds for the code to be decrypted. The screen opened and greeted with a melody. Ryan grimaced and turned off the sound. Immediately there was a knock on the door. Ryan didn't move.

"Hello! Doctor Hollister!"

Then it was quiet.

No steps.

"Doctor Hollister? Are you there?"

Ryan bit his lip and looked at the shadow in the crack underneath the door. He hoped that this person with the female voice would finally understand that Hollister was not there. She didn't seem to have given it up yet and knocked again. Then finally Ryan heard the footsteps moving away. He immediately opened the files and searched. He opened calendar, notes, addresses and many other too, possibly important things. Ryan sighed. The search would take hours. He did not have this time. Ryan inserted a stick into the computer and transferred the data. That alone would take a long time. Meanwhile he systematically searched the office. In the meantime, he had developed a feeling for quickly finding important things for him. Ryan grinned when he found a bottle of the finest Scotch Whiskey behind the files on the shelf, leaving everything exactly as he found it. When he came across a locked pigeonhole in the closet, he opened it with the tip of his knife. There was a small, white box, no bigger than a deck of cards. Ryan looked inside. There were six amber glass ampoules, each containing two milliliters of liquid. Just as many were missing or would still fit in. He picked up one of these and looked at it more closely. According to Keshia's description, these were exactly the ampoules. *Morphin* was written on it, as well as numbers and a barcode. Ryan pulled a plastic bag out of his pocket, the way the people from the evidence security department used it, and pocketed everything. Then he searched the loose sheets that were in the compartment. They were accompanying notes for the medication. He also pocketed one of them.

Ryan paused as he heard footsteps from a single person. The sound of the steps ceased. Someone must have stopped at the door. The doorknob moved slowly. That someone finally seemed to accept that it was closed and went on.

Ryan locked the pigeonhole again. Of course Hollister would immediately notice that something was missing.

But then the evidence is in a safe place, Ryan thought.

He continued to search and dealt extensively with the desk. The drawer was locked here too. No obstacle for Ryan. But he didn't find what he was looking for. Hollister's phone rang. After the fifth tone it fell silent. Ryan wrote down Hollister's number. The calendar on the desk was almost empty. Ryan flipped back to the month of June and took a closer look at all of the records before. There was only one entry on June 21st.

Exam nurse Keshia.

Ryan put the entire calendar in one of his bags. Hollister would also notice that immediately.

Ryan smiled.

Then he glanced at the PC. The data transfer was just finished when he heard the hasty steps of two men in the corridor. He heard them talk to each other and recognized Hollister's voice. Ryan pulled the stick and plug from the computer. It had to go quickly. With a few leaps he jumped to the door and opened the lock from the inside.

At the same moment the door was pushed open and Hollister came in with a colleague. The two men were so engrossed in their conversation that they did not notice how a black figure scurried out from behind their backs. The door closed.

Ryan stayed outside for a moment. He breathed quickly through the half-open mouth and the adrenaline made his heart beat fast. The blood pounded violently in the veins. Ryan clearly heard Hollister's words.

"May I ask you for a favor, Fisherman. You finish your duty earlier than me. My brother urgently needs his medication and I..."

Ryan couldn't risk more because he heard footsteps in the corridor again. Whoever came, the space in front of the door was empty.

*****

Ryan drove straight to Jimmy's snack truck in the Northern Cheyenne Reservation. He parked in front of the door and hurried in. Keshia and Jimmy stood behind the counter and immediately looked at the Lakota. Apart from a few young people, there was no one here. They chewed pizza and hamburgers and ignored him.

Ryan nodded to Jimmy.

"Come with me a second!", he asked Keshia.

She hesitated for a moment.

"Go", said Jimmy finally.

Ryan silently avoided Jimmy's skeptical looks. Keshia went out with Ryan.

"Do you have electricity?"

"At home, yes."

"Then we go there."

It turned out that Keshia lived at the other end of Cherry Groves, in one of the usual thin-walled prefabricated houses that only differed in color. She cleared the table in the living room, which was not very large, and opened towards the kitchen, as usual.

"Do you live here alone?", Ryan asked.

"No. With my father. My grandparents also live here in winter."

"Matthew Black Snake."

"Yes, but from where...?" Keshia did not finish her sentence. After all, it was his job to find out everything.

"Your grandmother told me a lot. After all, we spent a lot of time together", Ryan grinned.

Keshia laughed softly.

He put his laptop on the table, turned it on and put the stick in it. Then he took out the small package with the ampoules from his backpack and showed it to Keshia.

"Do you know that?"

She nodded.

"It has always been exactly that."

"Hollister continues to work. A young doctor is his courier. If I hadn't had to run away, I would now know where he wanted to send him. I will search his files for something useful. Your name is in his diary, on the twenty-first of June. Did your father reach the lawyer?"

"Yes, he has. They both come here tomorrow. Do you want a coffee?"

"Better a whole jug full. The night can be long."

"Okay."

Ryan sat down at the table and started working. When

Keshia had made the coffee, she sat down with him. "Thanks, Ryan."

He just smiled and took a sip of coffee. Only after a while did he say: "He disguised you here several times as an appointment. A jealous wife would have pursued other thoughts." Ryan turned his eyes to Keshia and grinned.

Then he took a sip of coffee. Keshia moved closer to Ryan and looked at the screen.

"Can you still remember all these dates, Keshia? I would like to know if the guy forgot one or added it after-wards."

Keshia went through the listing carefully.

"Everything is correct."

"What was the name of the one you brought the stuff to?"

"Allen. He said that and that was also on his apartment door. Not more."

Ryan nodded and marked any points that might be important. He searched meticulously. Until well after midnight the two of them put their heads together, read all the words without exception and spoke quietly to each other. Keshia was obviously tired. Ryan's eyes burned. He rubbed it several times. It only made them more irritable.

"If this continues, I need glasses", he said.

Keshia laughed softly. "Maybe we should go to sleep", she murmured.

Ryan drank the last sip of coffee that was already cold.

"Yes, you are right. That will be the best."

He took a deep breath, stretched his back, and turned to Keshia. Their looks met and nobody tried to avoid them. Ryan slowly extended his hand to her and stroked her hair back. Then he gently pulled her head closer to him.

Instead of kissing her, he leaned his forehead against hers. Keshia tentatively fingered his face and touched his lips.

"I can't ...", she whispered ".... believe that you are doing this for me."

"I'm a hunter and I never asked what and why someone did what. But you, Keshia, touched me and aroused a feeling in me that I thought was dead in me. I will love you."

"Nobody has loved me yet", she replied barely audibly.

Ryan got up, pulled her up and took her in his arms.

"I have not yet fulfilled my mission. Trust me whatever happens", he whispered.

Keshia snuggled up to him and nodded.

Keshia was still asleep when Ryan was back on his laptop. Jimmy had released her until the day of the trial. Around noon Keshia's father came back with the lawyer, Russel Broken Hand. Ryan gave him a detailed account of what he had learned. After Russel got an insight into the case, he said that it would be advantageous to have witnesses.

"This Hollister has a pretty clean slate and if no one testifies against him it will be difficult. The evidence has illegally gotten into our hands. Keshia is a young, inexperienced nurse and Indian on top of that. I'm sorry, Keshia, when I say that. We don't only want to defend you we also want to attack. This doctor should and must not get off scot-free from that", Russel said.

Ryan nodded.

"I take care of it. Today and tomorrow I have time before the deadline has passed. You can use my laptop. Everything that I copied from Hollister's PC is on the stick."

"I hope you know your limits, Black Hawk." Russel looked worriedly at Ryan.

"Of course."

Russel nodded.

Ryan finished his coffee and got up. Keshia followed him out the door to his parked sports car.

"Take care of yourself, Lakotaman", she said softly.

"I do. So we'll see each other the day after tomorrow, on the day of the trial."

"Will you take me .... me there?"

"That's the order."

Ryan noticed her fear. He felt the slight tremor running through her body as he pulled her towards him. He took her head in his hands and forced her to look at him.

"I gave my word on it to someone. Trust me, Keshia, whatever happens."

Her eyes gleamed treacherously when she nodded.

"If not you, who then?", she whispered.

Ryan smiled. He looked at her face as if trying to memorize it exactly. Then he let his hands drop. With a short *bye* he turned and got in the car.

*****

It was afternoon when Ryan parked in the parking lot at the Medicine Health Center Forsyth again. At first, he looked around the staff parking lots carefully. Then Ryan went in and asked at the reception if Doctor Fisherman was in the house today.

"He is far from being a doctor", grinned the old man. "He wants to be one. Who are you?"

"Hawk. I rammed his car into the parking lot, but I'm not sure if it was his. I'll have to wait for him outside."

"The little light green? Looks like a frog", the man laughed, amused. "Nobody here drives anything like that."

"Yes. Thanks Sir", Ryan said and went back to the parking lot. He lit a cigarette, leaned against the half-height wall, and smoked. Then he got behind the steering wheel of his Corvette and waited patiently. For a long time, nothing happened. Ryan fought the fatigue that gave him work last night. Some people came and went. Not fisherman.

It wasn't until five in the evening that Fisherman finally got to his frog-green car. The young doctor was tall, slim, had very short hair and horn-rimmed glasses.

An inconspicuous average person and maybe he's just as clueless as Keshia had been, Ryan thought.

Fisherman got in and drove out of the clinic parking lot. Ryan follow him. The green car drove west.

    St. Labre Indian School. 22 miles ahead

was written on a signpost. The car turned in this direction. Ryan's face darkened. After about eight miles, pouring houses appeared between the trees. This collection of houses could hardly be called a place.

Ash Springs, was written on a nondescript signpost. It seemed to be only one road that led through here. Fisherman stopped and parked the car on the side of the road. A dense, high hedge hid the property. He actually seemed careful enough not to park directly in front of the house. Ryan waited. Fisherman got out.

Ryan too.

He watched Fisherman go to one of the houses while opening the car door. Silently, quickly and invisibly, as he had learned in training, he ultimately followed the target person. Fisherman was terrified when he saw the strange man who was suddenly right behind him before he rang the doorbell.

"One wrong move or wrong word and you're dead", Ryan hissed.

Fisherman took his hands up to his chest. They trembled. He was trembling.

"Who ... who are you?" he stuttered.

"Your guardian angel, Fisherman", Ryan said softly. "Give me the package and wait for me in your car."

"Why should I..."

"Because otherwise you are dead", Ryan hissed impatiently. "So do what I tell you!"

His words looked like a warning shot. Fisherman immediately turned and ran to his car.

Ryan grinned.

He glanced at the door sign. T. Miller was written on it. Then he knocked on the door. A middle-aged man opened it. He was a little shorter than Ryan, had a wellgroomed beard and stared at Ryan questioningly.

"I have a package from Hollister."

The man looked around suspiciously. Then he nodded and cleared the door.

"Okay. Come in."

Ryan entered and looked around. The man who was just closing the door behind him seemed to be alone.

"How much?", he asked.

Ryan turned to him.

"As always", he replied.

"Really?", he asked astonished. "The last courier says that Hollister wants ten percent more."

"The pale-faced young doctor wearing horn-rimmed glasses?"

The man nodded.

"He's probably taking it out on himself. That's why Hol-

lister sent me."

A smile appeared on the man's face.

"Is anyone else here, Miller?"

The smile faded from Miller's face.

"No names, damn it."

"It says on the sign outside", Ryan defended himself.

Miller snorted angrily.

"Give me the ampoules and beat it."

Ryan grinned smugly.

"My price is much higher."

Miller stared at Ryan with wide, amazed eyes.

"What do you want?"

"You."

"Who the hell are you?", Miller croaked as his face turned powder red.

Ryan took out the handcuffs and put them on the
surprised man before he understood what was going on.

"Fuck! You're a cop", Miller grunted.

"And you will accompany me."

"Forget it. I will tell you nothing!"

"You will talk."

"They'll kill me", Miller growled.

"If they don't, I'll do it."

Miller swallowed hard.

"You are not from the police."

"No", Ryan replied shortly. "So ... who are you selling the
ampoules and when?"

Miller was obviously scared, but he said nothing. Ryan
pulled his gun and pointed it at him. Miller narrowed his
eyes.

"What do I hear", said Ryan.

"I ... I'm just a ... a ... even a courier", Miller stammered.

Ryan let the trigger tap click clearly.

Miller raised his trembling hands. Ryan looked at the open palms he was holding protectively in front of his face. The man was afraid. He was not a professional.

"I don't even know these guys who pick up the parcels from me."

"Are they always the same?"

Miller wriggled. He didn't want to continue talking. Ryan pressed the barrel of the gun to his temple.

"Good bye. I hope you are worth it", Ryan hissed softly in his ear.

"No! ... No, wait! They are always the same. They pay well and in cash immediately", Miller said hastily, gasping for breath.

"When?"

"Even today. Around eleven."

"You know their faces. You can describe it to me."

Miller nodded and slowly lowered his hands. Then he blinked at Ryan. Sweat had formed on his forehead and was bubbling over the skin in slow motion.

Ryan took a step back and looked expectantly at Miller. He still had the pistol pointed at him. Miller seemed indecisive to search for words.

"They come in pairs. The driver waits in the car in front of the door. One is tall, slim and black. He is about thirty and has a smooth-shaven skull. His arms are tattooed. He never talks. The other is about the same age, white and half a head shorter. He almost makes a serious impression like a businessman and always wears a white shirt and a dark gray jacket with jeans. He has brown hair, a mustache and scars on both cheeks that look like several bullet holes. He always wears sunglasses. I could never look him in the eye. They left me alone, but I was happy when they were gone. Now they're going to kill

151

me, damn it."

"You have to reckon with this if you engage in such businesses. They shot the last guy of your kind in his own bathroom. Looked bad."

Miller suddenly turned pale. Ryan grabbed his arm and urged him to the door. "Move!"

The man reluctantly surrendered.

When Ryan turned around the hedge with him, Fisherman's green car was still there. Ryan grinned triumphantly. The doctor was sitting behind the wheel and didn't move. Ryan led Miller right there. The passenger door of the green car opened. A big, bearded man got out.

"Nice to see you Baxter."

"You're actually still alive", Baxter said. "I already believed in a hallucination when I heard your voice on the phone."

"Red medicine", Ryan smiled.

"Oh... tell me! What can i do for you my friend?"

"Grab the two guys and don't let them out of your sight until tomorrow. Not even in the toilet. The court hearing begins at ten o'clock. I'll give you the address. Bring them to me on time and as safe as possible."

"Are you serious that i should spend the night with them in a hotel room?"

Ryan nodded. "Haven't you always wanted to...", he smiled.

Baxter grimaced and slapped Ryan on the shoulder.

"Thank you my friend. And you?"

"I'm having a cozy evening here in Mr. Miller's house. He expects visitors and it would be rude if no one opens the door."

"And you can manage alone?"

"I am quick and invisible."

"Never underestimate your opponents. That could be your undoing."

"You use my words. Don't you have your own?"

"Make sure you get your ass dry before I have to drag you out of the mess", Baxter growled.

Then he laughed. "And don't get caught by the cops."

Ryan shook his head, grinning, and put Miller in Fisherman's car.

"You'll testify against Hollister and his friends, tomorrow morning if you want to survive. Until then you are under mine and Goodman's protection",Ryan said, withdrawing from the inside of the car without waiting for an answer.

"Don't you think the two sausages prosecute us for the unlawful imprisonment?", Baxter doubted.

"Unfounded evidence. You, Mato, will convince them."

"Me!?"

Ryan grinned. "Yes, you can be very convincing."

Baxter grunted and squeezed into the passenger seat. Ryan slammed the door. Fisherman started his car.

Ryan followed the frog green car, picked up his phone, and dialed Thompson's number.

"If I am caught and arrested by the police this evening with three men and Hollister's morphine ampoules, can you get me out of pre-trial detention that night?", Ryan asked straightforwardly when Thompson called.

Thompson actually seemed to be speechless. Ryan clearly heard his deep breath.

"Do you think I'm a magician?"

"Yes I think so. I gave my word to someone to get Black Snake to trial tomorrow morning."

"Hell, Ryan, what are you up to? You´re bringing me into

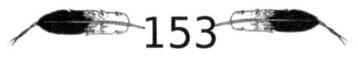

the devil´s kitchen! Why don't you call the Police Department Lame Deer, Forsyth or wherever you are right now? They can send their men for reinforcements."

"I will do that too. Only these three men, whom I mentioned at the beginning, are professionals. You will not enter the house when there is no one in and you have nothing with you to burden. Consequently, even an arrest would not be justified, and even if they were, they would be released in an hour. The local police must catch us in the act. Me too, because in that case I'm the one who opens the door."

Ryan heard Thompson's deep breath again. Then it was quiet. He seemed to be thinking.

"I can't start the helicopter until after midnight", he finally said. "That means we will hardly be there before three in the morning. Where?"

"Ash Springs, so Lame Deer."

"It's going to be a sleepless night", Thompson groaned.

"I trust you."

"I'll be there. See you."

"See you then", Ryan said and hung up.

He looked at the Corvette, strolled there, and took the small, black backpack out of the trunk. Then he took a deep breath and headed back to Miller's house.

*****

Ryan looked around the house. He inspected every room thoroughly and memorized everything exactly. It could make a decision about life or death, because it was obvious that the men who would soon enter this house were armed. Then he switched on the television, just so that he could hear the voices, and sat in the armchair. It

was now a quarter to nine in the evening. Dusk covered the street. The light in the house remained off. Much before eleven, Ryan heard the sound of a car. He jumped up from his chair and looked out of the window. The car stopped right before the entrance. The headlight went out. Two men got out. As they went to the front door, Ryan took Millers phone, dialed the emergency number, and put the receiver under the armchair.

There was a knock.

Ryan went to the door and opened it.

A black and a white man stood in front of him, just as Miller had described. Ryan took a step back and nodded that the men should enter.

They eyed Ryan suspiciously.

"Where's Miller?", the white man asked.

"They caught him. That's why I'm waiting here. I have the package."

Ryan's looks roamed the street and the garden carefully. Only the black limousine with the driver stood in front of the house. He clearly felt the distrust of the two. The white man nodded at the bald man, whereupon he indicated that he was carrying a weapon. Ryan showed his palms.

"They can watch us. So come in", he said.

"I hope for you, you are alone in the house. Switch on the light", the one with the mustache demanded. He spoke softly and not rude. He actually seemed to have a certain amount of style. Ryan switched on the light.

„I don't trust anyone except myself. That's why I'm alone."

The man smiled coolly.

Both entered.

Before Ryan could close the door, two black-clad figures

155

appeared, preventing him from doing so. They had come out of nowhere silently and quickly. The inscription on their vests let Ryan know that it was a Lame Deer police force.

"Drug investigation. Immediately put your hands over your head!", ordered a female voice.

Ryan stepped aside, hands over his head.

Get out of the line of fire, Black Hawk!

A shot fell in his mind.

Ryan instinctively threw himself to the ground. Then he felt the thud on his head. He felt dizzy. The images blurred before his eyes. Two more shots were fired. People's voices moved further and further away from his consciousness.

He felt that someone was kneeling near him and taking his head in his hands. There were soft hands.

"He lives! Fetch the emergency doctor!", he heard a woman's voice from afar and opened his eyes. But the shadowy shape became a black, opaque wall. A waterfall roared in Ryan's ears.

Then suddenly it was quiet.

*****

Keshia waited in vain for Ryan's return after a sleepless night. He was not available on the phone. Father tried to calm her down. In vain. He had to say goodbye to her. It was hard to have to leave at that very moment. Keshia understood him and smiled bravely. Her voice trembled when she said: "Don't worry Dad. Russel is with me."

They hugged each other. Matthew kissed his daughter's forehead.

Keshia paced restlessly and anxiously in the living room

when her father left. She dialed Ryan's number several times. His phone seemed to be off. The uncertainty tortured Keshia. Russel was sitting on Ryan's laptop. He was deep in thoughts too. Without testimony against Hollister, it would actually be difficult to get his client out of the lawsuit unscathed.

Neloa and Adam held back indecisively. It was only a quarter past seven.

An hour later, Keshia's phone rang.

Ryan!

Finally!

Her heart pounded against the chest as she answered. But another voice spoke to her.

"Thompson here. Good morning Miss Black Snake."

Keshia swallowed.

What happened?!

"Yes", she whispered.

"You called this number several times. I will pick you up and bring you to trial."

"Who are you and why do you have his phone?"

"Actually it's my phone. I am… ", the voice stopped abruptly. Keshia took a deep breath. "...his client."

"What about Ryan? Why doesn't he report himself? He wanted to be here long ago. He promised me", Keshia hissed desperately into the receiver.

"Something came up."

"What happened?", she whispered.

"Did you contact the lawyer?"

"He's here."

"Well. Then you come with him. In time. I trust you."

Keshia gasped. She was missing the words.

"Can I rely on that?"

"Yes, you can", Keshia replied softly.

There was silence in the receiver. The strange man had hung up. She turned to her lawyer and stared at him as if he were a ghost.

"Any word from him?"

Keshia shook her head. "He doesn't come", she said softly. "Something came up."

"Did he leave a message for us?"

Dejected, Keshia shook her head.

Russel took a deep breath. Then he turned off the laptop.

"I'll take him with me to safety", he said and finished his coffee.

Then he packed up his things. "It's time for us to leave", he said.

"I'm scared", she whispered.

Russel smiled.

"He did a lot for you and did a good job. I can do something with that. But now it's my turn to do my job, Keshia. You'll have to trust me now and I'm really good", he said proudly.

Keshia smiled bravely.

"Well. Let's go", she said.

Cold, damp air struck Keshia as she stepped out the car. The wind messed up her hair and made it flutter across her face. It didn't seem to bother her. The morning was cold and gray. The wind hurriedly drove the clouds. They hung deep in the mountains. There would be rain. Things didn't look better in Lame Deer either. The parking lot in front of the courthouse was quite full. Russel found a gap strait in front of the stairs to the entrance. They got out.

Keshia looked around. Hope did not escape from her. Her mind brought her back to reality.

A black commander stopped on the opposite side of the street. The driver got out and went to the car parked in front of him. The drivers spoke to each other. Keshia turned and went up the stairs with her lawyer to the entrance.

*****

Harsh winds whipped rain against the gray walls of the courthouse. Some people hurriedly struggled with their umbrellas, although it seemed pretty useless. The wind had brought the cold of the north, which was to herald the approaching winter. The mild and sunny autumn days finally seemed to be a thing of the past.

Hours later, Keshia came out of the big door on her side, Russel Broken Hand. They slowly went down the steps. The wind immediately loosened a few strands of hair from her braid and blew them over her expressionless face. Even the rain that was slowly drenching her seemed to ignore her. Although she had been acquitted of the murder charge, she had been given probation for life on drug-beating. As a nurse, she should have known that. Two strange men, a young doctor from the Medicine Health Center in Frosyth and a teacher from the St. Labre Indian School, testified against Hollister. An investigation against the doctor has now been initiated. Keshia felt neither satisfaction nor joy.

She felt a strange emptiness in her.

She had been registered as a criminal record because of the drug offense. It was a very bitter experience that she now carried with her.

Russel Broken Hand had noticed immediately that her eyes were roaming about again. His young client looked nervous.

"Come on, Keshia. There is my car. Let's wait there before the rain completely dissolves."

Keshia nodded and followed.

Dark clouds clouded the day. The rain pattered loudly on the car and obscured the view through the windows. The windows steam up. The fog made the human figures on the street and the lights of the cars passing by blur.

"Do you need a probation officer", Russel asked a little amused and grinned mysterious.

"Don't you trust me?", she asked indignantly. "I'm already off my job as a nurse and maybe someone will never hire me again with the criminal record. So no more opportunity. Besides, I wouldn't be that stupid again."

Russel nodded.

Keshia looked at him briefly and smiled weakly. Then she took her phone out of her pocket and looked out on the street before dialing a number. Her expectant look faded from disappointment when no one answered. The sound of the rain on the car mingled with the monotonous sound of the wipers. Russel took a deep breath. Keshia stared at the phone in her hands and struggled with tears.

"I'll drive you home", Russel said finally,

Keshia sighed and slowly loosened up from her stiffness. She put the phone away. "It's a big detour for you."

"Right. But I'm Cherokee." He laughed.

"Okay. Thank you Russel. Thank you for everything."

"Are you waiting for him."

"I thought he was coming. I hoped so much... but ...", Keshia stammered sadly.

"He's a headhunter. His order has ended."

Keshia swallowed hard and remained silent. She felt like crying.

Russel started the car without saying a word.

*****

Keshia was tired, depressed and sad when she arrived at her grandparents' house with Russell Broken Hand. The rain had subsided. The haze hung in the mountains. Politely and gratefully, she invited the lawyer to stay. It was already six o'clock in the evening. The front door opened when they both got out. Her grandparents also asked him to stay. Dinner smelled in the house. Russel thankfully accepted the invitation.

While grandfather Adam was talking to the lawyer, Keshia strolled to grandmother Neloa in the kitchen.

"Nice that you are here. You will be hungry. I cooked for us. It will be ready soon."

Keshia nodded sadly. She did not dare to say that she had no appetite. The two most important men in her live were missing. They were not here and they would not come to eat. Father had already gone into the mountains with hunters in the morning. He hadn't been able to wait because the order would take them all through the winter. Keshia knew that.

The time of the hunters, she thought.

Keshia's father had no regular job. He took on all sorts of jobs to take care of his family. Sometimes he also looked for lost people for the Rocky Mountain Rescue Service. He was rare at home. She hardly knew it any other way. She and her brother had grown up with it since the death of their mother.

And the other hunter? Ryan? She didn't know where he

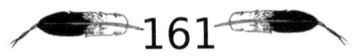

was. He had left no message.

Will I ever see you again, Lakotaman? Keshia doubted.
Will you stand by your words?

Compassionately, grandmother hugged her. Keshia could no longer hold back her tears.

The next day Keshia reported back to Jimmy. He didn't ask. Keshia said nothing. She looked absent and sad. Late in the evening when he closed, Jimmy hugged her and gently squeezed her. Keshia didn't resist. She held on to him for a while and cried silently. Jimmy had noticed that. He was her friend and he understood her without words.

Had Ryan ever said he would return? He hadn't promised anything. *I will love you*, he had said.

His voice and his words accompanied Keshia in her thoughts and dreams and the hope that he came to her was born. This hope waned with every day, week and month that started. The first snow fell. Nevertheless, Ryan was haunted by her thoughts and did not let her come to rest. When Keshia closed her eyes, she saw his face in front of her. It hurts.

Where are you?
When are you coming?

But she didn't want to forget. She couldn't. She loved him and it hurt. She sensed that he was alive and hunting somewhere out there.

Jimmy hadn't missed Keshia's longing to look out for every sports car that came by. He also noticed the traces of disappointment on her face. Every time. He was silent with concern.

*****

The snow finally covered the country and enchanted the forests and mountains. A long, hard winter, which always brought worries and hardships, had come. Hunger and the cold made people troubled. In the houses, which were not insulated, the walls glittered with cold and often cost the life of many. Snow and cold still clung to mother earth as the days grew longer. The second month of the new year ended. Keshia was still looking, day after day, out of the street.

"He's a headhunter, everywhere and nowhere. A hunter who roams a large area needs his freedom", Jimmy finally said quietly to her one day.

"Or he has to take care of his wife and children and didn't tell me", she replied just as quietly. "Then it's better if he doesn't show up again", she added sadly.

And yet she listened to every car and hoped that it was the dark blue Corvette.

Neloa and Adam also watched with concern. Grandmother knew exactly what was going on in Keshia. With her confident smile, she tried to calm her granddaughter.

Every evening after working at Jimmy, Keshia drove her father's pick-up truck up to the spot where through summer stood her grandparents' teepee. The horses pricked up their ears between the trees. Three piebald and one black belonged to them. Keshia's father had been out in the mountains for two weeks. This time, however, he had left the horses behind. That was rare. She had to promise to take care and look after them herself every day. The animals were in good hands up here and lived almost like wild horses. They had large terrain, shelters and protection. The horses knew the engine noise of Matthews pick-up truck. It promised them food

and a few pats. Keshia often sang to them as she unloaded the hay.

That evening when Keshia stopped the truck at the
fence, she stared in confusion at her grandparents'
teepee, which was usually not here during the winter
and had not been here until last night. She eyed the tent
suspiciously. A strange horse was pegged in front of the
tent and a narrow column of smoke rose from the smoke vent. Keshia still believed in delusion. She closed her
eyes for a moment and opened them again. Everything
was as before. She slowly opened the driver's door, got
out and called: "Dad?"

Nobody answered. Even though she knew the teepee
very well and it was in the same place where it usually
was in summer, she took the pepper spray out of the
glove box. She already had a knife with her to cut the
hay bundles open. Keshia climbed onto the bed to throw
the bundles over the fence. Again and again she looked
around suspiciously. Then she pushed the loose hay off
the bed. The horses came up trustingly and nibbled without suspicion, as if everything were as usual.

Finally, Keshia jumped off and closed the loading area.
She kept sending her gaze to the tent. She shook her
head barely noticeably. She still couldn't believe what
she saw.

Suddenly a rider appeared.

Startled, she jumped back to find cover behind the truck.
She watched him with a pounding heart.

The stranger directed a dark brown horse to the tent
and stopped next to the other. He was wearing a black
cowboy hat that he had pulled deep into his face. The
fur collar of his denim jacket was turned up. At first it
looked as if he hadn't seen the truck. But then he turned

the horse on the spot and looked closely at her.

Keshia held her breath. Her scalp began to tingle. The heart was beating too fast. She opened her mouth. Suddenly she felt hot. She was unable to move. She had waited so long for him, hadn't heard from him for four months, and now he was sitting there, motionless on his horse. Without greeting, without making any effort to come to her.

He waited.

Keshia pulled herself together and emerged from behind the tailgate.

"Hey stranger! What are you looking for?", she shouted.

"I am looking for a black snake", he replied.

"What do you want from her?"

"I want to get her."

"What did she do to you?"

"She stole my senses." Ryan set the horse in motion and came up to Keshia. He stopped in front of her. "And my heart", he said softly.

Keshia gasped. She trembled all over and tried to control herself.

"My name is Keshia Black Snake", she said in a trembling voice.

Ryan jumped from the horse. "I thought so. Were you scared?", he smiled.

"For four months! Every day", she hissed.

Ryan laughed softly.

"Come with me!"

He reached for her hand and pulled her to the tent with him. There he pegged his horse next to the chestnut.

Keshia felt dizzy when he pulled her into the tent with him. Small flames lashed around the logs in the middle and filled the room with pleasant light and warmth. Ryan

took off his jacket and threw it on the floor. The Lakotaman stood very close to her and looked at her.

Keshia felt the flush on her face rise. She thought she
was dreaming. As if under a spell, she could not move,
could not look away from him, and could not speak. Each
of the two looked at the other in the light of the fire.

Ryan slowly raised a hand and brushed Keshia's hair
from his face. Stroked her cheek with his fingertips and
touched her lips. His fingers were freezing. Keshia trembled barely. Both hands groped for her neck. Stroked the
skin gently while his gaze seemed to pierce her. His face
looked hard. Keshia could not see a trace of a smile. The
Lakotaman looked tense and breathed violently as he
pulled her towards him with both hands and kissed her.
Uncontrolled, almost rough, he stuck his tongue into her
mouth. Keshia gasped, startled. His breath became even
fiercer and faster. Meanwhile they slowly sank to the
ground and stayed kneeling in front of each other. Ryan
took the jacket off Keshia without detaching from it.
Then his cold hands went under her sweater. Keshia's
skin contracted in a flash. She sucked the air sharply
through her nose.

Now she felt Ryan's smile.

She was trembling, not only because of his cold hands.
Regardless of that, he undressed her. Keshia let it
happen. Finally, he loosened his lips from her and looked
at her naked body.

Keshia swallowed hard. How much she had wished for
that moment. The man she loved so much had finally
come to her. And now she was afraid. When Ryan
touched Keshia's breasts, she trembled more than she
already did.

"Nobody has loved me yet", she answered, barely audible, his questioning look.

His facial features softened. A smile appeared around his lips.

"I will do it. Have no fear. Trust me."

Ryan's gentle words filled her body with warmth. She watched Ryan as he undressed himself. When she saw his erect penis, she felt a strange tingle in her abdomen. She had never felt that before. The man gently pressed her onto the soft blankets. His hair stroked her skin and followed his kisses. She was still trembling. Finally, she carefully began to explore his body with her hands. She heard his sharp breath on her ear when she felt the tip of his penis. This brought the man to the limit of his self-control.

"Not", he hissed.

With gentle but relentless pressure, Ryan's body shifted between Keshia's thighs. She felt his cold fingers, which touched her most sensitive spot.

Keshia trusted him.

She loved him.

Her heart beat faster and faster. Keshia felt every blow in her head. She took a deep breath when she felt the cold fingers on her. She closed her eyes while her feelings were all mixed up. As if by itself, she raised her pelvis. Keshia's fingers began to dig into the shoulders of the man above her as she gasped. Then she no longer felt the fingers playing. She blinked and recognized Ryan's face.

He smiled. There was a strange shimmer in his eyes. Suddenly Keshia felt him deep inside. A short pain made her groan. Then she felt things that she had never felt before. Intuitively she moved with and against him. She was getting hot. So hot that she thought she was going to burn. As if from afar, she heard his and her own quick breaths. For a moment, Keshia opened her eyes. In the flames she saw the face of the man she loved. His eyes shone feverishly. Then he closed his eyes and pressed his lips together. His rhythmic movements became more violent. Keshia opened her mouth as if to scream. Her whole abdomen contracted. She closed her eyelids and sighed while her muscles vibrated. Then she heard Ryan's tight breaths. Suddenly he seemed to hold his breath and paused.

„Oh, Keshia", Ryan whispered hoarsely and slowly slid onto her body.

Two hearts beat against the chest in the same rhythm, as if they wanted to burst. They slowly calmed down.

It was quiet.

Only the fire crackled softly. Their looks met at a short distance. Keshia smiled happily at Ryan. He smiled and kissed her, this time tenderly. The damp, naked bodies stuck together. At some point Ryan slid next to Keshia and put his arm under her neck. With the other hand he stroked her cheek. His fingers were no longer cold.

Keshia turned to him and clung to his body.

"I love you", she whispered.

Ryan raised his head, supported himself with his elbow, and looked at Keshia.

"I brought two good broodmares to your father. They are both pregnant, four horses. That's why he gave you to me as a wife."

Ryan grinned when he saw the surprised face.

"Men!", Keshia hissed and shook her head angrily. "What? Only four horses? Am I not worth more to you?"

"Possibly. Your father was happy with it."

"Did you have to negotiate with him for a long time?"

Ryan smiled.

"Three weeks. I promised him that if I should send you back to him he could keep the horses."

Keshia gave him an indignant bump.

"And I thought you loved me!" she hissed angrily.

"I do. If it weren't for that, I would have got the horses from him to take you."

Ryan was obviously having a hard time staying serious. When Keshia giggled, he laughed amused. Then he leaned down and touched her face with his lips.

"What had happened four months ago? Why didn't you bring me to trial?"

"I was hibernating?"

"I want to know the truth, Ryan!"

Ryan stopped kissing Keshia, leaned on his arms and looked at her. "It's the truth."

She carefully felt over the light streak that went up to his ear over his left cheekbones.

"Please. Tell me. I almost died."

"An accident at work. I was in the hospital."

"The scar?"

Ryan nodded. "Yes."

"You did not call. Nobody said anything to me. This strange man, your client, who called me on your cell phone on the day of the court hearing, only said that something had come up. He also didn't call again. Why didn't you do it?"

"Because I couldn't, Keshia. I was passed out for a long time. Someone shot at me."

Keshia stared at Ryan in horror.

Yes, he had a dangerous job. But how should she cope with that? Waiting for him, always in the uncertainty that he was still alive?

As if he could read her thoughts, he said: "I want to go back to my ranch with you. I want a family, children and above all you. That's what I'm fighting for, all year round, every day. I want to live where I'm at home and where I can do the job, what my heart is attached to."

Keshia smiled.

"I was so worried about you", she whispered. "Afraid that I'll never see you again."

Ryan kissed her on the forehead, then on the nose, on her cheeks, chin and neck until he felt down to her breasts. As light as a feather, he slid onto her body while her lips hung on his.

"I love you since the first day, Keshia. But now I can", Ryan finally said softly.

Keshia's eyes gleamed in the faint glow from the fire.

"Me too. But now I can", she replied.

Lovemaking started all over again as if they couldn't get enough of this feeling of happiness. Again they sank deeply, gave and took each other. Let themselves fall together to get drunk on it. Gradually their senses returned, perceiving details inside the teepee. The wood was now burned. Only the embers were still shining.

*****

Keshia smiled, pulled the blanket over her and rested her head on Ryan's shoulder. He was lying on his back with his free arm under his head. His eyes followed the smoke vent and continued up to the stars.

"Where did you leave your Corvette?", Keshia asked.

"With a friend."

"You came with the horses."

"Yes."

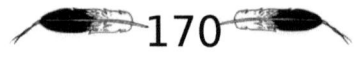

"And you set up my grandparents' tent."

"Yes, it was her suggestion."

"And when did you meet my father?"

"I had been with him in the mountains every day for the past three weeks. An order", he grinned. "I asked him for help because I didn't know anyone who knew up there better than he did."

"Now I understand. So you talked about me."

Ryan laughed softly.

"I asked him if you can cook well. I brought a white-tailed deer. It will be enough for both of us for a while."

"How long can you stay?"

"I signed off from my client for a week."

Keshia sighed.

"And then? You have to leave again", she said disappointed.

Ryan turned his head to her.

Keshia's eyes gleamed treacherously.

"Yes, Keshia. And I'll take you with me", he replied resolutely. "I came to get you. I told you. Don't you want to go with me?"

"My place is by your side wherever we will be and my heart will always be with you, no matter where you are and what you do."

Ryan smiled contentedly and nodded. Then he slipped out from under the blankets and crawled into his pants. Keshia watched him until he slipped out of the tent. It was quiet and cold, in here too. The fire had gone out and the warmth was only under the blankets. Keshia pulled her over her bare shoulder. Her husband came back shortly thereafter.

A strange thought. My man....

Keshia smiled happily at the thought.

He had an armful of logs and pushed a few of them into the embers. He stoked the fire with the branches.

"It's better if it burns all night. Is damn cold outside. Are you hungry?"

"I don't know. And you?"

"Yes, I am very hungry."

Ryan unwrapped a pot from a blanket and set it up over the fire. Keshia sat up.

"What's that?"

"Succotash, said your grandmother. She probably gave it to me in wise, because she knew exactly that we would not be able to get anything to eat today."

He grinned and gave her a large wooden spoon. Then he gestured to the pot and said: "All you have to do is stir it so nothing burns."

Ryan laughed as he skewered a piece of meat, seasoned it, and slowly started spinning it over the fire.

"What do you think so amused?"; Keshia asked while she dressed.

"I had to think about what your grandmother told me this morning when she gave me the pot", he grinned.

Then he started to tell. "It has always been common for women to prepare food. For a man it didn't work out. At least not in the village. Only the warriors and hunters did so when they were on the way longer on their forays and there was no woman who could have done this for them. However, a young warrior who had no wife was cared for by his grandmother, mother, sister or another relative. But someone was unlucky enough to be alone. So he roasted a good chunk of his prey alone late at night because he was very hungry. Now he was sure enough that no one could surprise him or watch him, smile at him or feel sorry for him. That would have been

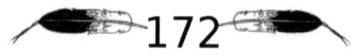

a shame for him. Even before the piece of meat was cooked, the entrance to the tent suddenly opened quietly. It was his adored one. In terror he didn't know what to do. He threw the hot piece of meat on his bed and lay on his back with it. She came and lay down with him. He had no chance. The young man miserably burned his back and endured the pain without noticing anything."

Keshia giggled. "Didn't she smell it?"

Ryan shrugged. "Maybe she had a stuffy nose", he said and laughed.

"And what's about you, Lakotaman? Can you cook?"

"Of course! What do you think what I'm doing here?"

"You roast a piece of meat."

"And I will definitely not throw it on our bed."

Keshia giggled.

"It smells too good for that", she finally said. "And besides, I got hungry like a bear."

It was night when they ate together. They praised Neloas stew and both soon realized that it was too good because the pot was empty. Keshia rose laboriously, groaned deliberately, and stroked the belly. She behaved as if she were very pregnant.

"I have to check on the horses", she said, when she crawled out of the tent a little awkwardly.

Ryan watched her grinning. His stomach also tightened. Then he got up, took the jacket and crawled out of the tent. Outside he lit a cigarette. The dozing horses he had pegged in front of the tent slowly raised their heads and snorted softly. Keshia came back from the truck. She had her arms full of hay and gave them to the two strange horses. They immediately began to nibble on it. Keshia stroked the dark brown mare along the neck.

"It was a good idea from your client to send you to me", she said.

Ryan pulled at the cigarette and smiled.

"No, it was not a good idea from him to give me this order. I don't think it was."

"Everything makes sense and I'm grateful to Maheo for coming", Keshia replied.

Ryan pulled at the cigarette and kicked it out.

"Let's go inside."

The young couple finally undressed crawled back under the covers. Keshia hugged her husband, who wrapped her arms around her. In this way, their bodies warmed up quickly and the blankets held this body heat. A few minutes later, Ryan pushed the blanket back because it was getting too hot. Keshia turned to Ryan, looked at him and smiled.

"When I was waiting for you, I dreamed twice that I was an eagle. It was wonderful. I was able to fly and saw our mountains, forests and lakes from far above. Saw buffalo and horse herds and finally a lonely wooden log house from which a column of smoke rose, but never people. The third time I saw another eagle. I saw the wind brush through his plumage and followed him. But the view of the earth was denied to me."

Ryan didn't smile when he said softly: "You scare me, Keshia."

"Trust me, Lakotaman, whatever happens", she replied.

Ryan pulled her closer and hugged her tightly with his arms. Silence finally accompanied the two people to sleep with gentle, even breaths.

*****

The morning light woke people and animals. One of the horses snorted softly in front of the tent. The fire had gone out and had left a pile of ashes in the recess. It was a test of courage to leave the warm blankets. The sun's rays encouraged Ryan and Keshia to do so. Both pulled their skin together. Ryan grinned when he prevented Keshia from getting dressed.

"Stop that!", she said and giggled.

Without mercy, Ryan pulled her out of the tent into the freezing cold of the new day. Her protest was of no use. She giggled and snorted as he unloaded her in the snow and rubbed her with it.

"You're crazy!", she giggled.

Then she shoveled snow towards him with both hands. Ryan laughed as he tried to dodge. The skin had turned bright red. The horses watched suspiciously the strange activity of the bipeds.

"You look like a snowman", Keshia laughed. Ryan shook himself. Snow flew out of the hair.

"Just wait!"

The high-spirited play in the fresh powder snow almost made them forget the cold. Her happy laugh echoed through the forest. Keshia tried to avoid Ryan's attack and plunged into the snow. Ryan pulled Keshia to her feet.

"Too much is unhealthy", he said finally and went to the tent entrance.

Barely two steps further, a load of snow landed on his neck. Then he heard Keshia giggle. As he turned, he saw the snow flying toward you from her hands. He ducked quickly, grabbing a new load. When he straightened up, however, he got the snow right up close in his face.

"Unruly woman!"

Ryan jumped to her, grabbed Keshia and threw her over her shoulder. He ignored her screeching.

"I surrender!", she gasped.

Ryan put her down in front of the tent entrance, shook his head, and pulled her inside. The crimson skin started to tingle. Soothing warmth flooded the body and became heat. Neither of them froze anymore.

When they were dressed, Keshia took the blankets and disappeared outside. She spread them out in the snow, patted and shook them, and then directed them back to the night camp. Ryan lit pine chips and made the fire blaze. He stayed in front of the fireplace and played with one of the branches. He blew it out whenever he started to smolder. Keshia sat down with him and leaned against Ryan's shoulder. He gave up the game.

"The coffee will be ready soon."

"After that I have to see Jimmy", she said.

Ryan nodded. "I'm waiting for you here", he smiled.

Keshia kissed him on the cheek.

"I can't wait, Lakotaman."

Ryan laughed softly.

"Jimmy won't be thrilled if you tell him you're leaving."

"Right. But he will understand. Jimmy is my friend."

*****

A short time later, Ryan looked after the truck that Keshia had come with last night. When he disappeared from his view, he turned to the two mares he had pegged in front of the tipi. Ryan smiled as he loosened the rope and led it to the other horses. You should get to know your new herd and your new home. He opened the gate and led her inside. He spoke a few Lakota words to them quietly and stroked their necks and noses. The sound of the words and his voice seemed to please them. The horses raised their ears and listened. When Ryan had taken the halter off, he sent them to the other animals, who were watched with curiosity. Ryan closed the gate, crossed his arms on the top board, and rested his chin on it. For the first time in a long time, he felt that the world and his life were in balance again. Ryan watched the little horse herd. While on the one hand they greeted and sniffed carefully, a power struggle broke out next to it. Every new, unknown being messed up the regulated order in the herd. The chestnut mare and the brown just started to clarify this order. Ryan remained motionless at the gate for a long time and watched what was going on until the cold rose in his consciousness. He turned and went. The smoke from his breath quickly vanished into thin air. Ryan brought firewood into the tent and packed a supply next to the entrance. The fire should not go out. The temperatures were well below freezing. As he pursued his thoughts on the night before, he heard engine noise. A car came up the path.

Ryan paused.

It wasn't Matthews or Adams truck. A ford pickup appeared. Ryan remembered seeing him before, down on Jimmy's trailer. He hid behind one of the tree trunks and saw a young man get out. He had met this Cheyenne at Jimmy before. He wore his long hair in a braid. Ryan could remember that this strange Cheyenne was not friendly to him. That is why he preferred to stay behind the tree trunk. The stranger greeted the horses that seemed to know him. Then, without hesitation, he went to the tent entrance. Ryan heard him shout something.

They were words he couldn't understand. He watched the stranger open the entrance and crawl into the tent.

As if he were at home here, the young man sat down by the fire and warmed his hands. He looked around. His eyes caught on the thermos, which didn't quite fit into the picture of the tent. He grinned and took one of the mugs. The coffee was hot. A pleasant smell brushed his nose as he sipped gently. The Cheyenne grew warm so that he took off his jacket. He had crossed his legs and now rested his elbows on his knees while enjoying the coffee. Suddenly he stopped and listened. Someone came.

Soft steps were heard. A delusion? But the cracking of a branch was unmistakable, as if it had been done on purpose. Slowly the Cheyenne turned to look at the entrance someone was just opening. Calmly, as if that couldn't touch him, he stayed seated and watched the tall figure of the other man who came in.

"I see I have a guest",Ryan said.

He took off his jacket and sat opposite the guest. Just the fire was between them.

"I've been waiting for you", the stranger said, looking openly at Ryan.

"My name is Ryan Black Hawk, Lakota. Who are you?"

"I know", the stranger smiled. "My name is Jerry Lee Black Snake."

"Then you are not my guest, but I am yours", Ryan stated.

"I told you, don't touch Black Snake." Jerry Lee paused while he seemed to pierce Ryan with his eyes.

He nodded skeptically.

"Maheo wanted it that way and sent you to protect my sister. You had more power than me. When you were helpless in fever, I took you to this tent with grandfather. I had no idea who you were. Now I wanted to get to know the man I want to call my friend and who wants to take my sister away as his wife."

Ryan nodded again. "And Wakan Tanka, whom you call Maheo, wanted Keshia to bring me back from the other world. I was an Air Force Sergeant and a headhunter, but I'm a Lakota."

Jerry Lee dug out a box of cigarettes from his jacket pocket. Then he grinned when he offered it to Ryan and said: "A pipe would be appropriate now."

"We'll catch up on it, brother-in-law", Ryan replied relieved. Now he grimaced and smiled and lit the cigarette.

When they had done a few puffs, Jerry Lee remarked: "You brought magnificent mares with you and they are pregnant, as I have seen."

"Yes, they are. The foals will be born in about three months. Fresh blood in your little herd."

"Father needs animals to change for the mountain tours. Sometimes he borrowed horses. When it got calmer in autumn, we often went up into the mountains with him. We had a small tent with us and were on the road for days. He said you have a ranch?"

"An old wooden log house with a shed and a piece of land in the Pine Ridge Reservation, at Potato Creek, in a valley that crosses a creek. There are our horses. Two stallions, four mares and sometimes foals. The dealers pay poorly. For Indian horses or less. Your father rides in the mountains as a hunting guide or with tourists. Maybe this is also a possibility for us, a future for our ranch."

"Yes, why not? It brings good money in the season. In the spring he is sometimes at home when there is hardly anything to do. Tourists come in summer. In autumn and winter, he travels with hunters quite often. Occasionally he takes on orders for the mountain rescue service. He knows his field better than anyone else."

"That's the way it is. And you?"

"I love the mountains. They taught me a lot. But I study because I want to be a teacher and will teach at our St. Labre Indian School in two years. Sports, art, English and Cheyenne."

"This is the better way you go."

"Why do you think that, Ryan? Being a guide or a horse-man is a good way too."

Ryan nodded. "Yes, that's my goal, Jerry Lee. Together with your sister I want to go this one. She grew up with the horses."

"That's her and she has a good sense of it. You made a good choice", grinned Jerry Lee.

Ryan reached for the thermos and placed the mug between his legs. Before pouring himself in, he filled Black Snakes' mug. Then Ryan threw the rest of the smoked cigarette into the fire.

"There will be snow soon, lots of snow", Jerry Lee said and grinned. "You may be snowed in here."

"I agree. I will make all arrangements."

"Do you have a hunting rifle with you?"

"An old Winchester, but fully functional."

"That's a good hunting rifle."

"We're not going to starve", Ryan laughed softly.

"This is a game-rich area. Sometimes the wild rabbits run back and forth in front of the tent. We often watched them as children. Most of the time we were up here with grandfather and grandmother all summer when father was out. They have taught us a lot, much more

than has ever been possible in a school. We lived in our world. I hope one day I can give my students some of it."

„I would have liked to know more of these things at school. But now we also have the Lakota language as a school subject. Hardly anyone speaks our language, let alone fluent. The children learn them like a foreign language today. My grandmother only spoke Lakota to help me find my way in life better, to recognize and understand my task, she said. She refused to use an English word even though she could."

"Yes, that's what I mean. It is our language that enables us to understand our way of thinking better. And the children are our future, the future of our people. Only they can make us survive."

Jerry Lee's eyes lit up as he talked. He spoke from the bottom of his heart, carried a fire in his words with which he could start a fire.

Ryan listened to him carefully. Jerry Lee Black Snake would be a good teacher he was sure of that. If he spoke to the children as he does now, they would hear him. Then they would also hear the unspoken, feel and understand it. Ryan instantly thought back to the grim face of the young man. The gloomy, devastating look he'd given him at Jimmy. He had to smile. Now Ryan saw a completely different man sitting across from him. Jerry Lee's features were anything but grim. But the determination remained. They were related in every way. Ryan carefully pushed a few branches into the embers. The flames immediately licked up on them. Time had no meaning, no rule over him and the world was far, far away. Ryan felt the inner calm deep inside, the satisfaction to live with the moment. His path had finally led him back to enter the circle that should make him who he was again. At some point a faint motor noise mingled in his mind. Jerry Lee also listened.

"Keshia", he said. Jerry Lee's gaze stuck at the tent entrance. "I haven't seen my sister since Christmas."

Ryan stared into the flames. He did so when Keshia asked if she could come in because the tent entrance was closed. Ryan looked up as Keshia gave her brother a warm hug. Ryan thought of Carry and the kids and smiled. Keshia sat down with him.

"Jimmy let me go with a heavy heart", she said.

"He'll find someone quickly", said Jerry Lee.

"Yes, but I'm his friend", Keshia replied.

Both her brother and Ryan laughed softly.

"You will stay that way!", Ryan replied. "Everything else is too dangerous for me."

"Why dangerous?", Jerry Lee asked in astonishment.

"He threatened to kill me if I touch a hair on Black Snake."

"Jimmy doesn't harm anyone. He's too good-natured and peaceful", grinned Jerry Lee.

"Are you sure?", Ryan asked skeptically.

Jerry Lee's grin turned into a laugh. "Were you scared, Lakota?"

"Yes, a black snake almost strangled me at night."

"In your fever dreams!", Keshia interfered. "Incidentally, I'm glad that you two are sitting peacefully by the fire."

"Did you expect anything else?", Ryan asked in surprise.

Keshia answered his question with a subtle smile. Ryan twisted his mouth and shook his head. "You never told me you have a brother."

"I have two brothers. Sammy has been severely disabled since his polio and live with our father's sister since the death of our mother."

"Then we will go to him and tell him."

"He is going to be happy."

"He's sixteen. I'm going to see him today. I want to be back before the snow comes", said Jerry Lee. "Sammy is always happy to see you."

"But before you go, you eat with us. Jimmy packed me something."

"Hot dogs?", Jerry Lee asked.

Keshia laughed. "No. Meat pies."

"Okay. I stay", he grinned.

*****

After eating together, Jerry Lee Black Snake said good-bye. The three of them stood by his car. Ryan put his arm around Keshia when her brother got in and started. They watched the one driving away until they could no longer see him. Then it was quiet again.

"What do you say to a ride? I want you to show something before the next snowfall sets in", Keshia broke the silence.

Ryan agreed.

The sun still sent its cool light through the bare branches. But heavy, snowy clouds were already moving towards the mountains. Keshia chose two mares. Ryan got the black one. He thought involuntarily of his black stallion when he stroked her nostrils and felt her warm breath on his hand. Then she snorted contentedly, as if she agreed that he would swing on her back. He smiled because he was happy. Keshia went ahead with a piebald mare, one half of the head of which was white, the other of which was brown. So she had a white and a brown ear. The forest became thicker and continued uphill. The air was cold and clear. It was quiet. Countless wild trails crossed the path of the riders. Then the forest gradually cleared. The horses walked side by side. Keshia smiled at Ryan. The feeling of happiness was also reflected in her eyes. The path ended on a rocky plateau. The wind played with the hair of the people and with the mane of the horses and made the dry branches rustle. Keshia stopped her mare and pointed with her hand over the valley that stretched at her feet. A broad, stony bank ran along a river. It led through the valley like a snake. Endless mixed forest stood bare in the valleys. The evergreen conifers formed a splash of color. They also stayed on the rocky ground, on the slopes further up, to the tree line. In front of them rose the treeless, snow-capped peaks of the Rocky Mountains. Wandering wispy clouds envelop them. It already seemed to be snowing heavily there. On the opposite side of the plateau on which the riders stood raised a jagged rock face. In this region the trees had already given way to the more robust shrub that grew out of crevices and boulders. Keshia looked around and listened. She waited patiently, like a hunter. After a while he came. Overpowering, like a big black shadow, the eagle spread its wings and sailed towards the rock face. His scream echoed through the valley.

"Up there in the rock that stand out like a tower from the wall, there is its nest", Keshia whispered.

Ryan looked exactly there and watched the eagle stick out its claws on the approach. The big bird balanced with its wings until he found a stop and finally put on its wings.

"A really beautiful animal", Ryan said softly.

"My grandfather once told me that one day he would be

reborn as an eagle to spread his wings protectively over everyone who needed his protection", Keshia smiled.

A second eagle circled the nest, keeping a close eye out. The two were watching him. At some point the eagle rose from the nest, spread its wings and took off with a few strong wingbeats. Then the mighty animal screwed itself up to the sky. His scream could be heard widely. The other eagle replied. They approached, circled in glider flight and moved away from each other. Their bodies became small dots and disappeared from the observing eyes of their audience.

"A couple", Keshia said and smiling at Ryan.

He also smiled and nodded.

Keshia let her mare start moving. "Let's move on."

They rode along the precipice of the steep slope, descending downwards. A faint rushing reached their ears. It got louder the closer they came to the waterfall. After all, the noise was so loud that the two should have screamed to understand each other. But the Indians were silent. They understood each other without words. With a huge roar, the water plunged down over a ledge. Thousands of small drops rushed through the air and enveloped the waterfall in a mysterious fog. In places, the color spectrum of the rainbow appeared in winter sunlight. The horses carefully put their hooves on the narrow path that now led steeply down into the valley. The shade of the trees and the sunlight conjured up dark and light stripes across the path. The snow in the forest reached over the pastern. When they reached the plain, Keshia put her mare into a light gallop. The loud roar of the waterfall became quieter and finally fell silent. They stopped the horses and let them slowly walk across the snow field to the river. The animals fought their way bravely through the powder snow, which reached up to their bellies. At a shallow point they crossed the river, which murmured peacefully over boulders at this point.

On the other side, Keshia and Ryan rode side by side, following the course of the river. Ryan looked at Keshia and smiled. When she noticed it, she smiled back. Their looks met and spoke without words. The cold wind that blew their faces, bit their noses and ears and reddened their cheeks, didn't seem to bother them. In the loneliness and silence of the valley you could feel the heartbeat of your mother, mother earth, from which all life rise. Even time seemed to stand still here.

*****

Dusk had already dawned when the young couple got off the horses again at the grandparents' tent. The breath evaporated as smoke from the noses and nostrils. They quickly unsaddled the horses and supplied them with hay. Keshia lit the extinguished fire in the tent, while Ryan brought a substantial supply of firewood into the tent. Then he threw his jacket and hat on the floor, sat by the fire and took off his boots and stockings. He rubbed his hands carefully and played with his toes.

Keshia undressed.

The fire burned evenly and spread its warmth in the tent. The branches cracked softly. Keshia wrapped herself in one of the woolen blankets and sat down with her husband, who was pushing a twig into the flames. The glow of fire lit up the face of the young man who sat in front of it and looked inside as if he could read it.

"What do you think, Ryan?"Keshia asked quietly.

"Whether the branch that I have just set on fire burns

faster than the log under it, which is already burning."

Keshia smiled. "Once it catches fire it will burn like hell."

"He's doing it right now. Do you see?"

"Yes." Keshia crawled behind Ryan, wrapped her arms around him and rested her head on his.

"He has no chance of escaping the flames", he added.

"It was his destiny from the beginning."

"To burn?"

"Yes."

"He feeds the fire so that it keeps on burning."

"It will always burn", Ryan said.

Keshia put her hands under his shirt and gently stroked his chest.

"Your hands are ice-cold", he said and grinned.

"They are Looking for something."

"After what?"

"After the fire that can warm it."

Keshia unbuttoned the shirt and pulled it back over his shoulders. He let it happen. He was still sitting upright, looking at the flames. "Are you no longer afraid?", he finally asked when she kissed him on the shoulder.

"From what?"

"To burn."

"No, I have`nt. I will rise again from the ashes like a bird called phoenix to burn again and again."

"Was it his destiny?"

"From the beginning", Ryan heard her soft voice directly on his ear and immediately felt her bare skin on his back. He reached for her arms, turned his head to the side and saw her face directly in front of him. She did not hesitate for a moment to keep the fire going. Her lips touched the Ryan's to show him her desire with no shy. Heat flowed through his body as her tongues touched. Slowly

she pulled her arms back. Ryan felt her cold fingers on his face. He turned completely to Keshia and pulled her close so that he felt her breasts on his skin.

"I love you, Lakotaman", Keshia whispered.

"Thechi hi hila. Me too", he whispered. "Thechi hi hila."

Ryan gently pushed Keshia back so that the Cheyenne woman fell backwards on the blankets with him. She smiled mysteriously, expectantly, and lovingly. Ryan felt Keshia's hands slide over his back and on. He sighed softly.

The fire they carried deep within them began to burn and seized their bodies.

Outside it was dark night and large snowflakes fell silently from the sky onto the tipi, so that it sank deeper and deeper into the white.

Chapter 4
The last order

It was late evening when there was a soft knock on Baxter's door. He grinned, put his beer down and rose from his TV chair. Even though he was expecting a visit, he left the chain on the lock and initially opened only a crack.
"Who there?", he asked bored.
"Of course, someone is there", replied a familiar voice.
Baxter opened the door fully. He eyed the woman standing next to his friend and grinned even wider.
"Come in!"
Ryan entered the apartment. Keshia stayed close behind him. Warmth hit them. Baxter slammed the door shut. The flickering television and a table lamp illuminated the living room. It looked cozy.
"Good evening", Baxter said. "Welcome to my cave."
"Bear cave", Ryan corrected as he and Keshia took off their jackets. "Hello Mato. How are you?"
"Great. And you too, I see."
Ryan nodded.
Baxter held out his hand to Keshia. "I am Baxter"
Keshia eyed the bearded man suspiciously. Hesitantly she shook hands with him.
"Keshia", she said.
"Beautiful. I like it", Baxter replied, meaning more than just the name. Well then. Take off your jackets and make yourself comfortable. Baxter took two glasses from the cupboard and placed them on the coffee table.
"Water, Coke, Beer?"
"Coke", Ryan replied and sat on the couch with Keshia.
Baxter brought two large bottles of Coke, assuming Keshia wanted Coke, and a beer for himself. Then he

turned the TV down. Keshia watched her husband's friend. He poured Coke into the glasses.

"Thank you. What's new, Baxter?"

"Everything with the old. I have been to the junkyard for the past few weeks and worked my way up warmly. Business is moderate. Ronny says that experience shows that not much is going on in winter. But now spring is just around the corner and things are looking up again. Has reached you ... well, you already know who?"

"Yes, he has."

"And?"

Ryan said nothing. He took a sip of Coke. Then he calmly pulled a cigarette out of the box and placed it on the table in front of Baxter. Even here in the apartment, Ryan held the lit cigarette down and covered it with his hand. It had long become a habit.

"That's why we came to you, Baxter", Ryan finally started. „Keshia is my wife. It is time to go home. But I still have an order. The last one. It currently seems too dangerous for me to bring her to my family."

"But isn't it the best place to be?", Baxter asked in surprise.

Ryan shook his head slowly. "No, my friend. I am looking for a Lakota and probably in my own area."

Baxter stared wide-eyed at Ryan as his jaw dropped.

"We need your help, Bax", continued Ryan, pulling on the cigarette.

Keshia didn't move. She hadn't even drunk.

Baxter nodded. "Of course. At any time. You know that. To cheer up something other than depressed old scrap cars." Baxter managed to smile and took a sip from the beer can.

"I combine", he said then, "...you're looking for a place

to stay for her", Baxter cleared his throat, "...for Keshia, until your dance is over. And since you could use me as a life insurance, I just remembered a little, lonely lady who would be very, very happy about Keshia's visit."

"You hit it right on the nose, my friend", nodded Ryan.

Baxter turned to the young woman. "Olivia Goodman. She's my mother, Keshia. Nowhere will you be better off than with her. She only talks a little, at least more than you do. But with her you can steal horses."

Keshia smiled.

"I look forward to meeting your mother. Thank you."

"I'm glad", Baxter said.

"You have to take her to Olivia, Baxter. Tomorrow morning, before the sun comes up, I'll leave. I can't wait any longer."

"Okay. I will." Baxter smiled kindly at Keshia. It looked almost embarrassed. Something warned him to hold back. Perhaps the fear that the Cheyenne woman might misunderstand his jokes, so he remained silent and leaned back in his armchair. Ryan put his arm around his wife and pulled her towards him. Keshia rested her head on his shoulder. They watched television together.

Later Baxter prepared the couch in the living room for his guests and wished them a good night. When Ryan and Keshia came out of the bathroom, they heard Baxter's steady breathing. The door to the bedroom was only ajar. They looked at each other and grinned. Then they went to sleep too. Ryan released the light from the small lamp and pulled his wife towards him. He felt the velvety skin under his lips that kissed her face. Then he felt her lips on his. It was difficult for him to control himself, because his body naturally reacted immediately and asked for more. "Good night", he whispered.

"Good night. I love you. Don't forget that", she whispered.

"Never, Keshia."

Then it was quiet. Only Baxter's clock ticked softly,
telling Ryan that the time was running. A short night lay
ahead and he tried to sleep. He had to gather his
strength for the next day. But his thoughts about the
next day did not let him go. His patience and calmness,
that of the hunter, were lost as long as his wife lay next
to him. Suddenly he felt a strange restlessness, as if he
had to climb onto a previously undefeated rodeo horse
the next day. His victory would be the decision about life
and death.

*Have warriors ever felt that way before fighting their
enemies*, Ryan wondered. *The exit was always an open
question and no one knew if he would return home alive.
Maybe I was never aware of it before. And now I feel
fear for the first time. Afraid not to see Keshia again.*

Ryan took a deep breath and shook his head, horrified
by his own thoughts. He tried in vain to wipe away his
self-doubt.

Ryan was aware that Keshia wasn't sleeping either. She
lay still in his arms and breathed noticeably. Maybe she
was scared too. Ryan sought her look. The eyes had long
since got used to the darkness in the room and
recognized the furniture, the television and the glasses
that were still on the table. In fact, Keshia blinked him in
the eyes. She smiled. Keshia looked at her husband for a
long time, as if she wanted to memorize his face very
precisely. *I see you,* said her look. *I see your heart, your
thoughts, your feelings and I am by your side. Trust me.*

His look said the same thing. No word left their mouth.
The soft ticking of the clock reminded that the time did

not stand still. At some point sleep closed her eyelids.

Keshia woke up when Ryan tried gently to pull his arm out from under her neck.

"Is it time to go?", she asked quietly.

"Yes. The sooner I leave, the faster I'll may be back."

Ryan gave Keshia a quick kiss and disappeared into his friend's bathroom.

Baxter was still asleep when Ryan came back.

While Keshia went into the bathroom, Ryan shook his friend vigorously.

"Hey Mato! Do you hibernate? Wake up!"

Baxter finally moved, yawned, lifted his head and blinked around. "What's up?"

"Time for departure."

Baxter dropped back onto the pillows exhausted and closed his eyes. "Hm", he growled. Then he threw off the blanket and stood up. "Morning", Baxter murmured, stretching with a strange cry.

Keshia giggled.

Startled, Baxter whirled around and was suddenly awake. Ryan switched on the coffee machine.

*****

About an hour later, three people said goodbye at twilight on the dawning day. Keshia got into the commander. Ryan slammed the door from the outside. Baxter followed his friend to his Corvette.

"Get in touch when you need me", Baxter said worriedly.

"Possibly. But this time it will be better for both of us if I go alone."

"Did Thompson tell you what the guy did?"

"He has done several times. Smuggled cheap Brandy and

193

drugs into the reservation. The guy walk over corpses. Hunting Wolf is not a bail jumper. He's a killer. As soon as I caught him, he goes to jail for a very long time. This time the FBI is after him, not just our tribal police.

Baxter gasped. "Do you know what you're getting yourself into?", he hissed.

"I wish I didn't have to do it, Baxter. And even though I was hired by Thompson, I do it for my people too."

Baxter put his hand heavily on Ryan's shoulder.

"I will tell you anyway! Take care of yourself, my friend."

Ryan's lips twisted, nodded, and got in. He raised his hand in greeting and drove away.

Baxter walked slowly to his jeep.

"Well then let's go", he mumbled and started.

Baxter remained unusually silent on the ride, so it was not apparent that the young woman next to him was silent. Country music played softly in the background. Baxter didn't feel the need to sing along now. At some point he automatically picked up the cigarette box. Before he lighted her, he remembered that someone was sitting next to him. He looked at Keshia.

"Do you mind if i smoke?"

"No."

Baxter lit the cigarette and blew the first smoke into the air. "You have a very nice voice, Keshia", he said.

Keshia just smiled.

Baxter cleared his throat and drag on the cigarette. He hadn't searched so hard for words for a long time. Not even when he met Ryan for the first time. That seemed ages ago. Almost five years. A damn long time. Ryan was right. It was time to get out. In every sense. Ryan would live with Keshia on the Pine Ridge Reservation, start a family and breed horses. And Baxter Goodman?

Maybe I'll finally fulfill my dream of working in a racing stable. I want to tweak horsepower racing cars and engines, the smell of gasoline, oil and hot tires in my nose ....and hot girls... Baxter grinned at this thought.

Maybe it's time, his thoughts said, without a word leaving his lips.

There were car races near Pierre on the Missouri River. A racing stable, north of the city. Baxter knew that and he had researched it.

Maybe the good people need a good mechanic, like me. Maybe it is a good idea to go there and have a look.

Baxter was so preoccupied with his own thoughts that he didn't notice Keshia watching him closely.

"What do you think?", he heard her voice and let him winced.

"Maybe I should shave my beard after all."

Keshia grinned.

"Well", he laughed. "For the sake of Dian. She is my best mate. Without my beard she would marry me."

"If she loves you, then certainly with a beard."

"That makes me feel better. The beard remains where it is. He belongs to Baxter Goodman."

"That's why Ryan calls you Mato", she smiled.

"Hm. And some of my friends call me Grizzly Adams."

Keshia laughed.

"A very good man. People like him."

"That's why my name is Goodman", Baxter enjoyed himself.

"You could see it that way too."

Baxter automatically reached for his cigarettes. He offered it to Keshia, but she didn't smoke. Baxter tosses the box back into the center console without using it.

"Where lives your mother?"

"In Black Hawk", Baxter laughed and waiting for Keshia's reaction.

"Where's that?"

"West Rapid City."

"Then we'll be right there", she noticed with astonishment. She smiled. Baxter liked that. He envied Ryan this wonderful creature. The envy, however, that he felt made his heart beat faster with genuine joy at the young couple.

*****

A little later Baxter drummed against Olivia's apartment door. It took some time before something moved. A small, well-rounded lady in a dressing gown opened the door and narrowed her eyes.

"I hope you have a good reason, Baxter Goodman, to chase me out of bed in the middle of the night", Olivia growled wearily.

"Oh yes, Olivia, I do. Otherwise I would never have allowed myself to do that." Baxter looked at Olivia and started to grin. "You look lovely."

"Oh, nonsense! Don't try to twist me around my little finger. Come on in and close the door behind you. It is cold", she growled, turned and went ahead. With a friendly gesture, Baxter asked Keshia to enter.

"Do you see Keshia. This is Olivia Goodman. She's almost bubbling over with hospitality. If she had slept in, it would be unbearable."

There was doubt in Keshia's smile.

Baxter nodded encouragingly.

"Who are you talking to?", Olivia asked and spun around. "Oh!", she made surprised.

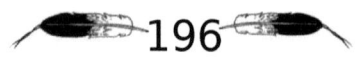

Her eyes grew big, round and curious. Immediately she smiled so that her teeth showed.

Keshia stood undecided next to Baxter.

"Good morning, Mrs. Goodman", she said.

"Good morning", Olivia said gently, smiling bravely. Then she immediately disappeared.

"Come and sit down, Keshia. That can now take a little longer. Wash, iron and smooth. She's pretty picky about it."

Keshia grinned in amusement. „I think that was just embarrassing to your mother. We just came over her."

Baxter cleared his throat.

"Coffee?", he asked.

"Yes, please", Keshia answered and took off the jacket.

Baxter searched the kitchen cabinets.

"You will see when she comes out of the bathroom, in about two to three hours, this woman is a completely different personality."

Keshia laughed.

"Believe me. If it weren't for this, Ryan would never have thought of ... ehm ..."

"To park here?"

Baxter paused and looked at Keshia in surprise.

"Yes", he laughed.

"Ryan told about your mother. They seem to like each other very much."

"At the beginning he hardly spoke. She talked all the more. In the meantime, they are literally dueling and I sometimes have doubts as to which of the two has the sharper tongue."

Keshia smiled. The coffee machine bubbled until its work was finally finished with a last hiss. The coffee was ready. Also Olivia Goodman. That way she had undercut her time in the bedroom. She went straight to Keshia.

"Welcome. I'm Olivia."

"Keshia Black Snake", she introduced.

"What a beautiful name. Are you a Lakota too?"

"No. Cheyenne."

"Oh God! How long have I longed for the day when my son will bring a woman home", whispered Olivia.

Baxter cleared his throat.

"That's Ryan's wife, mom."

"I almost figured as much. Anyway, where is he?", she asked resolutely.

"He has an order", Keshia replied.

"At this time? I think the racing season doesn't start until May?"

"Mm... he's working over winter... as... a taxi driver", Baxter interfered.

Keshia looked at him in astonishment.

Baxter shrugged and grinned lopsided.

"But he will hang up his spurs anyway and go home with his wife, ehm ... Keshia", he added quickly.

"That is also more reasonable. The boy needs a regular family life. He is getting thinner. If he hadn't found his way to me now and then, he would have starved to death!"

"Did you hear that, Keshia? If you don't feel like cooking, you come to Olivia Goodman with your husband. This is a serious invitation."

While Keshia's thoughts revolved around the strange warmth of these two white people, Olivia kept talking.

"Well, definitely! I am always happy when you come. But now we've talked enough about food. Now I'm going to have a decent breakfast!", she said and immediately put everything she thought was part of a decent breakfast on the kitchen table. Meanwhile, Olivia kept talking. She had found an attentive listener in the young woman.

"You want to leave again, Baxter?", Olivia asked indignantly. She couldn't hide the disappointment when after the long breakfast she started clearing the kitchen counter.

"What do you mean, you want? I must! Business calls."

"But not the junkyard?"

Baxter laughed. "Jealous?"

"What makes you think that?" Olivia shook her head vigorously. "Now tell me! You´re up to something."

"Only when I know exactly."

"You see!"

Olivia eyed her son suspiciously as she pointed the bread knife at him as it would be her forefinger.

"Bye, you two pretty ones", Baxter said, took his jacket and opened the door.

"What?", Olivia asked.

Baxter turned to her and grinned.

"Don't even bother Olivia."

"A woman?"

Her voice sounded hopeful, but Baxter only raised his hands as if he had no idea and disappeared without another word.

"Oh, that rascal!", Olivia called and turned to Keshia with a smile. "That would be too good to be true. He should take an example from you."

Then she finally put the bread knife out of her hand.

*****

Baxter's path led straight to Interstate 90 East. Although he had not yet decided to dare a fresh start again, an

invisible force drove him to Pierre. The little nest, Eagle Creek Village, on the upper Missouri River, was not even a flyspeck on the map. At least Baxter couldn't remember ever being there. He turned up the country music and sang along. Then he lit a cigarette and drummed his fingers on the steering wheel. He had about three hours of driving ahead of him. With every mile he approached this racing stable, his hope grew and his desire that they might need a good mechanic there. He self-suffocated the self-doubts that crept up on him every now and then. Baxter finally left the highway and used paved country roads to his destination. Eagle Creek Village was actually signposted. A gas station appeared. A motel and a Trading Post with a tipi in front and a row of mailboxes. These gave reason to believe that there were also houses in which people lived. Baxter finally decided to go to the gas station. Besides petrol there was always information and gossip. He would certainly learn a lot about the racing stable and racings here. His heart was pounding faster. There was a young, petite woman at the cash register. Baxter looked around. She seemed to be alone.

"Can I help you, Sir?", she asked.

Baxter turned to her. She smiled so that her white teeth came out. Dark eyes blinked at him. It was estimated she was still at school, Baxter thought. *What the heck*, he thought.

"Yes, little lady. That would be nice. I heard there is a car racing stable here. I am very interested and I would like to have a look at it."

"Of course. Hell is going on here every summer", she replied eagerly, so that her hazel ponytail bobbed. "But at this time..." she grimaced thoughtfully. "I hardly think

you will find anyone there today."

Baxter sighed dejectedly.

"Oh. Just drive out. Maybe you are lucky. The season starts this year on the last weekend in April. Sometimes the mechanics are outside to get the mustangs out of hibernation. Haywood often hauls several scrap cars to them. He gets them for a ridiculous price, the stingy old one."

Baxter's eyes lit up, his eyes literally hanging from the little woman's lips.

She grinned. "They have a lot of wear and tear on racing cars, you need to know. The race track is hardcore. Not everyone reached the goal. This is probably the hardest race I know. You must have brass balls."

Baxter shook his head like a bathed dog. He was captivated by her talkative nature. He heard her giggle.

"Are you a race driver?"

"No."

"You don't look that way, Sir", she said cheekily.

Baxter blew up his cheeks and stared at her in surprise.

"Then what?"

"You're a typical freak. I could bet that you understand a lot of motors and are mechanic."

Baxter looked astonished. "Wow! I admire your knowledge of human nature, little lady. You're right on the button."

She grinned triumphantly.

"What do you think? Could they use a good mechanic?", Baxter asked.

The little woman tilted her head appraisingly as she eyed Baxter. "If you're really good... damn good... you may have a chance."

"Thank you", Baxter rejoiced, because he had heard

exactly what he wanted to hear.

"All together five dollars", she said unmoved.

"Five dollars?"

"That was a joke. But it would be nice, Sir, if you would buy something or at least fill up it so that I could have a sense of achievement. Out of season, people rarely come here."

"I understand", Baxter nodded.

He went and refilled his tank, bought cigarettes and a brown plush teddy. The little woman showed Baxter her white teeth again and said: "Thank you, Sir. Have a good trip."

"I have to thank little lady."

He gave her the teddy. "This is Baxter Mato. Please do me a favor and take good care of my little friend until I come back."

She giggled and nodded in agreement.

*****

The racing stable was outside the village, outside on the prairie. The asphalt road ended at the turn where the billboard stood. The colors had faded and were peeling off the wood. *Haywoods Flying Horses - motor racing* was written in large letters on it. "Flying horses", Baxter laughed. That was just legible. Three Mustangs seemed to fly out of the billboard. Baxter's blood started to move. He drove along the dirt road, hoping to find someone. A head-high fence appeared beside of the road. It was largely overgrown with bushes and prevented any prying eyes. Then a wide gate appeared. The dust road led directly into it. Baxter followed the path to the open gate. Three old, abandoned factory buildings stood here and immediately reminded Baxter of his time with the US Air Force. However, the gates were closed. Everything looked pretty deserted. Baxter drove on slowly. There were some trees behind the buildings. Baxter spotted a house under its spreading crowns. At least there was a car. A black Jaguar F Cabriolet. Baxter parked the commander next to it.

"Business doesn't seem to be going that badly here", Baxter muttered to himself as he eyed the sports car. Then he headed straight for the house entrance. Baxter took a deep breath and knocked. It remained silent. He knocked again.

"Hello?"

Finally, he carefully pressed the handle. The door was locked. "Hm", he growled.

The owner of the Jaguar may have been out somewhere on the site. Baxter had to find out. After all, his journey shold not have been in vain. First he tried the halls. In fact, one of the gates was only ajar. Baxter draw it back.

"Hello?!", he shouted that it echoed.

Nobody answered.

Baxter looked around. Two Mustangs were in here and two more that, it looked like, were only going to become one again. Spare parts piled up in abundance. Some were lying around. Someone had to be here. Baxter could clearly hear noises. Without hesitation he went in to the Mustangs and called again.

"Hello! Is there someone?"

A small figure jumped up behind one of the open hoods and bumped into it.

"Damn it! Where are you from? Who are you? What do you want?", the little man showered Baxter with his questions in quick succession. Baxter's eyes widened as he

struggled to understand the man. He opened his mouth unconsciously.

"What are you staring at me? Have you never seen a Ling Fu?"

Baxter laughed out loud. "A what?"

"Ling Fu Tajaki. I'm a mechanic here. Who are you looking for?", asked the dwarf unkindly.

Baxter immediately stopped laughing and answered shortly: "Mr. Haywood."

"Haywood is not there. Only the manager. In the office." The little Chinese gestured to the front of the hall. Baxter's gaze followed this direction. There was a door between two large windows reminiscent of shop windows. A few steps led up.

"Who is that?", Baxter asked skeptically.

The dwarf grimaced and repeated: "Lulel! Now go!"

Baxter went and knocked on the door. Since no one answered, he entered.

"Good day, Sir. May I come in?", Baxter asked the man who was deep in his work sitting at the desk.

"You're already in", he got an answer from a young blondie.

Baxter closed the door behind him. He paused indecisively. He no longer felt comfortable in his skin. The man paused and eyed the one suspiciously.

"What do you want?", he finally asked.

"Are you Lulel?"

The blondie grimaced with a sneer. It looked arrogant. Baxter immediately thought of turning on the heel and hurrying away. Before Baxter put his thoughts into action, the blondie asked him: "Did the slit-eyed one tell you that?"

"The little Chinese, yes."

"My name is Ruler. I'm listening."

With these words he turned his attention to Baxter.

"Goodman", he replied. "My name is Baxter Goodman. I heard that good people are still needed here."

"So? From whom?"

"The wind brought it to me."

"Rumors."

"Hm… so?" Baxter played the ball back.

While Baxter waited for an answer, he felt Ruler's staring look uncomfortably on him.

"Haywood is looking for a good racing driver. Is that you?"

"No, I'm a mechanic."

"There's already one out there."

"One. Are there only two Mustangs that go into the race here?"

"No. At the moment everything is still in hibernation. The season only begins. Then the hall is full."

"From out of town?"

"The poor idiots come from all over America. Everyone pays his entry fee as a stake, in order to then hit his head here." Ruler laughed and lit a cigarette. "Either you drive your car to scrap or you are so good that you arrive at the destination. Some stay here all season. Some try their luck elsewhere."

"Well. So everyone dances his own dance."

Ruler looked at Baxter in confusion as he slowly blew the smoke to the ceiling.

"All crazy guys", Baxter added.

Ruler nodded.

He didn't seem to be crazy. Externally, too, he seemed to value distance. Baxter had never met anyone in his life who had his office in a paddock that was a spare parts

store. In black classy jeans and a snow-white shirt, wrapped in an after-shave cloud, worked in a racing stable. The first impression might be misleading, but Ruler probably didn't seem to understand much about vehicle technology, Baxter thought. It also seemed as if he was afraid to get his fingers dirty. Baxter didn't notice himself shaking his head at the thought.

"Maybe I'll take a look at that. Have a nice day", Baxter said goodbye.

"Bye, Goodman."

Ruler raised the hand in which he held the cigarette slightly. With a nod, Baxter left the office. His way to the exit inevitably led him past the Mustangs the Chinese was working on. He didn't seem to take any more notes from the stranger who was in the process of leaving.

Instinctively Baxter Goodman had to grin, when he heard him swear.

"Damn piece of shit!"

He stopped, took a step towards the dwarf and looked over his shoulder. He didn't seem to notice. "Trouble with the new transmission?", Baxter asked finally.

The Chinese whirled around angrily.

"Piece of shit! I've already said that to Haywood, but he's deaf on the ears."

"Looks like he's saving in the wrong place. Try the oil spray. Maybe something will move. However, the grid could also be replaced. The gearwheels are too tight. This makes them easily get jammed. The driver will curse if the gear doesn't slide in. It's a lot of work, terribly. Oh, what am I talking about...", Baxter interrupted himself and sat up.

The little Chinese eyed the big bearded man thoughtfully. "Right. Haywood thinks Ling Fu can do magic and

he can save. The success lies in the art of keeping to yourself what you don't know."

Baxter grinned broadly.

"His racing stable is not that bad. At least your manager leaves the impression."

"The fool who does everything never gets rich. But a rich man will do anything to fool himself."

"Aren't we all somehow?"

A smile appeared on the Chinese face. "Just a little bit. And you?"

"I must also have been a fool when I imagined my dream could come true."

"What's your name?"

"Baxter Goodman."

"Are you a driver? You also understand quite a bit about motors. Are you looking for a job?"

"No driver. At least not on the racetrack. I'm a mechanic and sometimes I can do magic. In the junkyard, where I am now, it gets too boring for me. I need a new challenge. Something right, something creative and sometimes what makes sense. I've always wanted to tune racing cars. The Mustangs have to scratch their hooves right from the start." Baxter's eyes shone like blazing flames as he talked and talked.

"What does Ruler say?"

"There's already one out there."

The dwarf grimaced. "A lot of work is coming, a lot. Too much for just one man", Ling Fu hissed. Then he grinned mysteriously.

"Why did you say Lulel to Ruler earlier? I thought the guy jumped at me."

The dwarf giggled.

"It always happens to me when I'm angry."

Baxter grinned broadly. He liked the little Chinese.

"Bye, Ling Fu. Maybe you'll see each other again."

"You always meet twice in life. Haywood needs you. More than he thinks. He just doesn't know it yet. I will help him to wisdom. Don't give up, Baxter."

"I never give up, my friend", Baxter said when he left.

Baxter blew an icy wind around his nose and played with his curls as he stepped in front of the gate. Gray mountains of clouds moved to the southeast. Although it was already mid-March, spring was still far away. The air was damp and heavy and still smelled of snow. Baxter sucked it deep into his lungs. It was already midday. On the way back to the junkyard in Rapid City, Baxter let his thoughts play. Everything was open to him, as before. Only now he looked at the sober reality on the way to his dream with mixed feelings. The little Chinese had been pleasantly remembered. The manager, however, seemed out of place.

He fits into a bank rather than a workshop. Haywood must have good reasons to keep such an office stallion.

Baxter laughed out loud.

When the time comes, I'll talk to this Haywood.

*****

A few rays of sun came in bundles, like arrows, through the cloud holes. Harsh north winds swept across the undulating grasslands of the Pine Ridge Reservation. Fine ice crystals still drifted across the country at night. It was March and no trace of spring. The Lakota called him 'the moon of sick eyes' because the rough wind inflamed her eyes. The wind whirled up dust and carried it to every corner, right into the houses. The people who grew up here never knew it any other way.

While the children were romping across the schoolyard of the Oglala High School, various groups of young people stood together. The strange young man who had mingled with them was not particularly noticeable. Not even that he smoked. He had turned up the fur collar of his jacket. The black hair was tied in the neck into a ponytail and not covered. The wind tugged at it, loosened individual hairs and played with it. Hardly any of these children and adolescents knew him. It was important to beware of the teachers. Ryan smiled. He couldn't make out a familiar face. He had been away too long. Almost six years. The time when they knew him, the cliques called his name, was a thing of the past. He was where he knew. The time had hardly changed. Only faces and names belonged to the next generation that went the same way. Ryan Black Hawk was among his. But today he was behaving like a scout among enemies. He especially observed those who had drawn to the edge of the street. Nobody seemed to take any note of him, but he knew only too well that he was being watched. That's why Ryan kept moving. It would be less noticeable if he suddenly had to move in one direction. Ryan had smoked his cigarette and kicked it out. His eyes turned to a car that stopped on the road. A young man got out and joined the group of young people standing there. The car went on. Ryan quickly moved to them. The man who had got out of the car had buried his hands in his pockets. Ryan stopped behind him. The voices were silent.

"Do you have something for me?", Ryan asked softly.

"I don't understand what you want from me", the stranger evaded suspiciously.

"Show me your hands so I can choose."

The young man, roughly seventeen, turned a little and looked Ryan out of the corner of his eye. Finally, he took out a pack of cigarettes and held it out to him. Ryan examined the rolling cigarettes.

"Only joints? Doesn't Hunting Wolf have anything better for me?"

Some of the youth left the circle.

"Who are you?"

"A wind dancer", Ryan smiled.

The young man seemed to be considering.

"I've never seen you here."

"The last time I was here you were probably still in diapers. So what's up?"

The end of the break called the students back. The stranger and Ryan remained alone. Finally, he pulled a plastic bag out of his pocket. He took out one of the white pieces, which were individually wrapped in a film. Then he gave Ryan one of them. He unpacked it, cracked it and looked at it carefully. He smelled it before he bit into it. His opposite observed his every move.

"Dextrose with little dope", Ryan noted.

The young man did not respond.

"How much?"

"A gift", he replied skeptically.

"Okay." Ryan pocketed it.

"Where is hunting wolf?"

The guy contemptuously twisted his mouth.

"Everywhere and nowhere."

"I want to negotiate with him myself. Tell him!"

With these words Ryan turned and left the school yard. On the other side, behind the gym, he had parked the Corvette. He knew he would stand out with it, but he needed her. As for Hunting Wolf, he would be impressed. Ryan got in and drove slowly. He could see the dealer get in the same car that dropped him there. Ryan followed them, even at the risk of being noticed. It was not long before the Interstate to Nebraska, which was hardly used at this time, had been noticed. For miles these streets led straight, like a ruler through the prairie, and offered no cover. The car in front of him promptly got faster. Ryan too. The Corvette was far superior to the Chevy. As Ryan started to overtake, the one in front pulled to the left and braked him down.

Ryan wanted to see if Hunting Wolf drove the car himself. He faked a new overtaking maneuver. When the Chevy pulled to the left, Ryan hit the accelerator fully. The tires scraped the asphalt. Then the Corvette shot past to the right of the Chevy. When Ryan thought he had enough distance, he put the brakes on. The wheels locked and he pulled the steering wheel around. He could see the driver but could not recognize him. Hunting Wolf didn't seem to be. Since there usually had to be at least two men in the car, Hunting Wolf would have stopped because Ryan was alone. But the driver of the Chevy had different rules. He turned off the paved road and disappeared sideways into the area. A daring venture, this season. The underground was still frozen, while a greasy layer of mud had formed on the surface. Ryan stopped on the side of the road and saw the car swaying over the ground until it disappeared from view.

The guy was at least a good driver. While Ryan took the last cigarette out of the box, he thought. Most of the trading places were still known to him. Maybe some were new or relocated. It was unlikely that Hunting Wolf would show up there now. Not during the day. Hunting

Wolf was certainly entitled to his name. The hunting wolf was a creature of darkness.

*****

Three weeks had passed. Cold wind still blew across the country. It had rained, stormed and snowed until the beginning of April. The soil was muddy. The rain clouds slowly migrated south. The sun had been shining for two days. People heave a sigh of relief and came out of their houses. The sunlight reflected on the black paint and the Commander's pane. Baxter, though wearing sunglasses, had the visor down. He drove on Highway 90 at the permissible top speed to the Pierre exit. Then he turned north. Eagle Creek Village was his destination. Haywood's stable had a magical attraction for the Bear. Baxter was now finally certain that it was time to speak to Haywood. His heart beat faster when the area in front of him appeared. His dream was within reach and took shape. If everything went well, he would then go to Olivia and Keshia to tell them. So far, Baxter had kept his secret safe, even though Olivia had tried several times to get it out of him.

The jeep rolled slowly through the open gate. So there was someone there. As before, Baxter stopped in front of the house under the trees. Haywoods office. He got out, pressed the cowboy hat onto his curly hair and slammed the driver's door. As he took the first step towards the door, he took a deep breath. Then he knocked.

"Come in!"

Baxter had prepared himself. He knew well that Haywood wanted a driver, not a mechanic. So he had to do

it cleverly. Selling himself well, however, seemed very difficult for him and cost him some effort. Baxter opened the door and entered.

"Hello. Baxter Goodman is my name. I want to speak to Mr. Haywood."

The man looked up from his desk and eyed Baxter critically. "This is me. Sit down", he said finally.

Baxter cleared his throat, picked up the hat, and sat on the chair opposite Haywood. He was desperately looking for the first words. Haywood must not have missed this embarrassment. He smiled amusedly from his bright eyes.

Haywood could have been Baxter's father by age. His hair was white and his sun-tanned skin had wrinkles. Haywood wore the typical clothes of a man from the country and a light cowboy hat was at hand on the desk. The office was relatively small and looked like a living room from the past century. Nostalgic and somehow cozy. Baxter's gaze stuck to the picture hanging on the wall just behind Haywood. He noticed it as soon as he entered. A shiny chrome, red truck filled the whole picture.

"What can I do for you?"

Baxter cleared his throat again.

"Well. Your racing stable, the Mustangs and the Prairie track have probably impressed me too much. At least something broke out in me. An old illness, so to speak."

"A disease?", Haywood asked skeptically.

"Yes. Chronic and incurable." Baxter grinned obliquely.

"Maybe you'd better consult a doctor with it, Goodman", Haywood said.

"He can't help me either. But maybe you."

"Me?", he asked in astonishment.

"Yes. I think I have too much gasoline in my blood."

"Oh, now I understand. You came for the job."

"That's the way it is."

"When can you start?"

"Are you serious?" Baxter was obviously perplexed.

"Naturally! Do you think I'm kidding?"

"I don't think so, but to be honest ...did Mr. Ruler or Ling Fu tell you I was here before?"

"Oh! You already know the two?"

"Volatile."

"No. I'm sorry."

"Then you don't know that I'm a mechanic?"

Haywood stared at Baxter. "No."

"Well! I was with the US Air Force for four years and two of them worked as a workshop manager. I can disassemble a Mustang into all its individual parts and quickly reassemble it without a blueprint."

Haywood stroked his chin thoughtfully before nodding barely. "That sounds promising, Goodman."

Baxter said nothing and waited.

"Did the Air Force fire you?", he asked suspiciously.

"No. It got too boring for me."

"Here the cars are rebuilt differently so that they become race-ready."

"Tuning. My specialty." Baxter's eyes shone.

"Where do you work now?"

"In Rapid City."

"Workshop?"

"You could say", Baxter grinned.

"And why do you want to get out of there?"

"As I say, it's too boring for me. Tighten a few screws here, there a carburetor and maybe wipe a paint scratch and change tires day by day", Baxter growled. "As a little

boy, I sniffed exhaust air on race tracks and dreamed of being one of them one day. To one of the teams in the colorful overalls."

"Then why are you coming to me and not going to Chicago, the professionals?"

"I don't feel like playing the stirrup holder for them. The racing cars are delivered from the assembly line in a box. Except refueling and changing tires is not possible. If the electronics fail, they will be sent back to the sender. Well that's how it looks. I guess you still need real handiwork, creativity and ideas."

Baxter actually seemed to have impressed Haywood with it. The grin continued.

"But you will never get that much money here."

"Does that mean I have the job?"

"If you like. Get in touch with Ruler next week. He will tell you what to do. The last weekend in April is the season opening."

Baxter was surprised. He grinned triumphantly. His eyes lit Haywood up. "Thank you, Mr. Haywood. Now I just need a place to stay. At the moment I still live in Rapid City."

Haywood grinned smugly. With his eyes he fixed his face like a fox his prey. "Alone? Then I would know something", he said.

Baxter nodded.

"Perfect single household with housekeeping and one baby", Baxter grinned amused and enjoyed Haywood's baffled face.

"Baby?", he finally asked.

"Oh yes, Sir. A Jeep Commander. He's out there, outside the door.

"Aha", Haywood breathed a sigh of relief and smiled.

"Over there, above the garages, there is space under the roof for a small apartment. I had started to expand it. An outside staircase leads up to the apartment. If you're smart, you can get it ready."

"That sounds pretty damn good, Mr. Haywood."

"We can have a look at that right away", Haywood said eagerly.

"With pleasure!"

Baxter thought he was dreaming. He wouldn't just work in a racing stable! No, he would live here too. He would be part of this racing team and eventually he would be on the inventory list. Haywood shouldn't regret it. Baxter wanted to show him how good he was and that Haywood couldn't have found a better one. The joy was literally written on his face and Haywood must have noticed. He was obviously happy to have found someone who wanted to expand the loft, was always on the spot and brought him regular rental income. Finally, he got up. "Okay. Let's go."

Haywood took the key off the hook and went ahead.

The room was large but a little dark, as there was only one window on the gable end. Opposite was a room that was intended for a bathroom. It smelled musty, of color, wood and damp cardboard. Tools lay on the dust-covered floor. Baxter finally looked out through the smeared window. He couldn't see the vehicle hangars from here. He opened it and gasped for fresh air. He looked at a red stone wall with a closed gate. Grass grew through the cracks of the stones. Behind the wall stood several cottonwoods, undemanding trees from the steppes of North America, and a lantern next to the gate.

"Is that the emergency exit down there?", Baxter asked

jokingly.

"That's how it is."

"Perfect. Living in the country",Baxter said. "I think I could feel at home here."

"Excellent, Goodman. Then we agree on business", Haywood said happily and held out his hand.

Baxter shook on it. "Perfectly."

The Bear's heart leaped so much with joy that he couldn't ask about his wages or the rental price. In principle he didn't care at the moment. Nothing would have questioned his decision.

On the way back Baxter stopped at the small gas station. He had to fill up and talk. Whistling he got out and went inside.

"Hello little lady. How are you?"

"Oh, hello, stranger. Well, thank you, and your bear too", she smiled. The plush teddy sat directly at the cash register and blinked amused at Baxter. "Nice to see you again. What can I do for you this time?"

"I'm Baxter Goodman and from now on I'm no stranger anymore. Call me Baxter. In the future I will be able to fill up more often."

The young woman smiled. "Okay, Baxter. I'm glad. I'm Susan Carter. For you then Susan."

Baxter shook his head. He had a little girlfriend in foreign parts. She was sixteen at the most.

"What's up?", she asked irritated.

"I still can't believe it! The guy actually hired me. I will soon be working over there in the racing stable as a mechanic", he proudly reported.

"Congratulations! The old scrooge didn't want to afford a second mechanic. For this he employs a guy who doesn't do anything at all, as a manager that nobody likes here."

"So you know your way around", said Baxter.

"The old scrooge is my grandfather."

Baxter's mouth remained open.

"Why didn't you tell me right away?"

Susan shrugged. "Why should I? He hardly knows me. He doesn't like family and all that."

"What a pity. A family is very important to me."

"Do you have one?"

"A tiny one. Olivia, my mother and I are left. I move to Haywood, above the garages. Alone."

Susan grinned. "Then in the future we will be something of a family if you move in with my grandfather. Maybe that's good for him."

Baxter rocked his head.

"Do you ever go to the races sometimes?"

"Of course! This is a real event, like a rodeo elsewhere. Everyone comes here. You will get to know the whole village ... ten to twelve people", she giggled.

Baxter laughed.

"I'm looking forward to it."

"Fill up?"

"Yes, please. And a stick of cigarettes, a country times and a bottle of water."

Baxter added a bag of cashew nuts.

"Bulk purchase?"

"Almost", he grinned. "The small gas station fascinates me. If I didn't already have a job with your grandfather, I could get used to the idea of opening a small gas station. That would be perfect. Interesting people keep coming, I could talk to everyone and would always be informed about everyone and everything and could tow a broken-down car every now and then. But this only works in the outback. I'm not a man for the city anyway."

Susan was obviously enjoying herself.

"With the start of the race season it started off. There is little going on in winter. I only earn a few Dollars. After school I want to begin one`s studies."

"Wow! And what?"

"Veterinary medicine."

"I was thinking of a chemical lab technician for alternative fuels."

"Maybe I'll go to NASA. I dream of flying into space."

"Seriously?", Baxter doubted

Susan laughed. "Of course! But before that I would have to become a pilot."

"I know a few people in the Air Force", he grinned.

"Have you been there? Are you a pilot?"

"Yes, I was. Pilot? No I'm not. God forbid. I was with the ground staff. Mechanic for very special cases."

Susan leaned her elbows on the counter and eyed Baxter curiously. "Did they fire you?"

Baxter gasped.

Why does everyone ask me this?

"How do you get the idea?"

"You don't just give up such a good and safe job, Baxter."

"Oh, to hell. I quit. It's too boring to follow orders in the long run. At some point, every man comes of age to want to make his own decisions", Baxter replied gruffly.

Susan kept grinning.

"Right. You should."

"I'll go and fill up. See you soon", Baxter said, and went out. He was here alone. Far and wide no other car and no human soul was to be seen. All around the wavy grasslands. The wind swept over the withered winter grass, so that it looked like a moving sea of waves. Baxter hung up the fuel nozzle. While the sound of the pump came to his ears, he thought of his friend.

Where is he at the moment?

Ryan hadn't answered in five days. Baxter took a deep breath. Then he wrote a short message.

Yes, damn it! I'm worried! You are my friend, my kola and my little brother.

The fuel nozzle clicked. Baxter pulled it and hung it up. Then he went to Susan to pay his bill.

"Thanks, Baxter. I was really happy to meet you."

"Yes, me too Susan. So then ... see you soon."

"Don't you want to take your teddy with you today?"

"No. Take good care of him until I come back."

Susan laughed. "Okay, Baxter Goodman."

*****

The icy north wind blew continuously over the endless grasslands and the cold of the night had turned the drizzle into fine ice crystals. The wind drove evenly wispy clouds. Only now and then did the full, round moon appear. He brightened the faces of the three men who were standing and smoking next to an off-road vehicle. With every breath, smoke rose and evaporated in nothing. The one who hid the cigarette in his hand threw it to the floor and kicked it out. Isaak Hunting Wolf had come. He had his younger brother, Craig, with him. A duo not to be underestimated. Ryan had been watching Isaac for more than two weeks and was circulating to get to him personally. It was finally time tonight. Ryan's Glock was loaded and in his shoulder holster. Isaac knew that. He had searched him. But he and his brother were also armed. The Lakota's Corvette did not appear suspicious to him. She confirmed the Hunting Wolf brothers, just this man's business acumen. In summer, exactly eight years ago, they had competed against each other in a street race. Ryan was fifteen then. Isaac could remember it just as well. His mistrust of Ryan seemed to fade. He really couldn't trust anyone, and he didn't. For this reason, he never came alone. Ryan had noticed two shapes hiding behind his back. At least one other was posted somewhere between the trees, watching them. With the two brothers five or six. Too many.

"So you've stayed true to your business, Black Hawk. You were a fox even then. Where have you been all year?"

"Alaska."

"Alaska?", Isaac asked skeptically.

"I had to go into hiding for a while."

Isaac grinned broadly. "And now you want to get involved again?"

Ryan nodded briefly without answering.

"Do you no longer know the sources?"

His question sounded scornful.

Ryan grimaced.

"I want more than just Pezi Sica, bad grass."

"What do you want?"

"The white medicine that you stretch with Dextrose and sell at the schools. Dextrose for children. Do you need that?", Ryan asked sharply.

Isaac and Craig contemptuously grimaced.

"What makes you think that?"

"Sugar containing cocaine for sweet dreams. It was a gift." Ryan took one of the white pieces out of his pocket and held it up to Isaac's nose.

He shaped the eyes into small slits.

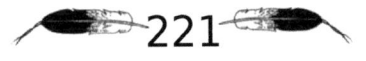

"What's your problem, Ryan? That gives the optimal drive for more and does not cost much."

"And immediately goes into the blood."

"You tried that?", Isaac laughed softly.

Craig laughed too.

Ryan grimaced. "I didn't even feel sick! What about brandy?"

"What should be with it?"

"Do you have one?"

"Enough."

"Well. Then let's drink together."

Isaac Hunting Wolf eyed Ryan skeptically. He was unable to see through Ryan.

The clouds shredded more and more. The fine ice crystals were gone. The phases in which the moonlight shone on the earth grew longer. Then the country around was clearly recognizable. The wind moved the dry grass and the branches of the bare poplar.

"Where are you living now? Here?", Isaac finally asked.

"Everywhere and nowhere", Ryan replied.

"Let's drive. Alone."

Isaac took a step towards Ryan.

"I determine the rules! Not you!", he hissed.

Ryan nodded. "It's up to you."

Then he turned and went to his Corvette. He opened the door and got in. When he tried to close her, Isaac prevented him from doing so.

Ryan waited. "Get in", he said finally.

Ryan noticed that Isaac was hesitating and mocked the corners of his mouth.

"Has the hunting wolf become a shy coyote?"

He did not answer, but gave his brother a sign to get into the off-road vehicle and to follow him. Then Isaac came

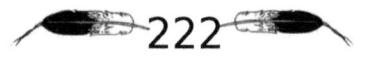

around the Corvette and got in. Ryan started. Isaac gave directions where to go. The off-road vehicle stayed behind them. The way through the night led south, beyond the border of the Reservation. After all, they were in Nebraska. They left the paved road to drive into the bush along a dirt road. Branches grazed the car. At some point the shadowy outline of a hut appeared. Craig stopped the Jeep and Ryan the Corvette. They got out. Without losing a word, the three men went to the wooden hut.

The wolf's camp, Ryan thought, and stopped in the doorway. He lit a cigarette while looking around. The eyes had got used to the darkness and the full moon sent its light into the open door. Craig opened one of the boxes and tossed a bottle to his brother. He turned it up and smelled it. Then he gave it to Ryan.

"Drink!"

Ryan took it and also smelled it, before he put it on and took a good sip. Isaac and Craig grinned broadly. The mistrust seemed to have melted and it seemed to Ryan like old times.

"And? What do you say?", Isaac asked, when Ryan put the bottle down.

"There are better ones."

"Way too expensive."

"He's good", Ryan nodded.

Isaac grinned contentedly and nodded.

Ryan held out the bottle. He took it and put it on too. A small, nimble shadow flitted across the floor and disappeared between the boxes. After a third was missing from the bottle, Isaac handed it to his brother. He drank too. It was quiet outside. Nothing moved except the wind, which made the dry branches rustle in the treetops. Ryan took a deep breath, sucked at the cigarette again and kicked it out half-smoked.

"A box. How much?"

"Sixty."

"Okay."

Ryan walked slowly to the Corvette, opened the tailgate and waited. Isaac sent Craig with the box to him and followed his brother. Craig put the box in the trunk. At that moment, Ryan slammed the tailgate down with full force before Isaak Hunting Wolf understood what was going on. But he reacted quickly. While his brother was incapacitated for a while, lying on the ground next to the Corvette, Isaak drew his pistol and aimed it at Ryan. Ryan, who was standing right in front of Isaac, grabbed it on the barrel with his left hand and struck hard with the right edge of his hand against the neck of his surprised opponent. Ryan disarmed and knocked him out in a second. Isaac moaned softly and lay motionless on the floor. Ryan pulled a thin wire from his sleeve with his teeth and quickly tied his wrists together. Ryan listened. From the way, quiet engine noise penetrated his ears through the clear night. Isaac grunted and sent Ryan a scathing look.

"You are a dead man, Black Hawk."

The coming car obviously drove very slowly, as if it wanted to remain hidden until it appeared. Ryan put the pistol in his belt and pulled Isaac on his legs.

"Get in!", he urges. "... and keep your hands still if you still need them in the future."

"Why are you doing this?", Isaac hissed.

Ryan pushed him to his car, in the passenger seat. Then he pulled Craig, who was slowly regaining consciousness, away from the car. He started. Slowly he drove past the

oncoming car. Ryan nodded to the driver. Hunting Wolf was sitting next to him. Ryan could see in the rearview mirror that the car was parked at the cabin. It would take maybe five seconds for Hunting Wolf's men to realize what had happened. Ryan drove on unwavering.

"Idiots!", Isaac cursed.

Ryan grinned.

A short time later, headlights appeared in the mirrors of the Corvette. The car followed. Ryan accelerated. The tires scratched on mud and gravel and hurled stones backwards. When Ryan reached the paved road and dashed the same way back, the pursuers were out of his sight.

"Who are you?", Isaac asked.

"One who claimed the territory", Ryan replied.

Isaac snorted angrily.

"What are you going to do with me? You could have killed me."

Ryan said nothing.

It was sunrise when Ryan stopped in front of the tribal police building. The time of the hunter was over.

"You'll have plenty of time to think about who you are, Isaak Hunting Wolf", Ryan said.

Then he got out, opened the tailgate and unloaded the box. Two police officers had already noticed the car and were standing at the passenger door. One opened. Isaac got out. He paid no attention to Ryan, but he spat at his feet before they led him inside. Ryan pretended not to notice, leaned against his Corvette and lit a cigarette. The wind played with his hair and blew it over his face. The braid had loosened. That didn't seem to bother him either. He felt empty and stared thoughtlessly at an imaginary point between heaven and earth.

225

*****

With a tired smile, Olivia opened the door where there was a knock. It wasn't Baxter's drumming.

"Oh! Our warrior has returned from his raid", she blurted out spontaneously.

"Tired and hungry." Ryan smiled weakly.

"I like that. Come in my boy!"

Olivia hugged him just as stormily and warmly as Baxter. Ryan had become her second son over time. Once Olivia Goodman has loved someone, then right. Ryan had liked it. Smiling he gave her a kiss on the forehead just as someone opened the door of the guest room. Olivia let Ryan go, grinned and disappeared into her bathroom.

"Ryan!" Keshia shouted and jumped into his arms.

He hugged her and kissed her before he could say a word. The kiss lasted a long time, just as if it had to make up for the lost time in which they had not seen each other. "Oh, Ryan", Keshia whispered. "I am so glad you are here. I was worried about you."

With his eyes he scanned her face. Then he nodded barely. "You are beautiful, Keshia. I remembered you in the same way."

She laughed softly. "And you look tired, my hunter. Come over! You can sleep in my bed."

She took him by the hand and led him into the guest room. He took off his shoes and threw the jacket along with shirt and Jeans on the armchair and crawled under the blanket.

"Sleep well", Keshia said.

"Hmmm", he murmured, breathing steadily in his sleep. Keshia smiled and sneaked out of the room.

When Olivia came out of the bathroom, Keshia was just switching on the coffee machine. She noticed her searching look and smiled.

"Where is he? I hope not gone again! Today you have to send someone else to the race."

"No. He's sleeping."

"What? Where?"

"In my bed."

"I see", Olivia said relieved. "But he hasn't even eaten anything..."

"He was very tired and fell asleep immediately."

Keshia went to the bathroom.

A minute later, Olivia heard the shower rushing as she made breakfast for the young woman and herself, watching the news on TV.

Keshia sat down with wet hair and took a piece of bread. Olivia poured coffee. Keshia immediately noticed that Olivia was more silent this morning than usual. That was unusual. Keshia also noticed that she was looking through the television. After a while Keshia said to Olivia: "I was only eight years old when I lost my mother. I grew up with my brothers with my grandparents. It's been a long time, but I know that she's always there for me."

Olivia moved out of her trance and looked at Keshia. She saw a happy young woman before her who seemed more alive than ever before. Her smile seemed to have a magical power. Olivia smiled back. Then she sighed.

"I will miss you, Keshia."

Suddenly Olivia grinned broadly. "Let me know if I become a grandmother. At Baxter I can wait until I go black."

"Yes, of course Olivia", Keshia laughed.

The wind had actually driven the clouds away. Bright

sunny shone in through the window. The winter now seemed to be finally over. Olivia called the pastor and canceled her ministry for today, because today was a special day. After breakfast, Keshia and Oliva made their way into the city to shop. Some things just didn't exist in the Reservation or they were far too expensive. Moreover, said the women, Ryan could sleep undisturbed. When they returned in the afternoon, the door to the guest room was open and the water in the shower rustled. While Olivia was unpacking the shopping bags, Keshia was making coffee. Then she filled the fruit bowl and put some sandwiches together for Ryan. She looked up and smiled when he appeared in the kitchen. Her eyes shone with joy to see him. In black boxer shorts and a towel around his shoulder, he greeted his wife with a fleeting kiss on the mouth.

"Slept well?", Keshia asked.

"Yes."

"Hungry?"

"Like a bear", he whispered to her.

Olivia grinned.

Keshia pointed to the plate with the various sandwiches, which she had decorated with tomatoes and pickles.

"Hm, thanks. I'll be right back."

With these words, Ryan disappeared into the guest room to appear dressed immediately.

He grinned. "How nice! Today there are two women to make me something to eat", he said as he reached for one of the sandwiches.

"Be careful with what you say!", Olivia warned, who was half in the kitchen cupboard.

"I'll put up a kitchen tent for you, Olivia. About a mile from ours."

Olivia turned to Ryan, blew her cheeks and put her hands on her hips. "You'd like that!"

Ryan laughed.

"You have a wife and she can cook and bake very well! I've also shared some of my secret recipes with her over the past few weeks."

"Wrong, Olivia. With Keshia I have three women who take care of me."

Olivia tapped her head clearly with her forefinger. "You have to take good care of this guy, Keshia. Sometimes he's mad."

Keshia shook her head and laughed amused.

Ryan chewed with innocence.

"Well. Then you could sing, Olivia", he said.

"What are you paying?"

"A horse."

"What am I supposed to do with a horse?", Olivia asked horrified.

"What do you think what you do with it?"

"Can I roast and eat it?"

Keshia watched them and giggled.

"No idea if you can."

Olivia took a deep breath. "Ryan Black Hawk! Would you take the mickey out of me?"

Ryan had eaten the sandwich, got up and went to her.

"If that's your wish, Olivia..."

Before she could have answered, Ryan put her up and carried her out of the kitchen. Olivia gave a short shriek and laughed. "Let me down, you crazy dog."

Ryan laughed, stopped in front of the couch in the living room and dropped her.

"Disrespectful! One like the other", Olivia puffed and fought his way around in a sitting position.

"Do you treat your mother in the same way?"

"How so?", he grinned defiantly.

Olivia waved with her hands, gasped, and threw a pillow at Ryan.

Keshia leaned against the kitchen cupboard, crossed her arms and grinned.

Someone banged on the door from outside.

"That can only be a Grizzly", Ryan said.

Keshia opened.

"Hello, Baxter", she greeted him.

Baxter entered and took Keshia in his arms, lifted her like usual Olivia and turned in a circle with her.

"Hey, you've changed, Olivia Goodman!", he shouted cheerfully and laughed. "First of all, you have become lighter, as light as a feather.

"I am not Olivia. I'm Keshia", she giggled.

"Oh, really. I was already thinking of a delusion." Baxter put her down. Do I get a kiss as a greeting?"

"No. I don't kiss beards."

Baxter grunted.

Ryan laughed amused.

"What do you think of that? Our little girl is mouthed."

Baxter bluntly put his arm over her shoulder and gently pulled her with him. Ryan leaned back in the chair and grinned triumphantly.

"Hi, Grizzly", he said.

"Hello little one", greeted Olivia, who was still grinning on the couch and holding a pillow ready to throw in her hands.

Baxter let go of Keshia and kissed his mother on the cheek. Keshia sat down on the arm of the armchair with Ryan. He pulled her onto his lap and closed his arms around her. Their looks met briefly. Both smiled happi-

ly.Baxter turned to them.

"Hello little brother. Nice to see you… and without scratches on the paintwork. Did you come to take my little friend away?"

"I don't need that. She will follow voluntarily."

"Show off!"

Ryan grinned deliberately.

Baxter plopped down on the couch and put his arm around Olivia.

"Well, I'll settle for you again, Olivia. My first big love", he grinned.

"Better take a woman your age, son, and see that I have grandchildren, at least a dozen. That is no longer bearable."

Olivia turned the television down.

"Let's see what can be done, old woman. Maybe one day I'll do you the favor."

Baxter got a side kick from his mother's elbow that he grimaced painfully.

"Have you already told your boss that he has to get by without you from now on?"

"Yes. He just doesn't want it to be true."

"I can imagine that. I will also quit. So no bronc bareback anymore."

"All life is a rodeo, Bax. Sometimes you sit up, sometimes you lie in the dirt with your nose. The question is not whether you remain above but how long. And when you are lying on the floor, the question is not how long, but whether you get up again."

Baxter nodded eagerly.

"I'm in the process of doing this, my friend", he finally said with a strange shine in his eyes. "From the week after next I'm a mechanic in a real racing team, up on the

Missouri River. In Eagle Creek Village, a godforsaken nest on the prairie north of Pierre. The owner is Haywood and he was actually looking for a racing driver for himself and his Mustangs. He already has a mechanic. A dwarf of Chinese. I was able to convince Haywood that he still needs me. Man! That's something, Ryan. You can take the speedster apart, right down to the last screw and when you have reassembled it, a racing horse is in front of you. And the best part! I'm moving in there. I will be one of them. Above the garages, under the roof, is a small apartment. Not quite finished yet, but I can renovate it to my liking. You have to come to my official opening!" Baxter had talked in euphoria. After his quick words it was suddenly quiet.

"And?", he asked uncertainly.

Ryan nodded. "Well."

"What? Nothing more?", Baxter hissed disappointed.

Ryan grinned.

"I hope you didn't hide the fact that you did it for the Air Force for a few years. if there is no racehorse at the end, but a jet in his shop."

Everyone laughed.

When Baxter got his breath back, he said: "Well, if you were to start as a pilot, Falcon, that wouldn't be a problem."

"Not for me. But maybe for the others."

"Don't you have something to drink in the fridge, Olivia?"

Olivia nodded. "Of course. We shopped today."

She got up and got glasses. Then she put two large bottles of Coke on the table and sat down. Baxter took it and poured it. Ryan watched him unusually closely.

"What's up?", Baxter asked uncertainly.

Ryan smiled mysteriously.

"I think Kola, today is truly a very special day", Ryan replied.

Keshia and he rose. Ryan went into the guest room without another word and came back with a bottle of the finest whiskey in hand. He put them on the table in front of Baxter. Baxter stared at the bottle with wide eyes and an open mouth.

He stayed silent.

He didn't move.

He didn't even bat an eye as if hypnotized.

Olivia and Keshia giggled softly.

Baxter was speechless, in the truest sense of the word. That was rare.

"A gift. Now open it already. Today is the day I drink a Whiskey with you, my friend. Tomorrow I'm going home with Keshia. Back to the ranch, back to my and our family."

Baxter closed his mouth very slowly. Stunned, he looked at Ryan and blew the pent-up air out of his lungs. Embarrassed, he stroked his hair.

"That I may live to see...", Baxter croaked finally hoarsely.

Olivia laughed as she placed four Whiskey glasses on the table. After all, it was she who reached for the bottle, opened it and poured it. Then they toasted themselves.

"To you, little brother, to Keshia and your future together. to the ranch and your family", Baxter said solemnly.

"And on you, Baxter. All of your babies and especially our friendship", added Ryan. ... "and on Olivia, our good spirit."

Olivia smiled emotionally.

As they emptied their glasses, Keshia smelled the glass

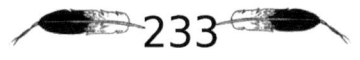

and sipped carefully. Then she made a face and put the glass back down, shaking her head.

Ryan smiled.

No one commented, not even Baxter. The whole evening was theirs. There was a melancholy feeling in the anticipation and happiness that they felt as their paths parted. But nobody wanted to be carried away by it right now. After all, they lived in one world, in one state, and this very special friendship shouldn't break in a few shabby miles. They laughed and joked while Baxter drank another whiskey and later another. The hours passed. It was night. The candle that Olivia had put on the table had almost burned down. The dimmed light of the standard lamp conjured moving shadows into the room. Time had no meaning. It was only in the early morning of the next day that fatigue let their tongues speak more slowly. Olivia said goodbye and went to bed. A short time later, Keshia and Ryan moved close together and shared the bed in the guest room.

Dead tired and his limbs as heavy as lead, Baxter shuffled to the window. He opened it and sucked in the cold night air as he looked up at the stars. Very quietly, so that only his lips moved, a single word left his mouth: "Pilamaya yelo." Then he dropped onto the couch and pulled the blanket over his shoulders. Seconds later he fell asleep.

Ryan was still awake. He smelled Keshia, her hair and skin. He felt the warmth of her body, felt it in front of his face and heard her steady breath. She was sleeping. It had a calming effect on him. Deep down he felt the joy that this woman had come into his life, that she loved him and was his wife. His dream was real. With these thoughts, Ryan finally found sleep.

A dream came to him at dawn. It led him into the valley through which the brook ran, to the old log house and the slope grown with pines. Ryan saw the grazing horses in the valley and there were more than ever. He saw his family, the sister with the children. The whole family was there. Ryan was looking forward to seeing them again and his heart started to beat faster and harder. He heard it himself. It woke him up, brought him back. Ryan kept his eyes closed tightly so that the faces of the people he was part of remained even when he was awake. Cante ma waste, said his thoughts. He was happy.

Keshia stirred.

Slowly she turned to him. Ryan opened his eyes and blinked. He saw her face in front of him at dusk and smiled. Keshia eyed him in silence. Ryan was unable to move and couldn't take his eyes off her face. It was like a spell that had caught him before when she sang magic songs for him that night in the tipi to heal him. Finally, his hand slowly moved to her face, gently stroking her cheek and touching her lips. She opened it and breathed through her mouth.

Keshia carefully pushed the coverlet away so that it fell to the floor. Silently, like two intertwined snakes, they let their naked bodies slide together. Ryan felt her lips, her tongue and her desire. He also felt his own and breathed harder. They had not seen each other for three weeks and had not touched them. His heart thumped against his chest as he stroked her breasts. He felt delicate, soft hands that went down over his back. She stroked his buttocks as the flames blazed in her kiss. Ryan was handed over. When he felt her hands on his penis, he moaned softly. *Keshia!*

Their hearts beat wildly, while they finally united in rhythm to one.

*****

The sun had already passed the zenith and was moving westwards when the cars were packed. Olivia had provided her children with plenty of provisions so that every storage space of the car was used. Baxter was amazed at everything that could be stored in the small sports car. He had noticed that Ryan stuck the Winchester, that old Sam had given him, behind the passenger seat. The small black backpack that always accompanied the headhunter was between his and Keshia's luggage.
"Will you meet him again?", whispered Baxter in astonishment.
Ryan shook his head.
"No. Everything is regulated between us."
Baxter nodded and put his hand on his friend's shoulder.
"I'm already looking forward to seeing you again."
"I guess my phone will ring this evening at the latest", said Ryan.
"Do you keep it?"
"Thompson left it up to me. However, he will turn the chip off. Then we can do smoke signals", Ryan grinned.
"I have problems with the spelling."
Ryan jokingly punched Baxter on the shoulder.
Olivia hugged Keshia firmly to her goodbye and bravely hid her goodbye tears behind a beaming smile. She was almost a head shorter than the young woman and stood on tiptoe. When Olivia broke away from Keshia, Baxter turned to her. He smiled a little sheepishly and cleared his throat. Then he was absolutely speechless when Keshia reached out and gently stroked his beard. An ice-

cold shiver ran down his spine. She smiled as if she had noticed. She quickly kissed him on the bearded cheek and got into the Corvette.

Ryan said goodbye to Olivia and also gets in. He raised his arm in greeting as the sports car drove away.

Olivia sighed.

Baxter put his arm around the small, round woman and hugged her and gave her hold. "That's the way it should be and that's a good thing", he said.

Then he got into his Jeep and pressed the horn twice in quick succession when he started. Olivia pulled out her handkerchief and blew her nose loudly.

"Now the gang is gone, Olivia Goodman. Now you can finally do whatever you want", she consoled herself, shaking her head.

*****

The wind blew over the hilly grasslands as he always did. The sun was deceiving about the cold air. She was already declining and making the shadows longer. While spring was coming elsewhere, April in the Great Plains still brought frosty nights and snow showers. The paved road, which cut the country in two, went straight as far as the eye could see. The wind had dried them. It was called Indian Route when Ryan and Keshia crossed the reservation border. The white towers of the badlands appeared on both sides. The evening sunlight gave them a yellow shimmer. Ryan drove south at a permissible top speed. In the prairie, the endlessly hilly grasslands, it seemed as if the sky was touching the earth. Keshia had grown up in the forested mountains.

After driving over a hill, the road gently descended again. Some trees appeared and a furrowed path branched off the asphalt road. Between the trees stood a couple of trailers in the shadow of the evening sun. All had satellite antennas. A horde of children played ball. A dog ran around barking. Keshia smiled. Ryan's cell phone rang.

Thompson!

Ryan accepted with his short, choppy "YES". Then his face darkened suddenly. He immediately stopped at the side of the road.

"He escaped, Ryan. Hunting Wolf is on the run! I'm in the police department in Pine Ridge, with your tribal police. You have to come right away. Only you can find him a second time!", he heard Thompson's excited voice. Ryan had never heard this man so stirred up and desperate.

"Damn!", Ryan hissed. "I am on the way."

Ryan put the phone away.

He pressed his lips together hard and was silent for a moment. Then he took a deep breath. Ryan noticed Keshia's concerned look at himself and turned to her.

"You can handle my rifle. It's easier to handle than your father's hunting rifle and has a targeting device."

Keshia looked pale when she nodded.

"You drive the Corvette. I'll tell you where to."

Ryan got out, opened the trunk, and dug out his back-pack. Keshia sat behind the steering wheel.

"You stay with the tribal police. I get into the car with Thompson", he continued, taking a seat in the passenger seat and slamming the door.

Keshia started.

"I'll ask Baxter to pick you up there right away. A killer has escaped and he knows my car. I leave my cell phone with you. Baxter's number is second."

Ryan called Baxter and briefly reported what had happened. Then he put the phone in the glove compartment of the car and tipped the contents of the backpack onto his lap. "Damn!", he hissed as he checked the pistols and loaded them both.

Keshia watched her husband out of the corner of her eye as she drove. The look on his face frightened her. She recognized the headhunter.

About forty minutes later, Keshia stopped in front of the police department at Pine Ridge. Next to Thompson's Dodge was a black FBI car. Ryan looked at Keshia and their eyes met.

"I guess we'll get home a little later."

"I'll wait for you to eat. Grab him."

Ryan smiled artificial.

"You're waiting here! Baxter is on the way."

"Okay", Keshia nodded.

Thompson already appeared next to the driver's door. Ryan got out.

"You're crazy!", Thompson growled as he nodded to Keshia in the Corvette.

"I was on the way home with her when the call came in, damn it!", Ryan snorted. "Did you want to pick him up here?"

"Shit, yeah!"

Ryan had never heard Thompson swear. He twisted his mouth and shook his head.

"When?"

"Just before I called you."

"Did he steal a car?"

"Not from here. He fled on foot. But before I called the cavalry into the reservation, I called you."

Ryan took a deep breath. Then he nodded.

239

"He cannot have come far yet. I think I know where we're going to look for him. Beyond the border, in Nebraska, outside the reservation and outside the area of responsibility of our tribal police."

"But not ours. Let's go! Let's get the guy back", Thompson said.

"What about the Van?"

"The transporter for prisoners. The inscription is too conspicuous", Thompson said, when he looked at the label 'FBI'. "My two men are on the road with the tribal police."

Ryan grimaced.

"Not just the inscription. Our people smell the FBI ten miles against the wind. Give me the key. Keshia is better off than in the Corvette or in the building."

"You think the guy is actually coming back here?", Thompson asked in astonishment and gave Ryan the key.

"I think everything is possible. Just the paradox."

Keshia took the rifle, got into the Van, and locked the doors from the inside.

Ryan and Thompson got into the Dodge.

Thompson was extremely restless and willingly followed Ryan's orders. He had every reason to do so because he had made the mistake of having Hunting Wolf delivered to the local police because it was the closest. He should have sent his FBI Corps' cavalry immediately when Ryan's call reached him. Thompson regretted bitterly and tormented himself with reproaches. It also jeopardized his hunter, who was fighting against one of his own people for the FBI. That was exactly what he wanted to avoid with his decision. He had not expected Hunting Wolf to break out of tribal prison. But he should have done that. A mixture of anger and despair rummaged through him. He accelerated.

"You stay in the Dodge. I'm going alone in the bush", Ryan ordered.

Thompson didn't argue. It was the first time Ryan spoke to him like that. It gave him fear that he had never felt before, so that it tingled under the skin. Thompson knew the situation was controversial, but now he felt it. Ryan stuck the two pistols, one in the holster, one in the belt and the knife in the bootleg. Then he stuffed a scrap of fabric into the empty cola bottle.

"There are many. There will be deaths", Ryan said while looking at Thompson.

He nodded.

"As long as we are not, I have no problem with it in this case."

Ryan grinned. "We hope so. In about two miles a gravel road turns right into the thicket. Wait there and make sure that nobody escapes and ...don't let your Dodge be stolen from under your butt."

Thompson laughed softly.

"You can count on it, Ryan."

The sun was deep in the west when Ryan left the Dodge. It was already dim between the trees. Ryan moved quickly and was gone after a few seconds of Thompson's gaze. Now the time of waiting began and attention was not allowed to wane even in the dark. Thompson took a deep breath. This did not release his tension in any way.

*****

Panting, a tall, muscular man ran through prairie valleys, jumping over fallen branches and trenches. He swirled up the old leaves as he slid down a slope. It drove sweat out of his pores and he fought against the fatigue of his limbs. Isaak Hunting Wolf had been running for his freedom for almost an hour. Nobody had stopped the fleeing man.

Breathless, he opened the door of the shed and put on a bottle of brandy to quench his thirst and to quench the burning in his throat. But it burned all the more. He dropped to the floor next to the door and leaned back against the frame. It was a while before his breath became calm and steady again. Isaac grinned as he thought of how quickly he had outsmarted one of the policemen. He hadn't had to bribe the other. It belonged to his Tiospaye, his family. Hunting Wolf listened when the sound of the engine of an approaching car came to his ears. The one who came was his younger brother.

Craig came in and sat with him.

"Next time you'll pick me up there! Then I don't need to walk that far", Isaac snorted.

"The next time? Brother! How often do you want to play your game?", Craig said and laughed. "Walking is also good for your fitness."

"I will kill him, this traitor. He won't rest to chase me."

"Do you think he follows you?"

"For sure and it is only a matter of time when he shows up here. As far as I know him."

"Then we should get out of here. The others are waiting for us."

"I won't run away from him! We have to settle the matter together. There is no place for both of us in the reservation. He will die as soon as he crosses my path. Do you have my rifle with you and the ammunition?"

Craig nodded.

"Everything in the car."

242

When suddenly something flew in at the entrance to the shed, the brothers jumped on their legs at the same time. At the same instant there was a deafening bang and a dull pressure. Splinters of glass shot through the shed, which burned in seconds. The first brandy bottles, which could not withstand the heat, burst and the escaping alcohol accelerated the fire. The flames hissed dangerously in all directions. The beams of the shed started to crack. Cursing, Isaac and Craig ran to the car. Craig started and went full throttle. The car moved with difficulty as if the brake had been applied. The car rolled forward a few feet with a rumble.

"It's him! He's here", Isaac yelled angrily.

He jumped out of the car and looked at two flat tires. "Show yourself, you coward!", he shouted angrily.

Nobody answered. The crackling and hissing of the fire grew louder. The shed was blazing. There was nothing left to save. Then the rest collapsed with a loud crash. Blind with anger, Isaac kicked the car and took out his rifle. A shot whistled past his ear as he straightened up. He spun around and fired blindly into the bush from which the shot had come. Craig ducked behind the car.

"Drop the weapon or I'll aim the next shot!", he heard Ryan's voice.

"Coward dog! Creep away and shoot from the ambush. You've been better, Ryan Black Hawk."

The engines of several cars roared from the gravel track.

"This is not an honest fight, Isaac. We both know that. You can surrender or prepare for your journey. The decision is yours."

Isaac laughed bitterly. "You'll be dead before the night is over, Black Hawk. I promise to you."

"Never promise anything you can't keep."

"We will see."

Ryan didn't answer. He thought it wiser to withdraw. The first of the cars appeared at the burning hut.

*****

Thompson's nerves were about to tear. Waiting was hell for him. Especially after he heard the explosion clearly. The glow of fire was visible far in the dark. Thompson wanted to warn Ryan about the strange cars. There were five! But Keshia called.

"Are you all right?", he asked, irritated.

"Yes, everything okay", she confirmed.

He hung up. "Damn it!", then he wiped the beads of sweat from his forehead.

Suddenly he heard gunfire. Thompson picked up his pistol, lowered the side window and listened. It remained silent. Even the engines of the five cars had stopped working.

"Damn it!", he hissed.

He was annoyed with himself. Just as he decided to get into the bush, the engines roared. The cars came shot onto the paved road and raced away at high speed in a northerly direction. They hadn't noticed Thompson's Dodge. He had to wait here. It was difficult for him. When the door of his car cracked a few seconds later, he turned around, startled, and pointed his pistol at a dark figure.

"Be careful, Thompson. Maybe you still need me", Ryan said and got in.

Thompson breathed a sigh of relief.

"Sorry, Ryan, but too many ghosts haunt the night."

Ryan laughed softly.

"They went there, back to the reservation and there are five cars."

"They got in my way. Now we're dealing with everyone", Ryan sighed.

Thompson twisted his mouth and remained silent as he started the Dodge.

Ryan's thoughts worked at full speed.

If the guys discover the Corvette before Baxter...

"All of the police officers' cars are on duty", Ryan said suddenly. "And nobody is in the building anymore!?"

"I do not know exactly. When I left there were two officers", Thompson said.

"Oh my God!"

Thompson took a noisy deep breath and let it out.

"I would rather have stayed in bed this morning."

*****

Keshia clearly heard the sound of an approaching car. It was a Jeep from which he wasn't Baxter's Commander. A second car followed and stopped right in front of the van. She watched the happening motionless and heard the voices of the men who got out. One of the men opened the Corvette. It seemed like he was looking for something. Finally, the guy triumphed because he seemed to have found something valuable. Keshia's handbag! She clearly heard the voice. Keshia gasped. She quickly slipped behind the driver's seat. The rifle on her knees pulled the woolen blanket over her and remained motionless. Finally, someone tried to open the driver's door of the van. She held her breath. She got hot under the covers, but Keshia didn't dare to move.

Then it was quiet.

Only her lips moved when she asked Maheo for protection and help. No sound left her mouth. Keshia carefully lifted the blanket and gasped. She winced noticeably when the FBI van door opened.

The killers!

Keshia heard her own heart pounding as someone pulled the blanket away. She carefully positioned the rifle.

"Hey, who do we have here?" The guy grinned diabolically. "Black Hawk gave us a generous gift..."

He didn't get any further. Keshia fired the rifle. The guy, hit up close, flew back a little and lay on his back. The men's voices got angry. A second grabbed the gun barrel and tried to snatch it from her. Keshia firmly held the rifle and fired another volley. Someone had to hear the shots!

And Baxter has to be right here.

*****

Thompson's cell phone ringed. His face froze when he clearly heard the voice at the other end.

"For you", he said in a thick voice and handed it to Ryan. He didn't speak. He only heard Keshia's voice.

"They are here", she said softly.

Then he heard Isaac's sneering laugh. "What a pretty little wildcat. Do you want to see her again?"

"Let's finish it. Where are you?"

"Rodeo. I'm waiting."

Ryan squeezed the phone out. Without saying a word, he made it clear to Thompson that he wanted to drive himself. Thompson nodded and exchanged places with Ryan. He just found a hold on the door handle when Ryan turned the car, almost from a standing start, at full

246

throttle. Thompson did not dare to loosen this grip as the Dodge continued to fly straight across terrain. Ryan pushed the Dodge to its limits when he turned the steering wheel at full speed and turned the car in the wished position. Thompson's beads of sweat stood on his forehead. He swallowed hard.

"You go to the police department. I stop right in front of the office door. There you jump out and disappear inside. I'm going to the rodeo place."

"I request reinforcements."

Ryan nodded.

"Baxter Goodman has to be here every moment. Tell him I need a scout and fire protection."

"Okay."

A wire fence surrounded the site. The gate was open. Ryan braked the car hard outside the door. Even before he stopped, Thompson jumped out and slammed the door. His black figure disappeared into the building.

*****

Ryan drove on to the agreed place. He saw the head-lights of a car flashing. He parked the Dodge between two trees and slid out through the crack in the driver's door. The strange car approached and came within range. A large, dark figure got out and put the rifle over the roof of the car. He aimed at the Dodge.

Ryan was no longer there. According to old war style, he crawled in an arch, looking for cover behind every bump and stone. The moon showed its sickle from time to time and sent moderate light to the earth. The smell of damp earth and grass roots reached his nose as he slowly cra-wled forward. Ryan felt the proximity of the men. Then he saw them. There were two. They stood upright with their backs to Ryan. A repulsive smell of sweat, cold cigarette smoke, and alcohol blew to Ryan's nose. He grimaced in disgust. The traces of her boots were clearly visible in the damp grass floor. Ryan felt it out by hand. The heels were heavy and deeper, so there were white people. Ryan was only an arm's length behind them when he straightened up silently. He quickly drew his knife over the throat of one. Even before the other could understand what was happening, he sank to the ground silently. Ryan immediately lay flat on the grass floor again. He cleaned his knife by sticking it in the ground and pulling it out again. Smooth as a snake he moved forward. The gang's wagons were his goal. Four armed men patrolled there. Trying to arrest four men without anyone noticing it was impossible. Ryan took his knife and cut the tires. He worked quickly and silently. In the cover behind one of the cars, Ryan finally sat up and looked around. Keshia was nowhere to be seen. Ryan went in search of her and Hunting Wolf, knowing that he would soon get reinforcements.

*****

Thompson immediately requested reinforcements from Rapid City and then explored the police building. The doors weren't locked and he was actually alone in here. His eyes had quickly got used to the darkness. The light stayed off. You never knew who was lying in wait to watch him. A single shot had been fired after Ryan let him out of the Dodge. Since then it has remained silent. Thompson looked at his watch. It could not be long before the reinforcement he requested came. The helicopters took about fifteen minutes. The adrenaline chased the blood through the veins faster, making him hot. Thompson was sweating and the air in there was stuffy. He heard his own breath and the pounding in his chest. Startled, he spun as it clanked behind him. With the pistol in the stop, he switched on the small lamp that followed the muzzle.

He carefully put one foot in front of the other. The door to the next room was only ajar. Thompson didn't dare wipe the sweat from his forehead. He kicked it with his foot and just saw a small, black shadow fleeing. The bundled beam of light illuminated a tipped metal bowl that bathed in a pool of milk. Thompson blew the pent-up air out of his lungs through his teeth and illuminated the small room that resembled a storage room. There was a crack on the back door as wide as his hand and twice as high.

Thompson shook his head.

"The night of the ghosts", he hissed.

At the same instant he heard a shot cracking outside. He hurriedly jumped to the window. A car drove across the site. Headlights glided across the wall and glowed briefly into the window. A bullet suddenly hit the window. Thompson jumped startled as the glass splintered and jumped to the side. Then he opened the door a crack. The Jeep was right in front of him. Only one of the two headlights was on.

"Goodman?", Thompson called.

"Give up! You have no chance!", Baxter's voice called.

Thompson listened.

A thud, a moan and a laugh. Then something dragged along the wall of the house. Goodman appeared in front of Thompson with a stranger. The big bearded man held the unconscious by the feet.

"A delivery, Sir. He shot my baby", Baxter growled.

„Let's lock him up."

"Where's Ryan? Where's Keshia?"

"Hunting Wolf got her. Ryan is alone at the rodeo."

"Damn it!" Baxter was angry. He roughly dragged the guy into the cell. Thompson locked.

"Now quickly", said Baxter.

"You drive. I'm saying where to", Thompson said.

Both jumped into the Jeep.

*****

Six men were off. Ryan didn't know how many opponents he still had to deal with. In his estimation there were maybe four. Silently and invisibly he crawled on the floor to find cover. He slowly rose behind one of the trees. The dim light of the crescent moon and the clear starry sky could be dangerous. It was quiet.

Ryan climbed onto the lower branches of the tree, behind which he found cover. Isaac Hunting Wolf was a coward. He had wanted the fight with Ryan, but he sent his men into it. It was exactly these words that Ryan shouted loudly and clearly through the night. At the same instant a volley was fired at him. They came from three different directions. Ryan clung to a branch. Wood splintered. It was silent for a few seconds.

Then Ryan's Corvette appeared. Isaac got out and pulled Keshia with him.

"If you want to have both back, then come and get it. But the price is high", he shouted.

Keshia tried several times to free herself from the grip.

"You are a miserable coward. Isaac, and a sore loser",

Ryan replied.

Hunting Wolf laughed out loud.

"You hide on a tree, fight from the ambush and your arrogance sucks. You are the coward."

Ryan regretted not having his rifle with him. He had left it to Keshia and certainly Hunting Wolf. To aim more precisely, Ryan gripped the pistol with both hands and placed it on one of the branches. There was no time left. The shot rang out in the instant as Isaac whirled around when someone called him in a loud voice.

"Give up! You got no chance!"

Baxter!

Ryan's well-aimed shot missed his target by inches. Ryan heard his own curse. Isaac smiled sneered. He put his pistol on Keshia's head. Ryan jumped from the tree.

"Here I am. Let the woman go", he said.

A shot was fired. Ryan immediately threw himself flat on the floor. Then he heard Thompson's pistol answer.

Ryan watched a dark figure approaching Isaac. Ryan recognized Baxter. Isaac must have noticed something and turned. That was the moment he took the weapon from Keshia's head. Ryan saw that she bit his wrist so that he howled in pain. At last she managed to tear herself away from him. She ran to Ryan. He lay on the floor and put his pistol on Isaac again. Ryan could have targeted Isaac with a shot, but his wife was on the line of fire.

Ryan listened.

Helicopters were approaching.

Thompson's cavalry.

Isaac had nothing left to lose. Furiously he spun his pistol around and fired a few shots at Keshia. Keshia fell. A satisfying grin flitted across his face.

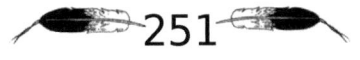

The headlights of the helicopters appeared in the night sky and scanned the country at low altitude. Isaac was about to jump into the Corvette. Baxter's shots prevented him from doing so.

"Freeze! FBI", Thompson called and fired two shots.

Hunting Wolf didn't think of surrendering and fled.

Keshia had fallen an arm's length in front of Ryan. Ryan knelt in front of her and took her in his arms. Breathing heavily, she sank into it.

"You're hurt", he said.

Keshia didn't answer.

Pure fear shot through his body like an electric shock when he realized that his hands felt something warm and wet. Blood!

"Keshia!", cried Ryan in horror.

He didn't want to believe it, but his eyes didn't betray him when he saw the blood on his hand.

"Keshia!", he shouted.

She didn't answer, but she was breathing very calmly now. Ryan jumped when a big, strong hand grabbed his shoulder. He immediately turned his head and looked into Baxter's face. Anger, despair and hatred were clearly on his friend's face. Baxter held a rifle in his hand. Ryans gun.

"One of the guys had it. It's loaded", Baxter said flatly.

Ryan immediately grabbed it while Baxter hold Keshia in his arms.

The helicopters circled over the rodeo area. One of the headlights followed the fleeing one. Ryan used the Corvette's roof as a support for his rifle and optimized the aiming device. The helicopter's headlight had fixed the fleeing wolf. Ryan fired without hesitation. Despite the exertion and his inner excitement, he managed to

keep his hands still. The dark shape was hit while running. Fell, overturned and lay motionless about three hundred yards away. The helicopter landed.

Ryan's eyes narrowed. He took a deep breath and grimaced. His skin tightened over the cheekbones. He looked petrified.

Baxter came up to him.

He stayed silent.

He was still carrying Keshia on his arms.

Ryan looked at Thompson, who was standing some distance away, watching the two men attentively. His stare held Ryan captive for a while. Then he felt his knees give in. He sank to the floor without a will and put the rifle away.

Baxter did the same and gently put Keshia down. She was no longer breathing. Her eyes were broken. Baxter grazed her eyelids with his hand.

Ryan shook his head slowly.

"Never again will I..."

His voice failed.

He felt the hot tears that could not quench the burning of his eyes and felt close to fainting. He carefully took Keshia in his arms and burled his face. Ryan didn't know how long he stayed that way. The time had suddenly stopped and the wind had stopped blowing. His heart cramped in pain as someone grabbed him roughly by the shoulders and tried to pull him onto his legs.

"Get up!", he heard the harsh command.

Ryan didn't respond.

The two FBI agents no longer waited and finally pulled the man onto his legs with violence.

Ryan's knees were stiff and painful. He heard the words unreal and from far away: "You're under arrest." Then

he felt the handcuffs on his joints. He let it happen ap-
athetically. Even though Ryan turned his eyes to the
ground, he noticed that the tribal police were there too.
Ryan heard Thompson's voice ordering that he be
transferred to Rapid City. Ryan let himself be led away
without will.
One slammed the helicopter door.

*****

Thompson rolled back and forth in bed. He did not come
to rest. The nightmare never ended. Although he always
managed to keep his distance from the cases, it was
different this time. His subconscious struggled against it.
He woke up weary and battered. The bed next to him
was empty. When he got up and shuffled to the window
as if in trance, his eyes narrowed. The daylight blinded
him. Slowly he opened it and sucked in the fresh air.
There was a note on the table in the dining room. He
read it and put it back. His wife had already gone to
work. He left the house without breakfast and drove to
the office. As if by remote control, he walked through
the anteroom, past Mrs. Dawson, and greeted silently
before disappearing into his office. His secretary watched him skeptically. She sensed what was going on in him.
They had been working together for decades, insepar-
able like an old couple. She brewed a very strong coffee,
put everything on a small tray and knocked softly on the
door. As her boss didn't react, she opened the door.
Thompson slouched in his office chair, staring holes in
the air. Finally, she carefully placed the tray on the desk.
"I think the coffee will do you good."
Thompson looked up slowly, forcing himself to smile

wearily. Tears veiled his eyes and he saw the old lady only vaguely. He blinked several times and lowered his eyes again when he said *thank you.*

Mrs. Dawson stopped.

"You would have wished that he had caught the other one too, the brother who fled."

Thompson was startled.

"How do you know..."

„I typed your report this morning. Unfortunately, I cannot avoid reading it."

"But that wasn't in the report", Thompson started, looking almost reproachfully at her.

"I know. But I know you well enough that I can see more than anyone else."

"That's all right", he murmured.

"Why did you arrested Black Hawk?"

"To protect him."

She cocked her head and looked blankly at Thompson.

"I do not understand. He worked for you. You send him there on behalf of the FBI to do his job. Your FBI agents arrest him for doing just that. That seems very illogical to me right now. Who is this supposed to protect him from?"

"From his own people, Mrs. Dawson. Ryan Black Hawk is a Lakota and has brought down Isaak Hunting Wolf's gang, alcohol and drug smugglers, mostly also Lakotas. He killed two white men and five Lakota on the Reservation. It was his last job. He wanted to go home, back to the Reservation. His people would despise him if it came out that he was acting on behalf of the FBI. I don't need to explain what that means to him."

The old lady slid into the chair opposite Thompson and sighed in a depressed voice as he sipped the coffee. She looked at Thompson anxiously. He, who could have been her son and who was now responsible for all of this. Maybe also about the young man who had tragically lost his beloved wife and who might be sentenced to death? She took herself a coffee.

"It's really good. Damn good", Thompson said, smiling wearily.

"Will you help him?", Dawson asked, hopefully attached her gaze to his lips. Her otherwise rough voice suddenly had a soft sound.

"I do everything I can to help him."

She nodded, reassured.

"I must hurry. Two men from the gang sit with him in the same prison. That worries me."

"But then he is protected by law as an FBI employee?"

Thompson nodded.

"Officially, Black Hawk never worked for the FBI, only for me."

Dawson's thoughts worked. Finally, she nodded.

"I understand. But how are you going to get him out?"

"I talk to the boss personally and vouch for him. It is pleaded in self-defense. I myself was a witness."

The old lady sighed heavily. Then she said: "Do you know that I feel something like pity. Why did he have his young wife with him?"

"Because he was on the way home with her when I called him. Shortly before the final destination. I feel complicit in her death because it was my fault that Hunting Wolf was able to escape."

Dawson nodded sympathetically.

Then suddenly she jumped up as if the milk in her ante-chamber had overflowed. She came back with two shot glasses and a bottle in her arm.

"Forget the coffee. Now we need something strong. My secret reserve for emergencies. He wakes up mummies."

Thompson watched Dawson fill the glasses to the brim.

"German Williams, Christ Obstbrand, with 60% alcohol," she smiled. A gift from my German relatives."

Then she gave her boss a glass.

"Cheers!", she said.

The fruit brandy that looked like water burned like fire on the tongue. Thompson felt like there were nails on the way to his stomach. But it felt good. He coughed a few times. Then he sniffled loudly into his big handkerchief, put it away and breathed a sigh of relief.

"And?", Dawson asked expectantly.

Thompson smiled over the rim of his glasses.

"I've always believed in good spirits, but I never knew what they looked like until the day we met, Mrs. Dawson. I don't know what to do without her. I would be completely in a fix and helpless", he said.

"Oh, Chief", she said embarrassed. „Now you exaggerate too much."

"Not at all!"

As if transformed, Thompson sat up in his office chair and rubbed his hands.

"Well then ... to work. There is a hell of a lot to do."

Dawson smiled contentedly.

"I immediately make an appointment with the big boss."

"I appreciate that."

She disappeared quietly through the door with the liquor bottle and glasses. The coffee was left on the desk.

*****

Baxter was no longer able to think clearly. He was angry,

felt helpless and powerless. He had been denied his friend's visit to the Rapid City's Remand Prison. After Baxter had hit the front wheel of his Commander with full force, he sat silently behind the steering wheel for some time. The memory of last night robbed him of his senses and paralyzed his limbs. He didn't want to go to his wrecks in the junkyard, nor to Eagle Creek Village. And not to Olivia either. Today he couldn't have endured her questions. He knew Thompson only briefly, so Baxter didn't dare go to him, perhaps to get permission to visit. And Sam? No.

At some point Baxter started his Jeep and drove off without knowing where. When he came to, he found himself in front of the truck stop, south of the city.

Dian!

Baxter smiled weakly. He got out and went inside. His destination was a bar stool at the counter. There he sat down weakly and rested his head on his hands.

"Hello, tired bear. Are you sick?", asked a familiar voice.

Baxter looked up and managed to smile.

"Hi Dian."

"Oh! It's serious. May I help you?"

"Hmm. A barrel of Whiskey for me alone", he murmured.

"So bad, Baxter?"

"Worse."

"Good lord. What you up to? Do you want to get drunk?", she asked amused.

"Drowning would be better", he answered tonelessly.

Baxter looked at Dian. Their looks met briefly. Baxter lowered her eyelids. He couldn't answer Dian's questioning look. Dian pushed a double Whiskey in front of Baxter's nose.

"Thank you", he murmured.

Baxter put the glass on and drank it all in one swig without blinking an eye. When he put the glass down, their eyes met again.

Dian was startled.

Never, as long as she knew the Bear, had she seen such an expression look on him. Never a tear. It laced her throat. She swallowed hard. Then she served the other guests before joining Baxter. She put her hand sympathetically on his shoulder.

"Ryan?", she asked softly.

"In prison."

"Oh my God! What happened?"

"He killed five men", Baxter replied sarcastically. "Smuggler, killer. One of them I have on the conscience and one Keshia, Ryans wife. Two are in custody with him. One has escaped."

"I didn't even know that your friend had a wife."

"Would have. Until last night", Baxter replied bitterly.

Dian audibly sucked the air through her teeth and was initially silent. "Oh no, Baxter. I'm so sorry", she finally said softly. Tears stifled her voice.

"Give me another double."

Dian filled Baxter's glass. Again he poured the Whiskey into his throat as if it were water.

"When I'm dead, you'll get the commander, Dian", Baxter said finally in a harsh voice.

"Than I can wait until I go black", he heard Dian's amused voice.

Of course he understood that she was just trying to cheer him up. The trace of a smile appeared on Baxter's face. Whoever decided that he had come here was a good decision. Baxter drank a third, double Whiskey, which did nothing to him. But he felt good and Dian felt good for him.

*****

When the sun sank that evening, just as it had the evening before, and nothing was as it had been before, Thompson leaned back exhausted but reassured in his television armchair. Even before the late news was over, his eyes closed. Two sleepless nights had left their mark. It was not easy to come to terms with things that one did not want to accept at all. The skill was to make the best of it. Thompson had tried and finally got what he wanted after a hard day's work. The overtime were merely peanuts.

The next morning, Thompson, more rested than the day before, did not drive to his office as usual, but went straight to the city remand prison. He wanted to deliver the message to Ryan himself. The FBI special agent was unlocked the door to the cell. When the door closed behind him and was locked, he shuddered. Thompson looked at the man who was lying apathetic on the plank bed and staring at the ceiling as if he hadn't noticed anything.

"Hello Ryan", he said softly.

The person addressed did not answer. He didn't respond either. Thompson froze in his track.

"I made my testimony. Your lawyer has quickly obtained acquittal for self-defense."

Ryan still didn't move. Either without even batting an eyelid. Thompson took a deep breath.

"You are a free man."

Ryan still didn't respond.

Thompson waited. Then he cleared his throat.

"Are you listening to me at all?"

"Thanks", Ryan said finally.

Thompson nodded.

"What will you do?"

Ryan crossed his arms behind his head and looked at him. "What does a wild animal do when it's driven into a corner?"

"Attack."

A bitter smile appeared on Ryan's face.

"That's what I did. But it didn't fix."

"Do you think of escape?"

"Hopeless."

Thompson nodded.

"Are you staying with me?", he asked carefully.

"No!" The answer came promptly and clearly.

Thompson said nothing.

He sensed that it was unwise and rude to continue asking. After a while he took a deep breath and said: "No matter what you do. It'll be right for you. I hope that you will find peace at some point. Do not give up hope. Farewell, Ryan."

Ryan rose slowly. He looked directly at Thompson for the first time in a long time.

"If once things settled down, i will go home."

Ryan shook hands with him.

Thompson agreed to.

"In spite of everything, we were a good team", he said.

"I will miss you and most of all I will never forget you."

Ryan nodded.

Without further words of farewell, their paths separated.

Thompson knocked.

The door opened.

*****

Ryan's expression was still taciturn when he was given his things two hours later and he acknowledged receipt. Then he went outside. Mild spring air blew towards him. The sun was shining. Ryan put on his aviator glasses. The glasses looked like mirrors and did not allow a curious look. She was his shield against the world out there, in which he felt lost and vulnerable at that very moment. The glasses hid him and made him invisible. People passed him without paying any attention to him. Ryan took a deep breath. He did not miss the fact that a car was always following him. The Jeep rolled along the footpath at walking speed. Ryan finally stopped and turned to face him. He hadn't been wrong. Baxter lowered the side window of the passenger door.

"Get in!", he heard his friend's voice.

Ryan did it without hesitation.

"Your Corvette is with me. Well ... at Haywood. I took her with the car transporter and patched her up."

Ryan nodded.

"By the way, there is also your backpack in there, Ryan. I was able to save the two Glock's. They just took the rifle away."

Ryan nodded.

"The Winchester is back. They didn't want them anymore."

Ryan nodded.

"Do you have a certain destination in mind before we go to my place?"

"Keshia. Where is she?"

"With her family. The funeral was yesterday."

Ryan felt the shackles around his heart, which suddenly tied it up, just like his dry throat. The pain overwhelmed him and took his breath away. He gasped. Then he pressed the jaws hard together and kept silent.

"Hm", made Baxter helpless and hit the gas.

*****

If Ryan had decided to remain silent, he could do it for hours. In the worst case, even for days. Baxter knew that. Since every word seemed inappropriate to him at the moment, he too remained silent. He felt the pain, the anger and the powerlessness just like his friend.

Baxter had handed over the apartment in Rapid City this morning and stuffed the Commander with the rest of his single household. He was on the run. Baxter no longer held anything in Rapid City or anything in his old life. He felt trapped and laced and that took his breath away. So he was driving into his new life, full of hope and euphoria. He didn't mind that there was no wallpaper stuck to the walls in his apartment and that the floor covering was still waiting in the shop. After all, electricity, heating and water worked. In the middle of the room there was already his worn out sofa bed and a table and chairs by the window.

The small town, Eagle Creek Village, appeared an hour later. Baxter felt the tingling in his stomach as he drove through the open gate onto the grounds of Haywood's stable. He stopped right in front of the outside stairs to his new apartment, grabbed one of the boxes and went ahead. Ryan also grabbed one and followed. He wasn't talking now either. He stared absently as Baxter closed the apartment door behind him.

"Pick a place, my friend. Feel like at home", Baxter said. "I urgently need to take a shower."

Ryan nodded and sat down at the table.

Then it was quiet again. The only sound was the running water from the shower. When Baxter re-entered the living room , Ryan was still sitting motionless at the table, staring at an imaginary point on the table. Baxter shook his head barely noticeably and finally signed up with Ling Fu. Then he rummaged in his boxes and swore when he couldn't find what he was looking for. When Baxter finally spoke to Ryan directly, he didn't respond. He didn't even flinch. His eyes were as empty as the point on the table he had been staring at for about an hour.

Baxter took a deep breath and his whiskey bottle. With a glass in hand, he sat at the table with Ryan and opened the bottle. Silently he poured himself a glass full of it. The bubbling noise came out relatively loud. Baxter immediately put the glass on and drank it all in one gulp. He made a face, shook himself, and sniffed the air deep through his nose. The grip on his cigarette box was already automatic and he would not have known where to put his hands.

Now something strange happened.

Ryan moved.

He took the bottle and the glass as a matter of course. Baxter could hardly believe his eyes. Ryan poured. Not to the brim, but at least a double. Without hesitation he also drank the glass in one gulp and then twisted his mouth down.

"Sometimes that's good", he said softly, pushing the bottle and glass away. "My grandfather, and also my

father, taught me to find the good in everything." He shook his head. "I've been thinking for a long time. But no matter how I turn it. I can't find anything good in the things that have happened. I fought and in the end I lost everything: Keshia, my life, my respect for myself. The first man I really killed with hate in my heart was a Lakota."

Ryan swallowed and stared at his hands, which he had clenched to fist on the table in front of him.

"He didn't deserve it any other way", Baxter said carefully.

Ryan didn't answer.

Baxter sighed indecisively.

"I'll have something to eat", Baxter said as he got up. "My kitchen will be delivered next week. But the coffee machine and the microwave work."

He put two sandwiches on the plate. "Do you want to bake it with cheese too? My Specialty."

"I'm not hungry."

"Hey! You have to eat something."

"Do I have to?"

Ryan's words sounded hard and a bit angry.

"Yes!", Baxter shouted.

"Why do I have to eat when I'm not hungry. That is illogical."

Baxter gasped and was obviously looking for the right words. "So that you won't go to the dogs, my friend. You live damn it!" Baxter tried to stay calm.

Ryan raised his head and looked Baxter straight in the eye. They glared at him and his face, which had turned to a petrified mask four days ago, had taken on a frightening expression.

"Someday I will live again. Then I will send my thoughts

far away so that they can no longer torture me."

Baxter gasped helplessly to say something but blew them out again. Then he took the cheese sandwiches out of the microwave and sat back down at the table.

"Did you talk to Thompson?", Baxter asked.

"Yes."

Baxter nodded and bit his sandwich.

"You could stay here. Haywood is looking for a crazy one", Baxter noticed with a full mouth.

A faint smile suddenly played around Ryan's mouth.

"There's more than enough of that", he said softly.

"But not like you."

"What?"

"Mustangs", Baxter grinned.

Indian Cowboy – Volume 3
The red Mustang

Mike Ruler, the manager, was in the office at Haywood. Haywood was neither pleased nor angry at the news that his indigenous driver in the red Mustang would start the first midnight race. Basically, he didn't care.

"So everything stays the same", summarized Mike.

"Come up with something", Haywood hissed.

"The stubborn Indsman doesn't play his part. He didn't want to understand that we are a team. He called me a cheater! And he won't take his foot off the gas. Today he won and tomorrow he will win again and so on … and I have to pay a fortune. It does not work like that. Then I can close soon."

"Why don't you just fire him?"

"Because he's the damn star here. Without him we are uninteresting. The spectators would go and with them their entrance fees and betting revenues", Haywood grumbled dejectedly.

Mike grimaced. He felt the anger against the Indian clearly within himself. His ego screamed for revenge.

"And take care of the missing parts from the ware-house", Haywood growled as he gruffly arranged papers on his desk.

"Yes, Sir", Mike said and left.

*****

An hour before the race started, the drivers had to be in the paddock. Ryan entered the hall two hours earlier that evening. The mechanic was expecting Ryan on the red Mustang. But the Chinese wasn't there. Ryan looked around and finally opened the driver's door of his racing car. He wasn't in the car either. When Ryan sat down in the driver's seat, the little Chinese rolled out from under the car.

"Hello my friend. Everything okay", Ling Fu whispered.

"What are you doing down there?", Ryan smiled.

"Only a fool sits down as a target, a good friend told me", Ling Fu grinned and got up.

"Correctly."

Ling Fu crouched and looked at Ryan.

"I want you to win at night too. Haywood doesn't."

"Yes, Ling Fu, I know it. Haywood is afraid that his betting shop will go bust. Meanwhile my victories screw up his business. He asked me to apply the brakes instead of the accelerator."

"Holy shit!", Ling Fu whispered in alarm and quickly put his hand to his mouth.

"He dreams of Frank winning. Then Haywood would be a rich man in one fell swoop."

Ling Fu sighed and looked worriedly at Ryan.

"Take care, my friend! Only two things are infinite! The universe and the stupidity of people. I'm not so sure about the universe", he chuckled softly. "Where is Baxter?"

"He will be here at any moment", Ryan said.

Ling Fu sat in the passenger seat and talked to Ryan.

The light was switched on in the vehicle hall. Baxter appeared next to the open vehicle door while the two men laughed softly.

"Well, it looks like you're fine!"

Both came out of the car.

"Yes, Baxter. Laughing is the best way to show your teeth to an opponent. That is the fuel that our hawk flies away from everyone."

"Don't overdo, Ling Fu. You turn our falcon into a jet plane."

Ryan picked up his cigarettes and pointed to the gate. Baxter nodded that he understood and continued to whisper with Ling Fu while Ryan went out. There he leaned against the wall of the old factory building and lit a cigarette. The setting sun cast long shadows on the grounds. From the entrance the voices of the people who were let in came to his ears.

The first drivers came into the hall. Baxter and Ling Fu got down to work.

Steve stopped at the gate, stopped in front of Ryan.

"I'm not falling for this morning's trick anymore", he warned.

Ryan smiled barely as he draw on his cigarette.

"You will swallow my dust tonight. You can't get past me. Not any longer."

Ryan shrugged. "If you like to be hunted by me", he said and stubbed out his cigarette.

He left Steve and went into the vehicle hall.

Steve grimaced as if he had just bitten into a lemon.

The drivers put on the overalls and took care of the preparations for the race car. A little later, Baxter gave them the instructions to leave. Mike was nowhere to be found. The drivers brought their cars to the start, in the position that Baxter assigned to them. Ryan was in the front row with his red Mustang. Steve and the third place from the previous race stood next to him. From now on, the drivers were not allowed to leave their car until the start. There were still ten minutes to go. Ryan leaned against his Mustang and waited. At 11.30 p.m. the cars started into the night of the prairie.

Steve actually managed to get in front of Ryan after the start. Instead, his light dazzled him in the rearview mirror. He swung it up. At full throttle he took the long left curve. Ryan stayed close to his back. Then the last curve arrived before the unpaved prairie route began. The cars braked hard to accelerate again immediately. The lights of the racing cars wrapped in dust clouds looked ghostly in the night-black prairie.

The steering wheel slid easily through Ryan's hands. He played with it. He also played with Steve. He had become braver and took the hill at full throttle. Without damage he even landed on the other side. Ryan was looking forward to the hairpin bend. But Steve's respect before that was too big. He didn't make the same mistake as the Texan. The moment Steve braked his Mustang, Ryan pulled past on the inside. He turned on the spot and drove Steve off.

When Ryan reached the paved track after the first round, his eyes started to burn. At times the lights blurred in front of his field of vision. He blinked several times until he could see clearly again. Ryan drove at undiminished speed through the track, which was blocked off with old, piled-up car tires. Mercilessly he felt leaden tiredness. The work of the last days took its toll. He took a few deep breaths. Steve had caught up.

Ryan braked on the right-angled curve to the prairie slope. For an instant everything seemed to turn as he drove the curve. He was dizzy. He took several deep breaths. Ryan stepped on the accelerator as if by remote control. The engine roared and the Mustang scraped the dusty ground.

The eyes burned so much that they started to water. Ryan blinked and pulled oneself together. He drove almost blindly up the hill. He knew the route inside out.

His feeling did not deceive him. Steve was close behind him. Due to the bumps on the slopes, Ryan stayed faster. After the start of the race, Ryan had easily played with Steve. Now it was getting difficult. Ryan looked at his hands, which were clinging to the steering wheel. He felt sick. It pounded in the head and the pictures blurred before his eyes. He shook his head.

For seconds he could see clearly again. Steve was still behind him and the hairpin bend was in front of Ryan. That was the last thing Ryan could see.

The blurry images in front of his eyes were spinning. He intuitively reached for the handbrake, but he was unable to think clearly, nor was he physically able to master it. What had to happen happened.

Ryan's Mustang flipped off the curve and overturned several times. The vehicle came to a standstill off the track, lying on the roof.

It became quiet in the dark of the night.

German language:
„Indian Cowboy" Band 1-6,
„Maggie Yellow Cloud" Band 1-2
„Die Farben der Sonne"
„Sheloquins Vermächtnis"

English language:
„The Indian Cowboy " Part 1
        „The night of the wolfes "
„The Indian Cowboy" Part 2
        „The hunter"

Comming soon:
„The Indian Cowboy" Part 3
        „The red mustang"

Buy now:
Twenty-Six-Verlag Online Shop
Amazon
Thalia, Weltbild, Hugendubel and
all online-book-shops in all formats

www.brita-rose-billert.de

More than just a book...